To Bubba

Live with ... courage!

The Boy with Golden Eyes

BOOK TWO

The Prophetic Journey

Enjoy the journey!
-Sam "Rupert" Wolf
Lucie (Lira)

MARJORIE YOUNG

ACKNOWLEDGMENTS

Once again, it truly required a village to raise this book.

Everlasting gratitude to Dilip and Carole Hiralal and their beautiful daughters Meera, Lea, and Tara, who were there from the beginning.

Profound gratitude to Helen Chamberland, Ann Butler, Michael Wolf, and Manfred Wolf for their endless patience and help.

Deepest appreciation also to Ann Brown, Rika Wakayama, Anne Dinning, Mimi Young, Glenn Young, Leslie Schneider, Shannon Buckner, Barbara Goulter, Paul Wolf, Dana Wolf, Lowell Young, Pat Domerofski, Scott Tsumura, and Sheila Boughten.

In cherished memory of Neil Young.

I love you all.

For Sam and Lucie–forever my joy and inspiration.

Chapter One

upert and his comrades descended from the mountaintop, making their way through the high waving grass and towering trees. Down, down the winding path they went, their steps light with joy. All were wrapped in their own thoughts, yet at the same time, united as never before.

The band of travelers had lived through miraculous events; of that there could be no doubt. The companions had fled the land of the Usurper-King Ryker - where Rupert was rightful ruler - and managed, after long and treacherous travel, to cross the border into Zurland. Rupert himself, though only eleven years old, felt he had experienced a lifetime in those days and weeks.

He recognized he'd already lived *two* lifetimes... his first ten years of isolation deep in the forest with his aloof grandparents and animal friends; and the other existence he'd led since. He'd discovered a hidden royal treasure and then endured the mysterious disappearance of his kin. Yet their cruel abandonment of the boy became a catalyst for leaving his forest home behind.

It was only then that his life truly had begun, Rupert reflected. For he'd encountered those he now considered his *true* family; Grandfather Liam and his granddaughter Lira, who had taken him in; Liam's son and Lira's father, Daniel, whom he had met while imprisoned; and Morley, a soldier of the wicked King Ryker, who had turned traitor to aid Rupert and Daniel's escape from a sentence of death. They'd all fled together, with danger at their heels. But at last, they had crossed into what they hoped would prove friendly territory.

The mountain air was crisp and refreshing, the tender azure sky pure and perfect. Rupert continued to savor the marvelous euphoria experienced soon after they'd crossed into freedom. What a joy to realize that, at long last, *all* his companions could see his golden eyes - the very symbol of his kingship! For a race of Golden-Eyed Kings had ruled their homeland for generations; ruled with justice and compassion, well-loved by their people. but the invader Zorin, father of the present despot, had betrayed and murdered most of the royal clan at what was to have been a conference of peace. The last of their race was thought dead these past thirty years or more… until it was discovered that Rupert himself possessed eyes of pure gold.

Now, though they'd fled into Zurland, their journey had, in fact, hardly begun. Their *true* destination was the far-away kingdom of Raja-Sharan, which lay several thousand miles to the east. A mysterious female, who had appeared to Rupert more than once, informed in a vision that this was where he and his friends should flee. Liam warned it might prove an impossible undertaking, but both Rupert and little Lira were exhilarated at the thought of such an odyssey; for who knew what strange sights and encounters might await them?

Furthermore, Raja-Sharan was the native land of Queen Khar-Shar-Leen. She was the wife of Marco, the last of the Golden-Eyed Kings. Therefore, she was a blood-relation to Rupert - presumably his grandmother. Surely the present royal family would offer Rupert and his comrades aid and shelter.

But for the moment, more immediate concerns loomed. They had been traveling in disguise for weeks – the males donning long skirts and cloaks, while Lira had taken delight posing as a boy. Though the men longed to end their masquerade, Lira would be less willing, savoring the freedom of masculine garb while traveling over hard country.

In their kingdom, the people were downtrodden, living under a harshly oppressive regime. Most sought anonymity, using the hood of their cloaks to conceal their faces as a matter of course. In such a dreadful atmosphere, few even dared look directly into the eyes of their neighbor. As a result, it was no difficult task for the fugitives' superficial masquerade to succeed. Now, however, they were entering a foreign land, where such devices might not pass muster.

It was late afternoon when the party arrived at the end of the winding mountain trail. Flatlands spread out before them, and in the distance, a road beckoned. Rupert and his faithful pup Raja, who as usual were leading the way, drew to a halt. His friends followed suit... along with the magnificent stallion Majesty, who had also been camouflaged as an ordinary pack animal. Rupert turned to his adopted kin.

"There lies a road directly ahead. But there is much to determine before we proceed."

"Of course," declared Liam. "It is imperative we discover the lay of the land. We know not what changes may have occurred of late. For so very long, we have been deprived of news of the outside world."

"Oh, I *do* hope the people will be friendly," chimed in Lira. "For how wonderful to perhaps sleep at an inn tonight! Not that I mind sleeping on the ground. But it *is* starting to get chilly."

"I'm sure none would object to a warm bed," said Daniel, smiling at his brave and beautiful flaxen-haired daughter. "Yet here is a situation we dare not approach blind. We are in dire need of information."

"Let us not forget the most important unknown of all," reminded Morley. "Will Rupert's golden eyes be visible to the populace here, or no? And how might we learn the answer without setting ourselves at risk?"

"Yes, for even if the populace proves friendly, surely the existence of a golden-eyed lad would not escape wild comment. Inevitably, word would reach King Ryker," added Liam.

"No doubt he'd send men after us again, no matter how far they had to go in pursuit," concluded Rupert.

"Well, what does that mean?" Lira wanted to know. "Shall we *forever* be in disguise and let none see our faces? All the way to Raja-Sharan?" Clearly, the idea found no appeal in her eyes.

"Lira has a point," admitted Rupert. "Let us get closer to the road and observe what we may. The tall grass should conceal our presence."

They were in agreement. This time, Morley led the way, taking up position as scout. He sped ahead, coming to a halt not far from the road. Sensing no danger, his companions approached. All knelt in the field of waving grass, and even the towering Majesty knew to keep his head down. In the silence, the only sound reaching their ears was the wind gently caressing the tall grass and swaying tree branches. Rupert felt a wave of peace permeate his being. Surely all would be well. And he continued to revel in an awareness of being somehow guided from without and within.

It was not long before a small party of travelers approached. Instantly, Rupert took heart. The appearance of the Zurlanders was a striking contrast to the citizens of their own beleaguered land. Their clothing was brightly colored, so different from the dark and drab apparel they were accustomed to seeing. There were three women, two men, and three children. The women wore long skirts of red or bright blue. Their blouses were white, with colorful embroidery stitched upon them; their cloaks were of lighter hues. All their faces were openly visible.

The men, as well, had donned cheerful tunics of white and green. The children sported colorful attire, and even from a distance, the comrades could perceive the sounds of laughter and banter as they made their way slowly past. They possessed a horse, pulling a cart heaped high with goods. Both were almost unheard-of luxuries in their own kingdom. The party appeared healthy and happy; the children romped playfully beside the cart. They soon were out of sight, yet the impression left behind was a momentous one.

"Why, these people seem so different!" exclaimed Rupert. "Surely, even this small glimpse may assure us conditions here are far better than we've ever seen."

"Not so fast, Rupert," cautioned Morley. "Yes, they looked well-fed and cheerful enough. However, we have no idea how they'd take to strangers."

"But look how brightly they're dressed!" exclaimed an enthralled Lira. "I do believe I wouldn't object to girl's garments again if they all proved so agreeable."

"Let's not confuse fashion with fact," observed her father with a laugh. "I agree they *seemed* charming enough…at a distance. So yes, this brief glimpse declares Zurland a veritable paradise compared to our suffering kingdom."

"Let us not forget the most important question of all," reminded Liam. "Will these beguiling citizens perceive Rupert's golden eyes? We ourselves, with the exception of Daniel, had been blind to them until this day."

Rupert regarded his friends. "Of course, we can never know until we are bold enough to show my face to those we meet. I hardly suppose we could journey through Zurland eternally concealing our appearance."

Just then another party approached…two men and a boy, each on horseback. They were also clad in bright attire, chatting amiably as they cantered by. The comrades were thus able to conclude that here, in Zurland, it was not unusual for ordinary folk to be on horseback; another sign of prosperity.

"Well, at least Majesty won't have to be in disguise any longer," remarked Lira. "For it seems horses abound in this happy land."

Her remark was greeted with laughter. "Yes, it is true, Lira," agreed her youthful grandfather. "Though he'll be bound to attract attention, even here." For Majesty was a huge, magnificent stallion…golden-brown with a flowing white mane and tail. He was almost identical in appearance to the legendary Rico, the favorite steed of King Marco.

"Well, it seems plain we cannot skulk about here. Either we travel openly or take to the hills and keep our presence secret," said Morley evenly. He believed, however, it was better to mix with the citizens and hope for the best. They couldn't hide forever.

"Dusk is upon us," observed Daniel. "Should we make for the nearest town, or decide our course in the morning?"

They instinctively turned to Rupert. He was not only their boy-king, but his visions had *usually* proven to lead them in the right direction. He smiled.

"I believe it is time to end our masquerade. Yes, let us become ourselves again." He decisively pulled the map from his tunic pocket...the mysterious document which led from his grandparents' forest home to the distant land of Raja-Sharan. They consulted it for a moment. "It appears the nearest town is about ten miles off. We could never hope to reach it before dark. So let us spend one more night in the open before we begin anew with the dawn."

Rupert's companions concurred. An intoxicating sense of relief mixed with a churning anticipation for the morrow. For in casting off their disguise, they were taking the most enormous of gambles.

Chapter Two

The night was spent cheerfully under a cold and starry sky. They had the comfort of a large fire to warm them and to provide illumination for their nightly study in the language of Raja-Sharan. But application proved a challenge. Rupert and his friends had lived as fugitives for so very long. When they had at last dared to travel openly, it was in camouflage. So the thought of what the new day might bring could not but dominate their thoughts.

When morning arrived, Rupert rose before the others. He always cherished the pre-dawn hour: to witness the night sky transform into the blush of day never failed to move him deeply. He summoned his beloved animal companions. Climbing astride Majesty and moving some distance from his sleeping friends, Rupert took off at a gallop. Raja had little difficulty keeping pace, and looking down at the mastiff pup, his master could not stifle a rueful laugh. Raja now, without question, weighed in the vicinity of one hundred pounds...and he was not yet many months old. Before he was done, he'd likely double his present mass. With perhaps the largest horse and dog in Zurland, it would be an even greater challenge to pass unnoticed here. Yet the greatest uncertainty would be whether citizens would apprehend his eyes' true golden hue.

Only Daniel had beheld them from the first, reflected Rupert. To Liam, Lira, and Morley, they'd appeared very dark brown...almost as dark as his waving black hair. Would the populace now become aware of them? Well, there was no way of knowing until they dared to walk about un-cloaked.

Rupert finally brought Majesty to a halt. He dismounted and sat between his horse and the ever-faithful Raja, transfixed by the glorious sunrise. He never failed to find wonder in the daily miracle, for each day created a masterpiece anew. And something in his heart was ever grateful.

Finally, he made his way back to his friends. They had already arisen, their morning repast prepared. While consuming the porridge, there was little conversation... an unusual occurrence for this lively group. For each comprehended what risk and promise the day might bring.

Finally, Lira sighed. "I suppose you'll return to your normal attire this day, so I must appear as a girl once more."

"Wise thinking, darling," agreed Daniel. "It requires the purchase of new garments so as to blend in more perfectly - permitting you to obtain those pretty frocks you so admired yesterday."

Lira blushed as the others laughed. For she *did* indeed covet the bright and charming garb the local ladies wore.

"May I pray the time has come to obtain horses at last? My well-trodden feet will be eternally grateful should that be the case!" declared Morley.

"Oh, *may* we truly get horses of our own?" cried Lira. "For though I do love Majesty, he is Rupert's horse now."

Daniel looked to his father for confirmation. He received a nod in return. "Why, yes, it does appear that our endless days on foot will be drawing to a close. It's not purely for sweet comfort's sake. We need proceed towards Raja-Sharan with haste. At least, that's what Rupert has always urged."

"By all means," confirmed Rupert. "Let us make for the next town. Then we'll learn whether we may travel openly or no."

"What if someone *can* see your golden eyes?" inquired Lira, echoing what was on all their minds. "What should we do then?"

"Well, in Zurland, golden eyes would not carry a death sentence at least," Liam reflected. "Should someone claim to see them we should react with puzzlement. Denial can be a useful tactic."

"We must be bold, proceed openly, and wish for the best," declared the young prince.

With that, they quickly donned their former garb…the men masculine attire of tunics and leggings, and Lira her last remaining dress…a now ragged, dark green one made from rough materials. Soon they were on their way, proceeding audaciously along the road.

It was not long before they encountered a man and woman traveling in the opposite direction. The couple passed by with a curious look. Owing to their drab garments, the comrades were likely suspected of being foreigners. Nonetheless, the party received a friendly enough glance. Yet Rupert felt this was not a true test; for out of fear and old habit, they still wore their hoods drawn down low. However, as the weather was chilly and breezy, that did not appear odd or exceptional.

The companions continued for approximately ten miles until reaching Zugan. Along the way, there had been several encounters with locals. Aside from receiving a glance or two, nothing remarkable occurred. Nonetheless, their hearts began to race as they passed through the town gates. Zugan appeared well-populated and lively. Though not a Sunday, which was traditionally the market day in their homeland, many shops were open for business. Rupert and Lira were alive with excitement to see the blacksmith, clothing and food stalls, and goods of all sorts on display.

The companions had formed no definite plan. Should they pause in their journey, or obtain supplies and quickly move on? It seemed an unwarranted risk to remain, no matter how Lira might long for a night spent under a roof.

"Shall we purchase clothing and then have a meal?" inquired Liam.

There were no objections, and Lira, taking her father by the hand, led Daniel to a small shop featuring attractive articles of wear on display. She quickly selected long skirts and brightly embroidered blouses, for tunics did not seem the fashion here. Her father reminded that warm cloaks, scarves, mittens, and leggings were not to be forgotten, as colder weather was already upon them. Lira was delighted with the chore of making more selections, and her happiness pleased the others in return.

The male members of their party, however, proceeded with a more business-like air, and soon obtained what was necessary. The purchase of horses would be their next task.

Then came the *real* test. It was something so very simple...having a meal in the open. They proceeded to a stall with several wooden benches. Cautiously taking their seats, they were nearly overwhelmed with trepidation. The mistress appeared to greet them; a pleasant-looking, slightly plump lady. The simple fact she did not seem worn or hungry set her greatly apart from many in their own land. Boldly, Liam took down the hood of his cloak. His message was clear; now was the time!

Cautiously, the others followed suit. Rupert held his breath; so much depended upon this outcome.

"Well, what can I get your family today?" inquired the lady to Liam, taking him to be the patriarch of this fine group.

"We prefer not to partake of meat," he answered with a friendly tone. "But otherwise, we're quite open to suggestions."

"Hmm...not eat meat?" she asked, puzzled. "Well, it takes all kinds, I suppose. I can gladly offer roasted vegetables, cheese, and my freshly baked walnut bread. Would that please you?"

Rupert brazenly spoke up. "Why yes, that should be excellent!"

The lady turned to smile in his direction. But suddenly, upon beholding his face, she gave a gasp. The others could hardly draw breath as Morley found himself reaching for his sword. It was but a reflex. For it would hardly serve to run the poor lady through for the crime of seeing Rupert's golden eyes!

"Why, bless me," she proclaimed. "I do believe I've never beheld such a handsome young lad! He looks quite like a prince from a fairy story. And such unusual dark coloring! You must be travelers from afar, I'll warrant you."

Rupert began to breathe again. Apparently, she could *not* see the true color of his eyes after all.

"Yes, he *is* so very handsome, I agree!" proclaimed Lira stifling a relieved giggle.

The lady turned towards the girl and caught her breath once more. "Why, you're quite as beautiful as a fairy princess yourself, little miss! And so blond and fair while the boy is so dark. Perfect opposites, I declare!" Her reaction forced the others to conclude that, golden eyes or not, Rupert would almost certainly attract a measure of undesired attention...as would Lira.

14

The mistress smiled again and finally hastened off...concerned she'd offended her guests by her outburst. Of course, it wasn't wise to tell children they possessed outstanding looks. It might swell their heads.

After she'd scurried away, the others exchanged bemused glances. Rupert attempted to suppress laughter. He'd always thought Lira to be surpassingly beautiful, and took it for granted her flower-like face would attract notice wherever they might go. Rupert's own supposed good looks meant less than nothing to him. His only concern was whether his golden eyes would prove visible or not. So far, so good!

The companions maintained a brief silence, allowing themselves to bask in their good fortune. They were content breathing in the sights and sounds of their alien surroundings. Before long, a tasty repast was placed before them. All were mightily hungry and inhaled the victuals with approval. Raja, of course, received his share. Keeping him well fed was a continual challenge, but he seemed to thrive on his meatless fare.

After the meal, they made inquiries of the proprietress. "We hope to purchase horses. Could you direct us to where some may be obtained?" asked Liam.

"Well, the blacksmith always has one or two for sale. But if you require enough for all, I'd suggest the Borgan farm at the end of town. He raises horses, and fine ones they are. Are you planning a long journey?" she inquired pleasantly.

"We are traveling to the east," replied Daniel, "a rather long way, I fear."

"Ah, then I expect you plan to winter here. For the snows will soon set in and the roads will prove impassable."

The companions realized this must be the case, yet took it as a matter of course they could continue on somehow. "I expect we'll take all necessary precautions," commented Liam with deliberate vagueness.

"Well, you could do worse than winter in Zurland," she declared stoutly. "For this is a prosperous and peaceful land thanks to the treaty between our fine sovereign and King Ryker!"

Rupert and his friend attempted to conceal their shock. King Ryker! Their greatest enemy! Was *he* on friendly terms with the rulers of Zurland? It took a moment for Liam to gather himself.

"Do forgive us, but we are strangers here. So your good sovereign and King Ryker are allies?"

"Oh, dear, yes," she went on pleasantly. "I presumed everyone knew that. The peace treaty was signed years since. King Ryker threatened to invade...there were all sorts of skirmishes and scares, let me tell you! But our wise King Kruger and King Ryker came to an agreement. There would be no invasion. Zurland would agree to pay a yearly tribute to King Ryker's treasury, and permit his men to pursue any traitors fleeing here. Or if our own soldiers found such types, we'd return the fugitives back where they belonged.

"Of course, that's hardly been necessary. No one has ever escaped that sad land as far as I recall. So it works out well indeed for us. But I'm astonished you know nothing of this. It's rather ancient history."

Rupert spoke up, his voice little more than a whisper. "Why, you see...we're from the North Country...the Northern Lands. We live quiet-like and somewhat retired. How fortunate indeed you live so peaceably here."

The lady gave Rupert another penetrating glance and then smiled cheerfully. "That's something we're all grateful for, I assure you. And I hope *your* journey will be without incident as well. Yet I again urge you to pass the winter in Zurland. No use inviting danger or trouble."

The comrades exchanged furtive glances. *'Danger or trouble'* indeed! For they'd had no idea that by crossing into Zurland, they'd entered a land filled with King Ryker's allies and spies. And if detected, the companions would once more face danger, capture, or death.

Chapter Three

Rupert and his friends remained mute after hearing such unforeseen and undesirable tidings. Liam paid for the meal, thanking the mistress for the fine repast as they took to their feet. The party moved back towards the vendors and continued their purchases; for food, blankets, and other necessities remained to be secured. For the moment, their funds were adequate to their needs. Liam's father had salvaged a portion of the family treasure when his homeland had been invaded years before. It would now serve to make possible their perilous odyssey to Raja-Sharan.

Soon, their tasks were completed. The companions continued to draw notice, but hoped that once dressed in the newly acquired garb, they might not prove as readily identifiable as outsiders.

They continued on foot towards the edge of town, where crop-filled fields and orchards greeted them. Liam led the way towards a cluster of trees, where they sat, appearing as casual travelers taking a moment's respite. All of them had been eager to speak since hearing the proclamations of their hostess.

"Indeed, I'd feared something like this could be the case. Deprived of word from the outside world and its doings, we've certainly been traveling in the dark," declared Morley with wry exasperation.

Daniel attempted to be philosophical. "Well, obstacles are hardly new to our condition. And things could be worse. At least we're not openly hunted in Zurland. Likely word is not known of Rupert's and my escape from High Tower Prison. Perhaps we may proceed without much ado."

Morley regarded him, a sardonic expression on his rugged features. "Ah, you must have truly slept well yester-night to be so optimistic today! As for me, I cannot help be convinced King Ryker has agents about who may *well* know of our existence."

"Should we not avoid guessing games?" intervened Liam. "Though this news is unwelcome, what are our options?"

Rupert spoke up. "Our path will never be easy. But we are for Raja-Sharan, and the way lies through Zurland. We must remain ever cautious, which is nothing new to our condition."

"Must we again take up disguise?" Lira wanted to know. "Yet how could we, when people here do not cover their faces? Unless Rupert can conjure up some magic spells enabling us to appear as trees or creatures of the forest!" she teased.

"Don't count on that," smiled Rupert in reply. "At any rate, our course is to obtain horses and continue as before."

"You make your usual sense, my boy. That Borgan farm should not be far."

Lira was overjoyed. "May I have a horse of my very own? One that I choose myself?"

"Of course," replied Daniel. "Our journey necessitates we indeed have our very own horses."

With that, the companions again set off. Their minds were yet filled with doubts and questions...but only one obstacle might be crossed at a time.

Within another hour, the horse farm came into view. There was no mistaking it; several dozen magnificent beasts romped and pranced in two corrals. Majesty gave a whinny in greeting, Raja whined in excitement, and Rupert was almost overcome with delight. The most profound of animal lovers, the sight of so many glorious steeds was something new to his experience. He felt a wave of communion with them. He had, since childhood, possessed the ability to exchange thoughts with his animal friends. He immediately intuited these creatures were well-contented, proud, and confident. This made Rupert take a sight-unseen liking to Mister Borgan, who was master here.

The party made the short walk to the farmhouse and barn. Before they could reach it, a large dog charged out to challenge them, followed soon after by a weedy, middle-aged fellow with flowing dark-blond hair. He whistled to his hound, calling him back to his side.

"I hope Morgan, here, didn't startle you. He's friendly enough." And indeed, the yellow guard dog wagged his tail in vigorous greeting. Raja eyed Morgan with curiosity, but would not leave Rupert's side.

"Oh, we could tell well enough he's friendly," exclaimed Rupert. "He's beautiful, as are your horses."

"Why thank you, young sir," replied the man, glancing casually in Rupert's direction. What he saw made him stare.

"We're here to purchase horses, if you please," intervened Liam hastily. He presumed the man fixed his gaze upon Rupert due to his unusual looks, not because the stranger could see something more.

"Why, yes indeed," replied the owner, "I have a large selection, as fine as might be found in all the kingdom. However, it appears you have *one* amongst you that has no need of a mount. For what a magnificent steed that carries your burdens!"

Rupert blanched. He could feel his companions tense as well; for this was the first occasion in which Majesty had drawn attention. He had been told by Rupert that once crossing into Zurland, he need no longer pose as a feeble, tired beast of burden. Freed from that role, the stallion allowed himself to proudly hold his head high. Moreover, the towering steed was an exact twin of King Marco's famous mount, Rico. Though it was highly unlikely any Zurlander would be aware of that particular fact.

"Yes, he is my horse," said Rupert speaking up. "As you observe, he's been unfairly weighed down, and it is time all be mounted and share the load."

The fellow finally tore his gaze from Majesty. "Well, I'm at your service. Borgan is my name. And you are…?"

Liam hastily introduced them only as a family of travelers. After all, if King Ryker's men *were* indeed present in Zurland, the names of the fugitives might well have become known to the populace.

"All my fine specimens are available. You may take your pick, then we'll have tea and discuss a price."

The companions felt inclined to refuse the invitation, but first things first. All but Rupert were immediately absorbed in the quest for the perfect mount. Lira examined a number of steeds, determined to obtain an impressive horse for herself, though hardly hoping for one to rival Majesty.

Before long, she found her ideal - a striking black stallion. She remembered well the tale of how her father had first encountered her mother Vyka, racing across a meadow atop a beautiful ebony steed. This horse could be ridden in tribute to her dazzling mother, who had perished of a fever at seventeen, when Lira was but a year old.

"This is just the one I've dreamed of!" the girl declared. Seeing her gallop outside the corral with her curling flaxen hair waving behind her in the wind, Daniel could not help but be reminded of his wife; the wife he missed and mourned every moment since he'd lost her.

The men had less emotional motives in their search. They merely sought a beast capable of great endurance. For who knew what challenges awaited on the endless trek before them?

It was not long before Morley chose a dappled gray mount; Daniel, one of dark brown with black mane and tail; his father, a white horse with a black diamond-like mark on his forehead. Finding themselves well satisfied, they returned to the side of Borgan.

"These are the mounts we've chosen. We shall pay and be on our way. For sunset will soon be upon us, and we must seek shelter before dark."

"Why, if you have no place to stay the night, you are welcome to be my guests. My wife has passed on, and I'm not much of a cook, but I've yet to let anyone starve." He seemed anxious for them to remain. That very fact made the others uneasy.

"You are most kind, sir," said Daniel. "Sadly, I believe we must be on our way."

Borgan was not easily deterred. "Please do reconsider, for it looks like rain or even snow may begin before dawn," he observed, examining the sky.

"We shall manage," asserted Liam.

Borgan shrugged, and began to calculate the cost of the four fine horses. He declared the total, but Liam instinctively realized it was expected he bargain, and so made a counter-offer. After further negotiations, a fair price was agreed upon.

"What of saddles, bridles, and the like? Surely you don't plan to do without them?" Borgan inquired.

"Oh, but it's ever so much fun to do so!" declared Lira.

"I suppose I could do with saddle and bridle," declared Morley. "It's what I'm used to," he confessed, almost apologetically.

"I believe all us grown-ups will avail ourselves," said Daniel.

"Just follow me to the barn, then," said Borgan, and they did so while Rupert and Lira remained with Raja and the other dog, enjoying a moment where they could romp like ordinary children.

Once they'd entered the dim building, the owner pulled out a selection of accoutrements, and the men chose amongst them. Once more, a price was negotiated. Daniel and Morley took up their purchases and retreated outside. Liam was about to follow suit, when Borgan caught his sleeve.

"Please, do not go, sir. I realize full well I am a stranger, and you have no cause to trust me. But you *can*...please believe me for that. I have but one question. Sir, are you and your kinsmen by chance fugitives from the land of the Golden-Eyed Kings?"

Liam attempted not to react, but he was certain a measure of astonishment had crossed his features.

"Do not be alarmed," continued Borgan. "For you see, that was my own native land long ago. My father served the good King Marco; he was keeper of the royal horses. I, too, helped my father when a child. I shall never forget that great and valiant king, nor his magnificent mount, Rico. Such a horse was never to be seen in all the world - enormous in size, golden-brown, with a dazzling, flowing white mane and tail. *Never* could I hope to see another such like - until this very day. You may pile your beast with baggage, but you cannot disguise from my eyes his true identity. If your boy's horse is not Rico, he is indeed his duplicate!"

Liam still continued mute. This stranger knew horses well enough; that was plain. He *claimed* to have served King Marco as a child, but with informers clearly roaming this land, how could Liam think to trust him?

Finally, words came. "We are wayfarers from the Northern Lands," he declared with some regret. "This horse wandered onto my farm many months since," he added with truth. "Where he came from, I know not."

"Oh, I see," sighed Borgan. "I was hoping you might have news of my beleaguered homeland. I escaped as a child, along with my father, but have obtained no news since; only of a vile treaty between King Ryker and the local liege. So even now, fugitives are not safe here."

"Are you in no danger yourself?" Liam inquired.

"No, for none know that I was not born here. I expect I am safe. But I would be honored to help any that flee the darkness that has contaminated my native land. Truly honored to help!"

Liam looked long and hard into the man's beseeching pale eyes. But something deep down warned against opening his heart. Not now, not yet. Not to this man. With a shrug, he took up saddle and bridle, then headed out of the barn.

"I thank you for your concern. We are simple travelers in need of horses, which you have now provided. That is all we require."

Liam returned to his companions, nodding tersely. They understood something was amiss, and hastened to depart. But for the first time on their entire journey, their party was not setting off on foot. They at last possessed steeds of stamina and beauty, and with an avid anticipation climbed atop their new mounts.

Yet as the party galloped off, they were filled with consternation, comprehending the seemingly affable horse trader might represent an ominous threat to them all.

Chapter Four

The comrades traveled along the road, seeming to fly now they were on horseback. However, when darkness approached, their usual sense of caution prevailed, and they sought a suitable resting place. The evening air had a distinct chill, and they hoped to discover a roadside shelter. Yet it soon became apparent they would sleep once again in the open.

An inviting grove of trees presented itself, and it was not long before they had built a sturdy fire, looked after the horses' needs, and hungered for their own repast. Soon bread and cheese were in their hands, along with welcome cups of steaming tea laced with honey.

"I hope you'll see fit to recount what passed between yourself and that horse trader," remarked Morley. "For you've seemed distinctly uneasy ever since."

"Indeed, I will hold back nothing. The man revealed he had fled from our homeland when a child, and claimed his father had been caretaker of the royal stables. He declared amazement that Majesty seemed the very twin of King Marco's mount, Rico. He begged to know if we were fugitives, and whether he might render assistance."

"By heaven, that must have given you a jolt!" cried Liam's son. "We learn that King Ryker has spies throughout Zurland, and now one of the first people we encounter inquires if we are fugitives! What are we to make of this?"

"He *could* simply be telling the truth," ventured Morley. "After all, how would he have recognized Majesty otherwise?"

"That *is* possible, I suppose,' said Liam. "But I confess to having been taken quite off guard. It required an instantaneous decision whether to trust him."

"Besides which, in exactly what way could he have proven helpful?" wondered Morley. "We possess a very adequate map. He could hardly keep the snow from falling, or prevent other obstacles which might lie in our path. I think it better to be discreet and keep our counsel."

"There's one way he might have come to our aid," Daniel pointed out. "He could tell us who might prove trustworthy hereabouts. Or what towns are likely filled with Ryker's agents. But of course, only if Borgan was an honest fellow."

Liam turned to Rupert, who had been uncharacteristically silent. "Well, my dear boy, what say you? What were *your* impressions of the fellow? Did I do well in remaining closed-mouthed?"

They all turned to Rupert. His head had been down for the last few moments. When he looked up, he seemed pale and troubled. "I cannot say," he whispered.

Morley chuckled. "Indeed, this is a remarkable event...our Rupert run out of words?" But the others did not take up the jest when they discerned Rupert's clouded expression.

"Rupert, are you quite well?" inquired Lira. "You've hardly eaten a bite."

Rupert sighed heavily. "I confess I do not at all feel myself. It is true I lack appetite, but that is of little matter. The fact is...you see...well, it's difficult to describe...but I seem engulfed in silence."

They stared in puzzlement. ""My dear boy, what can you mean?" asked Liam with a frown.

"You asked what I thought of the horse trader. I would, as a rule, make ready answer, for I am habitually feeling – 'communication'...or perhaps 'inspiration' is more accurate - from what source I cannot say. Something from within me or without. It speaks with clarity and truth, as we have seen."

Rupert regarded his friends, his huge, black-lashed golden eyes beginning to brim with tears. "But at this moment, I feel nothing...hear nothing. It is as if I awoke to find myself deaf. I cannot explain what has occurred, only that it *has!* I confess to feeling unnerved and abandoned - that something I have done has caused this to occur."

Liam and the others moved toward their prince. Daniel put a comforting arm about Rupert's shoulder and spoke. "Why, Rupert, I believe you are alarming yourself for no good reason. One cannot expect *always* to feel this guidance you speak of. As for you having done wrong, why, no one could be braver or more steadfast!"

"Of course, my father speaks true. You are most noble and resourceful, with or without your special gifts. So never fear. Besides, I'm sure they'll come back. You're probably just tired, as we all are."

"Lira is correct, as is my son. But tell me, do you feel quite well?"

Rupert looked up, thoughtful. "I *do* find myself with an aching head. It began earlier this day." His expression turned hopeful. "Do you suppose *this* could be the explanation?"

"To tell the truth, *my* poor head has been aching for some time now," consoled Morley with some humor. "So you're not alone. Wonder if we ate something strange at our noon meal?"

Liam smiled. "Ah-ha! I do believe there exists a very simple solution to our puzzle. For I, too, have a suffering head. And I venture that Lira and Daniel may as well?" He looked to them for confirmation, which they provided.

"Why, it's merely the mountains! I had forgotten that when one travels to higher altitudes, a headache often follows. It is quite natural, and nothing to cause alarm. Should we proceed slowly the next few days, allowing us to become habituated to the unaccustomed surroundings, I believe all shall be well."

Rupert felt a blaze of optimism. "Oh, do you really think that is the cause?"

Morley spoke up. "Indeed, it seems reasonable, Rupert. Your head aches…and your thoughts and intuitions run about in that remarkable noggin of yours. So why shouldn't a headache interfere?"

"Rupert," inquired Lira with a flash of inspiration. "Can you still speak to the animals with your thoughts?" He turned to her and smiled faintly.

"I shall endeavor to try." Rupert turned to Raja, who was, as usual, beside him. The young prince attempted to silently communicate with the mastiff pup, and almost instantly Raja responded by leaping up and dashing to where the horses were tethered. Rupert knew a measure of relief. "I believe that gift is yet intact," he enthused.

"There, you see!" smiled Lira. "Nothing to worry about. It's just a silly head pain. We shall all recover in a few days, right Grandfather Liam?"

"I believe so." All relied upon Rupert's 'messages' - for it seemed a sign of his kingship; that powerful forces were looking after him until the day he claimed his throne. Liam refused to believe those forces would abandon Rupert, any more than the boy's golden eyes might suddenly alter their color.

"Let us examine the map once again," suggested Daniel. "Perhaps we should take the path least challenging in the thin mountain air."

In a moment, the document was spread before them. It became apparent their most direct route through Zurland was the most mountainous. They could hardly avoid the towering peaks altogether, but the path which led southeast looked somewhat less daunting.

"What say you, Rupert?" inquired Morley. "Should the swiftest route be ours, or the less intimidating one?" But this time, Rupert did not have a ready reply.

"I can hardly say with certainty," he sighed. "For it is utterly strange not to receive guidance. How can I know what is correct?"

"Well, dear boy, you've always insisted we proceed to Raja-Sharan with utmost haste. We shall take up the more challenging path, that being the most direct."

That settled the matter, and soon they lay down to sleep. But Rupert felt a chill of apprehension, convinced something was greatly amiss. And the break of dawn would prove this to be only too true.

Chapter Five

Rupert's companions knew something was awry the moment their eyes opened. Firstly, it was well past the dawn, their usual hour of arising. Why, it must be near noon! Morley was the first to force himself awake, his head throbbing even more than the previous day. Noting the glaring sun nearly overhead, he became instantly alarmed. With difficulty, he raised himself to a sitting position, his sense of dread mounting. His companions were only just now beginning to stir. As he looked about, what sent a dart of fear through him was that Raja lay only a few feet away; Raja, who never willingly left Rupert's side. Yet Rupert was nowhere to be seen.

A dazed Morley staggered to his feet, bleary green eyes sweeping the scene. Majesty and the other horses were still tethered, eliminating the possibility that Rupert had gone for his habitual morning gallop. Besides, Morley knew, the pup always accompanied his master on those pre-dawn jaunts. It was just as those thoughts filled his head that Raja, as if sensing his human companion's alarm, suddenly awoke, leapt to his feet, and commenced racing in circles. The young hound was clearly unsettled, finding Rupert nowhere to be seen.

Raja began to howl, a strange, eerie echo that sent a chill of terror through Morley. And the wail brought the others, who had been fighting what seemed to be a heavy weight about their own heads, at last to their feet.

"What is wrong with Raja?" Lira cried. The hound continued to fly about, in ever widening circles, sniffing the air and earth, desperately seeking his young master's scent.

"Rupert is gone," announced Morley, buckling on his sword.

"Let us not leap to hasty conclusions," cautioned Daniel, though reaching for his own favored weapon, the bow and arrow, as he spoke. "Perhaps he has merely gone for a walk to clear his head. My own aches abominably, far worse than before."

"He would never have done so without Raja," protested Lira. "And look, Majesty is frantic as well!" For Rupert's powerful stallion was attempting to tear loose from his tether while snorting wildly and pawing the ground.

"You're right, Lira," acknowledged Liam, stricken and pale. "And why have we all slept half the day away? Something is amiss indeed." With that, he grabbed up his own sword. "Let us spread out and search. If he wandered off, he would leave tracks - as would anyone who might have taken him."

Lira burst into tears. "But, see Raja! He should be able to pick up Rupert's scent, yet he cannot discover it!"

"His senses must have been affected as Rupert's were last night; though I fear altitude cannot be the cause."

The others agreed with the dark assessment. For the pup had no inkling where Rupert had gone; and his wails of distress tore at their hearts. And Majesty, now let loose, was apparently stymied as well.

"We have no option but to search as best we can," Morley advised with fierce eyes. "Spread out in a circle and see what we may discover. For *some* clue must be found."

Heeding Morley's words, they began as methodically as possible. Raja continued his own investigation, but the comrades could not but observe he was as unsuccessful as they. Nonetheless, Rupert's friends continued fanning out farther and farther from their campsite. At length, dusk began to set in. It would be futile to continue once darkness fell.

They finally regrouped where they had awoken that morning; which now seemed a century ago. Time appeared to be frozen in place, so distressed were they. The men exchanged looks of near panic, attempting to keep their most dire thoughts from Lira. But needless to say, she shared their fears.

"We *must* keep searching, though night is falling," she cried. "Why, Rupert might be injured. And there are wolves that roam the hills at night. We *cannot* wait until dawn!"

Daniel took his daughter in his arms and attempted to console her. But there was no consolation to be found. Their Rupert, their boy-king, had vanished. "Come, darling, if anyone can be counted upon to be strong and resourceful, it's Rupert. We must believe we will soon find him, or he'll make his way back to us. We must by no means lose heart."

Liam and Morley added their own words of comfort, but the girl would not be cheered any more than Raja, who had run himself ragged searching for his master's scent.

"I still cannot comprehend what could have happened," insisted a stricken Morley. "How could he disappear without a trace? He would have either walked off or been taken by someone on horseback. A trail *must* have been left! How is it that we discern no sign of it? It is as if Rupert vanished into thin air!"

The moment Morley voiced those words it was as if a bolt of lightning struck the companions. Of course! That is exactly what must have occurred!

"By heaven, that is it!" exclaimed Liam. "How strange the thought did not present itself sooner. It demonstrates how far we have allowed frenzy to blur our vision. For we know only too well 'disappearing into thin air' is indeed a possibility."

With that, they recalled the mysterious lady from the Sunday market-day who had presented Rupert a basket containing the puppy Raja and King Marco's ruby ring. She had indeed 'dematerialized' before their disbelieving eyes; as did the three sinister beauties that had appeared during a savage storm. They somehow discovered the concealed cave where the companions had taken shelter, casting a spell over the grown men, though leaving Lira and Rupert unaffected. The children had saved the day when Rupert succeeded in ordering them off. The ladies then vanished before the astounded companions.

"At least, *now* we can begin to guess what has happened," said Morley. "Yet if Rupert was indeed abducted in this manner, how can we possibly reclaim him?"

When Lira spoke up, with something like hope in her voice, the others turned to her instantly.

"Wait! We have forgotten we have a witness to all that took place. For while we were caused to sleep, the horses appear to have been unaffected. Perhaps Majesty can tell us what transpired."

The men took heart. Daniel turned to his insightful daughter. "Lira, can you communicate with Majesty? I fear none of us grownups have that capacity."

"Oh yes! I could do it even before Rupert taught me how to be even better at it. Come, let us not waste a single minute!" With that, she ran to Majesty's side. The powerful steed had been agitated and restless all this day, joining in the search. Now he grew calm, as if comprehending his mission.

She approached and he lowered his head, enabling Lira to rest her forehead upon his. The girl closed her eyes as the men held their breath and was not long in obtaining the information desired.

"We were right, for Rupert *was* caused to disappear, as we feared. A single, cloaked figure came as we slept, took up Rupert in her arms, and promptly vanished."

"You say *'her'* arms. Are you certain it was a woman?" demanded Morley.

"That is my impression. That is what Majesty believes."

The men exchanged looks. "Can Majesty lead us to Rupert? Does he know where our boy has been secreted?"

"He showed me we will find him near water. He is not far. But I don't believe Majesty knows how to take us there. Rupert has been hidden away and neither Majesty nor Raja would be able to pick up his scent."

"That news is better than nothing," said her grandfather with a grimace. "We can do no more this night. We renew our search with the dawn. And trust we will recover our prince before the sun again sets upon us."

Having no alternative, they attempted to force down some nourishment while warming their chilled bodies by the fire, hoping against hope Rupert might return under his own power. But when darkness brought with it a heavy snowfall, their fears for the morrow grew. Raja, too, refused to be comforted.

Therefore, it was indeed fortunate they could have no way of knowing it would be a matter of tortured days, rather than hours, before the searchers caught sight of their vanished prince once more.

Chapter Six

Rupert felt suffocated by an enormous weight... as if buried deep underground. He struggled to move, but that seemed an impossible task. Neither could he open his eyes. He assumed he must be sleeping, but it was as if he were *drowned* in sleep.

He could see nothing, but he could hear – recognizing that a flowing stream was beside him. It was a comforting sound, familiar as the bird calls also penetrating his awareness. But where were his friends?

After a time of struggling for breath, he believed he might just be able to open his eyes after all. But before Rupert began the attempt, he grew aware of a very strange sound - as if he was now surrounded by a horde of bees. However, the buzzing was far more pronounced than he'd ever heard before. He gradually deduced it was not a hive after all, but rather human voices! And then Rupert comprehended someone was shaking him and calling out words. At last the fog cleared. His companions were calling his name.

It took a long moment for the young sovereign to acknowledge the presence of his friends, for the weight that was glued to his eyes was slow to lift. But at last he found himself staring into the face of Liam, who was cradling him in his arms. Rupert looked about with difficulty to see that Lira, Morley, Daniel, Raja, and Majesty were gathered round as well.

"Rupert, my dearest boy, are you unharmed? Can you speak?" demanded Liam in a hoarse whisper. Rupert sought strength to respond.

"I believe I am quite well, though very tired and thirsty," he managed to utter. His own voice was strange to his ears. But instantly, water was produced and he partook, slowly at first, then more greedily.

"Wait, you must not drink so quickly," cautioned Daniel. "But have you had nothing all these four days?"

Rupert regarded his friends in amazement. "*Four days!?* How is that possible?"

"First things first," cautioned Liam in his most soothing tones. "Are you able to stand? To travel? For snow is setting in once more, and we'd best seek shelter."

It was only then that Rupert was able to look about and note that a thick snowfall did indeed cover the ground. No wonder his limbs felt heavy and numb. "I think I shall be able to move. However, might I have a cup of tea? I am frozen to the bone."

"Let us build a fire at once," said Morley. "We could all use tea and nourishment before we set off. Rupert, have you eaten anything these many days?"

Rupert gave them a bewildered look. "I truly cannot recall," he admitted. The others exchanged troubled glances. Lira spoke after giving her friend a fierce hug.

"What *do* you remember? For we imagined the worst and were filled with fear every minute!"

Rupert's head was still pounding, but his strength was slowly returning. "I recollect we had camped and eaten dinner. I was alarmed I could not feel the voice that often guides me. Grandfather Liam said it might be due to the altitude. After that - nothing. Yet, you say that was *four days past!* How can that be so?"

"Do calm yourself, my boy," urged Liam. "There are many mysteries we have yet to unravel. Surely, the important thing is we are reunited. Now come, eat and drink something."

Very soon, tea and porridge were prepared, and they all partook and warmed themselves before the sputtering fire. Raja curled his body next to a shivering Rupert. Afterwards, Rupert changed into dry clothing, and these acts removed a measure of the chill from his body. It was clear the air promised more snow.

"We should seek indoor shelter this day. Rupert must recover his strength. I do believe, from the manner in which he downed his porridge, he has likely not eaten since his disappearance," observed Morley.

All agreed, and now that Rupert was with them, they could consult the map found to be still in his pocket. It proved a vast relief; for they feared whoever took their prince might have been after that document as well. They were reminded of the incident of the three mysterious beauties. They had appeared in their cave the moment the map had been discovered, hidden in a book from Rupert's home…but one which he had no memory of ever seeing before. Obviously, the parchment was of great value to others besides themselves.

After perusing it, they discovered a town was not a dozen miles distant. They should reach it before dark with any luck.

"But would it be wise?" Rupert wished to know. "Since we know not whom to trust, should we not endeavor to stay out of sight?"

"Yes, true enough," replied Daniel. "Yet under the circumstances, we should spend at least one night indoors. For you are deathly pale and not yourself."

"We have not slept even one night under a roof since that long ago day we stayed at Rupert's cottage!" Lira looked wistful, and the others smiled in fond memory of that memorable night Rupert showed them his royal treasure and revealed the astonishing secret of his golden-eyed heritage.

With haste, they set off. Rupert was barely able to sit astride Majesty, but insisted upon doing so. It was a fine thing to be back with his cherished stallion again.

Though their journey was not overly difficult, they traveled slowly for Rupert's sake, pausing once again to partake of food and tea before he was fit to continue. Yet they were cheered to see color begin to creep into his cheeks, and the sparkle to his golden eyes.

It was just before sunset that they reached the town of Korenth. The place was in no way imposing, hardly larger than a village, but the sight of an inn was welcome. After inquiries, it was found that a room adequate in size was to be had, and the mistress made no demur over Raja sharing the accommodations. They saw to their horses, and soon settled into a rustic chamber, featuring several large beds stuffed with straw. A rickety table, spindly wooden chairs, and an adequate fireplace completed the simple space, but it seemed wonderfully luxurious to the weary travelers. It was reasonably warm and dry, and they would dream of nothing more.

There was a dining room downstairs, but they hoped to avoid the gaze of strangers. The mistress agreed to serve dinner in their quarters, and soon a repast of hot vegetable soup, freshly baked dark bread, cheese, and butter was spread before them, along with cups of sweet tea and fresh milk. Lira and Rupert managed to keep out of her view and so attracted no notice from the lady. After serving the meal, she left her guests to themselves.

They ate with gusto, but Rupert most of all. It seemed clear he had gone hungry during his mysterious absence. The others could hardly fathom what had taken place in the interim. Since the boy claimed to have no memory of what had occurred, it seemed pointless to question him further; at least, for the moment. But they burned with curiosity - as well as the *necessity* of learning what had transpired. For in this case, ignorance might represent tremendous peril.

After devouring his fill, Rupert moved before the fire with Lira and Raja. He was still debilitated by his ordeal, and quickly fell sound asleep. Lira followed, as the girl had hardly rested in recent days. Indeed, all his companions were nearly as weary as their prince. Yet while the young ones slept, their elders were greatly troubled. They removed to the far corner of the room, conversing in whispers.

"It is a blessing beyond measure to have Rupert back with us," began Liam, "though it is also in some manner disturbing."

"I can only agree," said Morley. "It is the best possible news for us, and the worst. For we have no idea who abducted Rupert - or for what purpose. Or for that matter, what might have been done to him while captive."

"Yes, it troubles me also," Daniel admitted. "Perhaps he has been thoroughly interrogated. Perhaps he has revealed the secret of his kingship...or our intended journey to Raja-Sharan. We could be in greater danger than before."

"Indeed," agreed Liam. "I believe Rupert is honest in his claim of remembering nothing. Obviously, *something* extraordinary has occurred. I can hardly believe someone would take the boy, only to merely observe him in his unnatural sleep! Likely there was a sinister motive."

"True, unless she only desired to be with him?" ventured Daniel. "As we can see, no harm has been done. If the abductor was our foe, Rupert would have been totally at her mercy. The boy could have been tortured, killed outright. Yet we were allowed to recover him."

"That's undeniable," agreed Liam. "But who would have taken him for no apparent purpose?"

Morley shook his head, as if denying in advance the words he was to say. "Perhaps a loved one? A parent? Such a one might merely wish to spend time in his presence? Or is that too absurd a suggestion?"

"The mysterious lady with the basket at the village market?" ventured Daniel. "We know not who his mother may be…*could* it be that lady? Or perhaps his mysterious grandparents? We cannot claim to know who took Rupert, or what the objective might have been. Or even whether something was done to the boy… something that might affect his judgment. We rely on his clarity. If we can no longer do so, what course are we to take?"

The companions regarded each other grimly; for indeed Rupert was their liege, and his intuition had guided them through countless hazardous moments. If this unconditional trust was called into question, how were they to proceed?

"There must be some method to determine if Rupert's judgment is made unreliable," sighed Morley. "Perhaps time will tell. For now, we can only take note of what changes we observe. And let us not forget that whatever did occur, it is in no way Rupert's fault. So let us leap to no faulty conclusions. Surely, the truth will reveal itself before long."

Liam and Daniel could only reluctantly concur. For they could in no way determine whether their young king had been compromised. They could only hope this would not prove to be so, that Rupert had somehow remained unscathed, and still worthy of their unblemished trust. For upon this, all their fortunes would depend.

Chapter Seven

Liam awoke to the sound of pelting rain and a crackling fire. He and his son had somehow slept in...a most unusual occurrence. However, such a development was not to be unexpected, considering the fatigue caused by the past hellish days.

Liam grew aware of another sound greeting his ears; a whispered conversation between Rupert, Lira, and Morley. He sought to catch the gist of their talk, but could only hear muffled words accompanied by giggles from Lira.

In another moment, Daniel was also stretching awake. He sat up on the straw-stuffed pallet shared with his father – a great contrast to the cold, hard ground they'd endured of late. It had been so very long since he'd slept under a secure roof, he reflected. For nearly six years had passed since he'd been dragged away into the army to serve a despised usurper. That had occurred only a few days after the tragic death of his wife. Following that came the horrific daily struggle for survival, imprisonment after finally deserting, leading to a life as a fugitive after being rescued from a sentence of death. No wonder a few hours on a soft bed seemed a veritable paradise to Daniel.

Father and son sat up, and the hushed conversation among their three companions came to an abrupt halt. Lira, Rupert, and Morley glanced in their direction with seemingly casual smiles; but clearly, something was afoot. In a moment, the girl was at their side.

"Good morrow to you both," she exclaimed prettily. "I do hope you had a fine rest. Rupert and I did…so well that we spent the entire night by the fire, and never lay in the bed at all." She beamed at them innocently, but both men comprehended she was plotting mischief.

"Why, thank you for inquiring, my sweet daughter," Daniel replied. "Yes, it's clear you'll find our condition much improved since yesterday. I, for one, have no complaints."

Rupert sat himself down on their bed as well. "Speaking of such, may we not perhaps spend one more night under this roof? I confess to feeling a bit out of sorts, owing to my recent episode."

The Golden-Eyed Prince spoke with all the sincerity he could muster, but could not outwit Daniel or his father. The children were up to something! Yet surely, it was true enough that not only Rupert, but all might benefit from a chance to recover from their recent harsh ordeal.

"Well, I suppose that could be arranged. However, did you not wish to proceed rapidly on our way, Rupert?" Liam inquired.

Rupert squirmed at that. "Well, yes, but that was yester-night. Since I find myself still fatigued this morning, and I sense poor Raja is too, I believe one more day here is not a poor idea." He turned meaningfully to Morley.

"Why, yes, one more day should do the trick, and we can be off at sunrise."

Daniel and his father were more convinced than ever that something was brewing between the children and Morley, but agreed in principal. And so they gave consent, and the children jumped to their feet.

"We must check on the welfare of Majesty and the other horses," proclaimed Rupert. "Morley, do come with us, in case of danger."

Liam nodded sagely. "Yes, do go along Morley, and keep them out of trouble. Daniel and I will see to preparations for the morrow."

Almost before the words left his mouth, the trio, accompanied by Raja, was out the door, and their footfalls heard clattering down the stairs. Daniel turned to his father with merry eyes.

"Well, our friends are up to something. No doubt, we will be the wiser before this day is out."

"Very likely," replied his father. He regarded Daniel as his blue eyes suddenly misted. Their bond was extraordinary, but so much had remained unsaid. There had not been a private moment to discuss the horrors of the past years - years of separation and despair, hope and terror. From the moment Liam had broken his son and Rupert out of High Tower Prison, they had been forever on the run, with death and danger at their heels.

Thus, Liam and Daniel took advantage of these stolen moments to open their hearts. For the first time, Daniel recounted what he had endured as a slave of King Ryker, for a slave is what the soldiers truly were. No opportunity for escape, except under penalty of death, with daily horrors and agonies, kill-or-be-killed their only reality. Added to this was the torture of wondering if his cherished father and daughter were alive and well, had become fugitives from an oppressive regime, or had perished, as had his beloved bride, Vyka.

In his turn, Liam revealed what he and Lira had endured in Daniel's absence. They had fared better than most, having enough to eat, living in comparative safety on their isolated farm. But no one was *truly* safe dwelling in King Ryker's domain; security and peace being unknown blessings. And most of all, the unrelenting anguish over Daniel's fate. For Liam had feared they would never meet again; that Lira had indeed lost both her parents.

After opening their hearts, more than a few tears being shed, father and son found comfort in at last sharing their innermost thoughts, and their bond was even more perfect than before.

So deep had been their converse, they at first did not realize the others had been long absent. This fact might have caused concern, had they not then heard footfalls outside their chamber, followed by hushed words and muffled laughter. The door flew open, and Lira, Rupert, Morley, and Raja burst inside.

"Surprise!" they exclaimed. "And a very happy birthday to you both!" The four entered, Rupert and Morley carrying a number of parcels, while Lira conveyed a very large chocolate cake gingerly in her arms.

Father and son exchanged glances of bemused delight. They had entirely forgotten this was indeed the anniversary date of their birth - or at least, very close to it.

"Do forgive us, for we are several days tardy in remembering your day, Grandfather Liam. And we are one day early for yours, Daniel. However, with the recent gaps in my memory, it is fortunate we did not miss the commemoration entirely!" exclaimed Rupert. For Liam's true birth date was the eighteenth day of the tenth month, and Daniel's was upon the twenty-first day. This was the twentieth of the month. However, neither man was likely to take offence.

"Job well done, remembering at all," pronounced Liam. "Many thanks!" And with that, Lira put the cake carefully down upon the table, and ran to claim hugs from her father and grandfather. Rupert soon followed, along with Morley. Raja joined into the fray with excited leaps and barks.

Soon, they were seated around the wobbly table, partaking of the sweet concoction. "I bespoke to the mistress this morning, when we recalled the date, and a luncheon feast is soon to follow. But on birthdays, cake first, as we did on my day," explained Rupert with a grin.

And they hungrily partook of the chocolate treat, the most delicious ever tasted by the young prince. It was only the second time he had been privileged to do so, but he was enchanted for life. All consumed it with gusto, for none had eaten breakfast, and it was now nearing noon.

"Of course, we have something more as well," sang out Lira. "Morley accompanied us to the marketplace so we might choose in secret." With sudden shyness, she produced two packages. She handed the first to her father. He felt his eyes mist as he took it from her hands. Slowly, he unwrapped it. A smile of delight spread across his fine features.

She had presented him with a wooden flute, simply but handsomely carved. She looked up at her father with eager anticipation.

"Why, it's a perfect gift, sweetheart," said Daniel with sincerity. For he had, in days of old, delighted in playing the instrument. It had been many years, so many dark years, since he had held one in his hands.

Raising it to his lips, he began, a bit soberly at first, but within a moment, he commenced a merry tune. Lira was enchanted. Rupert and Morley as well were delighted at Daniel's abilities.

"Now, I believe we shall find our nights by the campfire more charming than before. And Daniel's tunes should keep dangerous wildlife at bay!" predicted Morley. They all broke into laughter at his remark.

Next, Lira presented her grandfather with a book of poems. After thanking her with all his heart, he regarded the girl in puzzlement. Perhaps she had forgotten that his failing eyesight no longer permitted him to read. However, those fears were allayed, for Rupert immediately handed Liam his own gift.

"This is something I meant to present you long ago. As you may recall, those plans were rudely interrupted," exclaimed Rupert as he reached into his pocket and drew out a large magnifying glass.

Liam took the offering with some joy as well as pain. For they only too well recollected the wretched night when soldiers of King Ryker had invaded his farm and dragged Rupert off to prison, on the false charge of stealing a similar object from the village market. Now at last, the gift from Rupert's heart could be presented to his adopted grandfather...who relished reading as much as Rupert himself. The two embraced.

"Thank you, dearest boy! This will truly bring more pleasure than you can imagine." They exchanged a look that spoke of the love and respect they held, each for the other.

"No solemn words," cautioned Morley, "for Lira and Rupert will have to go far to match my offering." That said, he presented his two friends with identical pairs of knit gloves, made extra thick to protect against the harsh conditions soon to be upon them. Daniel and Liam thanked their friend for the practical gift. "Very practical, indeed," agreed Morley. "For if each of you loses a glove, you'll still have a pair between you!"

This statement struck Rupert as very amusing, and his laughter inspired the others to join in

And then, Rupert produced a gift for his new brother Daniel, a ring he had found in the marketplace.

It appeared to be an antique, of silver with a small topaz in its center.

"I believe I have a ring from King Marco that should, by rights, be yours. You and your father insisted I keep it, so I'll give you this in its stead."

Greatly moved, Daniel thanked his prince. He placed it on his finger, and it fit very well. He swore to never once remove it until the day Rupert sat upon his throne as a true Golden-Eyed King.

"And now, there remains one more gift to be given," announced Liam, reaching for his backpack and slowly pulling out a crocheted scarf of finest wool, long and dark-brown in color, with a fringe of black silk hanging from either end. Father handed it to son, and Daniel took it up.

"This is something I have waited many long years to bestow, my boy. For it was made by your dear mother. She knitted it all the while she carried you in her body. And after you were born, when she became ill, she made me promise to give it you on your twenty-fifth birthday, and never before. It was a difficult vow to keep, but I have succeeded, and here it is now; a gift of your mother's love for you."

All were touched as Daniel held the wonderfully made object to his lips and kissed it. He felt connected as never before to the mother he had never known. The companions stared in wonder for a moment.

"I do not know why she would wish to wait until this day," Daniel whispered. "But I am very grateful to have it now."

Suddenly Lira gave a gasp, and all heads turned to her. "Why, I do believe I know *why*....though the reason amazes. Do not you see the color of the scarf - deep brown with black trim? It would have held no special meaning until just these past days. Father, think of the color of your new horse!"

They turned to one another in some surprise. It was true, the sturdy steed Daniel had chosen was deep brown in color with a long mane and tail of jet black... exactly the colors chosen by his mother twenty-five years before. *Might* it be happenstance? But why would she have instructed him to wait until this very day to present it to her son?

"This is all mysterious, indeed," observed Rupert. "I myself no longer believe in mere 'coincidence'. Life is always filled with much that defies our poor logic. Perhaps we should take this as a talisman - that Daniel's mother is somehow giving her blessing."

"Let us hope you speak true, Rupert," whispered Liam, mystified and moved.

Silently, Daniel wrapped the long scarf about his neck. It set off his dark blond hair, blazing blue eyes, and aristocratic features to perfection. "You look handsome as a prince!" declared his bedazzled daughter.

The solemn mood was interrupted by the mistress of the inn, bustling forth with a luncheon feast. The comrades found they had appetite still, though the chocolate cake had been devoured. They continued the double celebration with open hearts and great appreciation of their fellowship and good fortune – though knowing untold obstacles undoubtedly loomed before them. Moreover, the men could by no means forget the conundrum of Rupert's absence, as yet unexplained. Yet for the moment, they would partake of joy when they could find it.

Chapter Eight

They were off as soon as dawn broke, eager to make up for the time lost due to Rupert's disappearance. Luck was with them, for the rain of the previous day had washed away recent snows. The resulting mud presented no obstacle, for they were well mounted, and conditions which would have proved greatly disagreeable were they on foot, hardly posed a challenge to their trustworthy steeds.

The companions were exhilarated to proceed so effortlessly after weary months of difficult travel. Rupert felt as if he were indeed flying! Majesty took to the task of carrying his young prince with joy, and the two were united in spirit. Although Majesty could have easily continued without pause, his master knew the others were unequal to such a pace, and so called for rest at reasonable intervals. Perhaps Raja especially welcomed it, as he was now required to keep up with the trotting horses. Yet he proved capable of that, as he had so many other challenges.

The party determined to avoid villages unless strictly required. Having consulted their precious map and finding Zurland was not large, they might expect to reach the eastern border within two weeks' time if the weather continued to favor them. However, one heavy snowfall could disrupt their plans drastically.

They halted each evening just before sunset. The nights were cold. But all were now equipped with blankets and warm clothing, and they could build a hearty fire and prepare warm food. The only cause for concern was the ever-looming possibility that Rupert would be torn from them again. If he could be carried off by someone having the ability to disappear, they would be indeed powerless to prevent it.

Liam had decreed the men take turns remaining awake through the night. Rupert vetoed this tactic. After all, he pointed out, they all required sleep at day's end... and since none could fight against unseen forces, it was fruitless to try. But Lira was not convinced.

"Surely, there is *something* we can do. What if we bind you together with one of us? At least you wouldn't vanish alone!" She seemed delighted with the idea.

The others exchanged bemused glances. Perhaps it *was* a possibility! Yet Rupert only smiled at his enchanting friend.

"I thank you for the stratagem, Lira, but don't believe it very practical. If someone can appear and disappear at will, we must assume she could leave behind anyone she wished."

"We cannot know that," observed Morley. "Why not give it a go? What have we to lose? I'll volunteer my services for a start."

After further discussion, it was eventually agreed upon, but the next morning, Rupert again voiced objection. "Yes, it's true I did not vanish in the night, but I don't fancy spending future evenings lashed to a companion. Do not fear. After all, whoever took me did me no lasting harm. So let us reject constant apprehension over what may or may not occur."

The others concurred only in part, but the plan was workable only if Rupert agreed. The comrades must hope that Raja would give alarm if Rupert were again in danger. However, they desired to believe that whatever happened to Rupert was now in the past.

Their evenings were spent pleasantly enough, studying the language of Raja-Sharan, (which was known as *Veshti,*) listening to Daniel play upon his flute, or in lively conversation. Each morning they arose before dawn and were on their way at first light. They were making good progress, for the mountain paths had dried and hardened, and no new snow had fallen. There proved no necessity for pausing at the scattered villages they passed. Encountering no unforeseen obstacles, the comrades found themselves no more than three days' travel from the border marking Zurland from neighboring Martan.

Sadly, this happy circumstance was not to continue. For the very next evening, well after midnight,

Morley awoke with a jolt, as if aroused from a dreadful dream. Briefly, confusion clouded his thoughts, but he instinctively leapt to his feet while reaching for his sword.

A cold, starry sky shimmered above, and his companions slept peacefully under piles of blankets. But fear swept through him. Morley turned to his left, to where Rupert should be, and found only an empty mound of covers. He pulled them back to be certain. The Golden-Eyed Prince was gone. Fortunately, he observed another fact that made him take heart; Raja was also among the missing. He could not suppose the mysterious lady who had previously taken the lad would have troubled to take his dog. Perhaps Rupert had left under his own power.

Morley wasted no time in alerting his comrades, who, in turn, grew instantly alarmed. Then, when Morley pointed out that Raja was with his master, all were slightly reassured.

"Raja will protect Rupert," Daniel predicted, comforting his stricken daughter. "Perhaps we can pick up their tracks. Let us light torches at once."

They did so, wondering aloud if Rupert did indeed wander off on his own, and if so, why? They remembered to consult Majesty. With Lira's help, Rupert's stallion was able to confirm their theory - the boy and his pup had proceeded under their own power. Majesty, let free from his tether, guided the way. Rupert's friends were, though not without difficulty, able to discern their trail by torchlight. But it might have been hard going without the stallion's senses to aid them.

The search continued for the better part of an hour, when abruptly Majesty drew to a halt, ears pinned back. The men readied their weapons. The steed was giving warning; they could feel it clearly.

Motioning for Majesty to remain, the men proceeded forward. They'd signaled Lira to stay back as well, but she stubbornly shook her head, and there was no time for argument. She walked a few feet behind the men, and held her breath. They were without doubt nearing Rupert and Raja. But why did Raja not bark to alert them?

They proceeded cautiously, yet complete silence was impossible. Morley motioned he would go on alone, but after no more than a few hasty yards he came to a halt, and the others arrived at his side. They'd reached a small clearing, and the rescuers saw and smelled a fire burning.

The scene that greeted them made their hearts stand still. Rupert was with Raja, but they were not alone. There was also a man; a tall stranger, his back to the companions. Rupert was on his feet, struggling to move away, but his arm was held in the intruder's firm grip. Rupert tugged yet again, but was powerless to break free. Mystifyingly, Raja did nothing to protect his master from this menacing fellow.

Moving as one, Liam, Daniel, and Morley strode forward, their weapons drawn. Daniel, with his bow and arrow pointed at the stranger's back, spoke up first.

"Unhand the boy this instant!"

Slowly, the man turned, revealing his face for the first time, while maintaining his harsh grip on Rupert's arm.

Eerily, the lad did not acknowledge his friends. Instead, he continued mute, as if unaware of their presence.

"So, you must be the boy's family. Glad I am that you're here and high time too! But I'll trouble you to lower your voice, or you'll run the risk of awakening him. That would be far from advisable."

He spoke in a calm, reasonable, even friendly tone. There was also a hint of amusement in his voice. He appeared older than Daniel or Morley, but certainly younger than Liam. The stranger's strapping body was extremely tall and he had slightly waving, very long dark hair. Lira, stepping to the forefront to see that her prince was safe, immediately liked him. She thought him very dashing, with strong, bold, virile features. As the fellow stepped closer, pulling Rupert in his wake, she observed his eyes were long-lashed and a wonderful clear gray color. He smiled down at her.

"Oh, what a lovely little lass we have here! The right age to be the boy's sister, but I've hardly seen two young ones look less alike. Yet you're both passing beautiful." The fellow seemed all charm, but the men were not under his spell.

Daniel repeated his command to release Rupert. He did not trouble to lower his weapon, though by now the target was only a few feet away, better suited to striking with a sword than a bow.

"I'll not hesitate to do so, once the lad is awake. As you must know, your son is sleep-walking…a most precarious state. Glad this giant of a dog was here. He'd serve to keep even the hungriest wolf at bay, I'd venture to guess," he concluded with a grin.

"How can you be so certain he is walking in his sleep?" demanded Liam. "How do we not know you somehow lured him here?"

The interloper regarded Liam in surprise. "Do you mean to say this has never happened before? That would *indeed* be strange. I am not a believer in coincidence, so there must likely be great import to the boy venturing to this spot. My mother was right! It was *her* instruction that sent me hither to await events. I believe I will not be disappointed by the outcome."

The men were still greatly suspicious. They could not but wonder if this was some trick or trap. But the intruder appeared to be quite alone, and any weapons remained upon the back of his aging horse, tethered to a nearby tree. Their immediate thought, however, was for Rupert's welfare; for he did appear neither fully awake nor fully asleep. He repeated attempts to pull from the stranger's grip and move off into the woods. Liam came to kneel beside him.

"Rupert, my boy, are you well? Can you speak? Have you been injured?" But the stranger protested.

"Please, do not startle the lad. It would prove dangerous for him to suddenly awaken. I believe if we all sit quietly, he'll soon come to himself. Surely, with you here to guard him, you cannot worry for his well-being."

The men were not certain at all, but it would hardly do to drag the boy back to their campsite while in this strange state. And so, reluctantly, they lowered their weapons and moved by the fire.

Lira sat by Rupert's side, and firmly took hold of his other arm. It made perfect sense that Rupert was sleep-walking. Of course, the possibility that he may be under a spell was just as real. The girl wished to believe this amusing stranger was not the cause, however.

The men were as yet not won over by his open manner. Suspicion was very much in the air. Liam took Rupert's arm from the interloper's grasp and softly addressed the fellow.

"And to whom do we owe the debt of our lad's safety?" he inquired with irony. Liam received a ready smile in return.

"Since you introduced yourselves with arrow and sword, I did not find the opportunity for manners," he said mildly. "Yet as you now so politely inquire...my name is Drego. I belong to clan Gitan...from the land of Gitano. But I have never seen my homeland. It was overrun by wild hordes many decades since. My family fled, and we've long been wanderers...made refugees more than once, I fear. But who are *you*, if I may be so bold? For your accent, as well as the boy's looks, proclaim you are not likely natives of Zurland."

Liam was hardly in a mood to share confidences. But before he might manage a reply, Rupert began to stir. He slowly raised he face, which had been turned towards the ground ever since they had found him. And his eyes, which had been barely opened in slits, now began to grow wide. As if in response, Raja jumped to his feet and began to lick his master's face. Rupert squirmed, and a quiver went through his body. All present became silent as they observed his transformation from that strange semi-sleep to wakefulness.

Morley reached out to him, as Drego moved back a few paces, so the boy's family might reassure him upon his awakening. As Rupert shook his head attempting to clear it, Morley spoke. "Don't be alarmed, Rupert. We are with you."

Rupert looked up, first at Morley, then at all his companions. He wore a bemused expression, knowing something untoward must have occurred for his comrades to regard him with such concern. As he examined his surroundings, his eyes fell upon the stranger. At first Drego smiled at the boy, but his look changed from amused relief to one of greatest, most profound astonishment. He uttered a gasp as all eyes turned from Rupert towards this outsider.

Drego brusquely pushed the others aside until he stood before Rupert. The boy sat staring up at him in puzzlement. But Drego found the youth regarded him with eyes the likes of which he had seen but once in his lifetime…eyes of which he had heard spoken of in many bold and tragic tales - eyes of amazing, blazing, *golden color!*

Drego uttered an involuntary cry, swiftly falling to one knee before the youth. The others instantly comprehended that, once again, their journey had taken a most unexpected turn. Yet where it might lead, the untold consequences it might foretell, none could possibly predict.

Chapter Nine

Rupert was now awake, confounded and bewildered by what he comprehended. Though his family surrounded him, it took only the briefest moment to realize they were no longer where they had camped earlier that evening. Moreover, a strange man was kneeling before him; someone he had no recollection of whatsoever.

Indignation and anger, which was nearly rage, coursed through him. It must have happened again! Someone or something had manipulated his actions - carried him off. He could not know if he had been gone for hours or days, or what had occurred in the interim. Rupert took pride in determining his own path; as a prince he had even more reason to be master of his destiny. Yet at this moment, he felt more as a puppet on a string than someone hoping to rule a kingdom. He spoke up, firstly to determine the identity of this outsider in obeisance before him.

"Arise at once, good sir," declared the young prince, struggling for composure. As the dazed man did as he was bidden, Rupert turned to his friends. "What has happened here?"

Liam and the others moved closer, while Raja continued to prance playfully, reassured that his master was once again himself.

"Come, let us withdraw for a moment," whispered Daniel, "for clearly we have matters to discuss in confidence."

Rupert nodded gravely. Liam addressed Drego. "You will excuse us."

Drego could only nod wordlessly. He face still wore an expression of awed disbelief, and the chatty fellow now appeared incapable of speech. Stumbling slowly to where his horse was tethered, Drego gave the others their required privacy.

"Firstly, tell us what you remember," urged Morley.

Rupert shook his head in confusion. "I recall only going to sleep at our campsite and awakening here. I pray I have not been long absent, or caused you grief or alarm."

Lira sought swiftly to reassure her friend. "No, you were gone but an hour or two at most. Morley awakened to find you missing. We were vastly relieved to find Raja had accompanied you. Again, it was Majesty who was able to lead the way. When we discovered you, this stranger, named Drego, was attempting to restrain you."

Rupert could not conceal his deepening fury. "This is most dreadful, for I recall nothing. I *detest* this feeling of being manipulated. It must be some weakness within me that allows it to occur!"

The others could see plainly Rupert's distress. Liam spoke to reassure him. "We are all subject to events not under our command. It is how we rise to the challenge that determines our fate. We will yet come to comprehend these matters, of that I am certain. It is only because you *are* indeed unique that these episodes test you."

Though taking little comfort from these wise words, Rupert forced himself to address practical matters.

"What, if anything, have you learned of this Drego? Clearly, he beholds my golden eyes."

"Let us jump to no conclusions," cautioned a wary Morley. "We must not forget this cursed land is filled with King Ryker's spies. Perhaps Drego is one of those very agents. We have attracted attention whenever we've dared show ourselves. That woman who served us food, the horse-dealer Borgan...Rupert's presence did not go unnoticed by either. Borgan even questioned you, Liam, whether we were fugitives from the land of the Golden-Eyed Sovereigns. So perhaps they reported their suspicions to this fellow, and he is determined to catch us in a trap."

"Even if he suspected we were on the run, how could he possibly know of Rupert having golden eyes?" wondered Daniel. "What are we to do - deny their existence?"

"We can by no means trust him," declared Rupert. "We'll interrogate him closely, and afterwards make our determination."

"Well, I see you're back to thinking clearly," noted Liam with satisfaction. "Yes, let us do so at once."

With that, the companions moved back to the campfire, and motioned the intruder to join them. He moved cautiously, as if in a dream. Liam indicated they sit by the fire, for the night was indeed very cold. Rupert turned towards the woods and whistled, beckoning Majesty to his side. In a moment, the glorious stallion was by his master once more, nuzzling Rupert's flowing tangle of black locks in greeting.

Drego gazed at the scene before him. "By heaven, this is the very image of Rico - the mount of the great King Marco. I was but a lad of three when last I beheld them. But they were entirely unforgettable, please believe me for that. And now I see a boy with golden eyes and the very horse ridden by the last of your line. *How can this be?!*" Drego's emotion seemed genuine enough; he was either truly stunned, or else a very skilled actor. But the comrades were not ready to open their hearts, not yet. First, they had to hear more…far more.

"Do be so kind, good sir, as to tell us who you are. And do not scrimp on details, if you please," said Rupert, allowing himself to feel no good-will towards the fellow.

Drego bowed his head in Rupert's direction. And then he began his tale.

Drego's clan had its origins in the land of Gitano, located many hundreds of miles to the southeast of where they now stood. For years, his family had been wandering performers, until his grandparents had finally settled down to farming. But when Drego's father, Daro, was still a lad of seven, invaders crashed across the borders and began a brutal campaign of conquest. Having no more than an hour's warning of the coming attack, his family had grabbed what they could and fled towards the nearest friendly territory. They were able to make good their escape, though not without many harrowing moments.

Finding themselves safe but penniless, they took to their former profession. They took to staging plays in any town or hamlet they passed. Survival was difficult for the group of twenty, but Daro enjoyed the wandering life. Yet his family lived in sorrow for all they'd lost and the loved ones left behind.

For years, they drifted across many borders and into many lands. At last, after a more than a decade, they came to the land of the Golden-Eyed Kings. They found a prosperous country populated with warm-hearted citizens. They were greeted with enthusiasm wherever they chose to perform, for their reputation as entertainers of some skill preceded them. And indeed, they came to receive a truly unforeseen summons - an invitation to perform at the royal castle of High Tower.

The troupe was greatly honored, never before commanded to appear before a ruling family. Drego's father, Daro, now a strapping lad of almost nineteen, was as euphoric as the rest. And it was while being welcomed at High Tower that his life changed forever. He always would recall his first sight of King Marco, a towering figure with stunning looks - a noble face, with eyes and waving hair of pure gold. His Queen Khar-shar-leen was as petite as was the king tall, with tresses of rippling black silk hanging to her knees, glowing black eyes, and a face more exquisite than any the lad had ever beheld. He also glimpsed the Lady Meera, the queen's cousin, herself a dazzling beauty who strongly resembled her royal relative.

But it was another lady who took Daro's heart that day; a young girl who watched the performance with avid eyes, sitting at the end of the row where the royal family was seated. Her looks also proclaimed her to be from Raja-Sharan, the Queen's homeland. Her shining black hair fell in one long braid down her back. Her face had not the striking beauty of the royal ladies, but was unutterably charming to Daro. Huge black eyes, long lashes, a round, sweet face that lit with dimples when she smiled, and a creamy dark complexion. She was clad in the brightly-colored silks favored by the queen and her cousin, but her apparel was more modest. Still, Daro could not help but believe she was part of the queen's own family, and so concluded she could never be his - for the poor lad had lost his heart at first sight.

Summoned back to the castle day after day, the young man and the pretty lass finally had opportunity to speak. It was then that Daro learned the truth… the lovely one was not a royal after all, but instead a handmaiden to the queen, having served her since childhood, accompanying her from Raja-Sharan for the royal marriage years before.

Hope surged in Daro's heart. Drawing up his courage, he requested permission of the queen to court her servant. Daro was informed that the girl was an orphan and would bring no dowry, but Daro cared nothing for that. He admitted he had no home or wealth to offer Tara, but swore he would care for her and give her a happy life.

Knowing that Tara had fallen in love with Daro almost instantly, the match had been approved. The king and queen insisted the wedding take place at High Tower Castle, and not a month later, the happy day arrived. The celebration was a colorful mixture of the customs of Raja-Sharan, Gitano, and the Golden-Eyed Kingdom, and the perfect day was made even more so by the overwhelming generosity of the royal couple. For, far from leaving the girl without a dowry, they presented Daro and Tara with a bag of a hundred silver coins; sufficient to see them through many years of married life. Furthermore, they offered the newlyweds something even more precious...a gift of *land*...something they never dreamed of owning again. It was a goodly piece of property, no more than twenty miles from High Tower, ensuring Tara might visit her former masters and friends whenever she desired.

And so, Drego's parents began their life happily. Tara insisted on joining the performing troupe, and proved her talent as an actress, with a pretty singing voice besides. They decided against settling on their newly acquired lands, for the young couple was filled with wander-lust. They meanwhile ordered a home to be built upon their property. The existence as traveling players continued merrily, and their fame increased when citizens learned these performers had appeared before royalty itself; that one of the ladies had even been a handmaiden to the glorious and legendary queen Khar-shar-leen.

Drego's parents finally did settle in their new home after their son was born. They sometimes missed the roving life, as most of their extended family continued their wandering ways. Tara frequently visited the queen and her cousin Meera, with whom she remained on cordial terms.

However, these happy days were not fated to last. For when Drego was but a child of three, the horrifying news arrived at their hitherto peaceful farm. King Marco and his royal heirs had been slain at a 'conference of peace' by the invader Zorin, who now declared himself ruler. The kingdom was under attack! Again, Drego's family was forced to flee, able to take with them less than nothing. Tara and Daro were filled with disbelief that the incomparable royals could now have perished. Tara begged to go to High Tower, but her husband would not permit it.

"Thus, my family became refugees once more," concluded Drego. "We succeeded, after many harrowing months, to cross the border into Zurland, and from there, located other kinsmen who had also managed to escape. We were in mourning and shock. Yet there was no course other than to survive. Again, we became itinerant players, but the joy had departed. We eventually heard that Queen Khar-shar-leen had perished, her corpse put on display. But there was nothing we could do about that. Or, indeed, anything else.

"Years passed and I learned to savor the life of a wandering player. My father died not many years since, and my mother grew too ill to continue our old ways. We settled in a village not distant from here, where I performed in taverns and on festive occasions, and we made do.

"But it has been only two years since my mother revealed the secret guarded all her life. She had discovered, upon her final visit to High Tower Castle, that the queen was with child. It was the custom in Raja-Sharan to guard such news until the babe was safely born, so those who might wish it harm could have no opportunity to carry forth their plans. I was bewildered that my mother had kept her council all these years. And to what purpose? For the queen had died long since; and there had been nary a whisper of a royal baby."

Drego paused to regard Rupert with a radiant, awe-filled countenance. "Yet clearly, that child did survive! He must be your father, for you are far too young to be that boy himself. At any rate, my mother assured that *one day*, I would discover the Golden-Eyed Line had indeed *not* vanished, as all the world believed. That someday the truth would be revealed, and I, her son, would carry on serving the *true rulers*. To that very end, I had been born!

"Of course, I wished to credit my mother, but her revelation seemed too fanciful...indeed, impossible. Then, not two days since, my mother instructed me to come to this very spot and await my destiny. I have been here but one day and one night, and already the truth of her words has come to pass. For I, Drego, am witness to the revelation that *the Golden-Eyed Kings still live!* And I vow to serve you faithfully in whatever capacity you require."

Drego wished to kneel once more before Rupert, but his prince waved him off with a gesture of dismissal. Although yet skeptical, all had been moved by the stranger's tale. Indeed Lira seemed entranced, for she had taken a liking to the charming, charismatic fellow from the first. But far too much was at stake to be lured in by prettily-told sagas. After a pause, Liam spoke.

"Your mother appears to possess secret knowledge concerning the royal family. Since she came from Raja-Sharan and served the queen for many years, we would be most eager to make her acquaintance. As she instructed you so recently to proceed to this spot, she must be living nearby."

"Alas, if only that were so," replied Drego with a sigh. "For it is indeed a fact that my mother directed me here only a few days since. Yet she has been gone from this earth for more than two years."

Incredulous, Rupert and his friends regarded Drego in disdain. Rupert, flushing with anger, felt a shell of distrust harden about his heart. For how could he even *begin* to credit someone who so calmly spoke of something so outrageous? Thus, he now concluded that Drego could indeed prove himself a very dangerous man.

Chapter Ten

The companions were struck by a sense of betrayal. The man was clearly a liar, and a transparent one at that! They were not slow to express their outrage.

"Come, sir, you must take us for simpletons," accused Liam. "You expect us to believe your delusion of your long-dead mother communicating with her son? Such things are not possible, and all you have said is now open to deepest suspicion!"

Drego observed his contemptuous audience with puzzlement. "Do you mean to tell me you have never had such encounters? I assure you that in my dual homelands of Gitano and Raja-Sharan, such happenings are not at all out of the way. How can you disbelieve it when I have clearly been led to this unlikely spot to encounter my lost prince?"

The companions exchanged looks. "It is far more likely you've been following us, and seek our good graces. Perhaps it was *you* that caused the boy to sleep-walk," suggested Morley. The party seemed of one mind, and without further discussion, Rupert stepped forward.

"Sir, since you misguidedly claim me as your prince, you should not prove reluctant to obey my commands. And what I tell you is to depart away at once! We have our journey, and you are not to be part of it. If you delude yourself with fairy stories, that is your concern."

With those words, Rupert and his friends made to depart. Then, Drego's next exclamation brought them to a halt.

"But what of the *fortress?*" he cried. "Surely I was destined to help you find it?"

"Of what do you speak?" inquired Daniel with scorn. For he now believed this stranger would say or do anything to be taken into their midst.

"The young prince himself spoke of it. When I encountered him in his sleep-state, he attempted to pull from my grasp, whispering *'the fortress, the fortress'* - and that was all. But I trust it meant His Majesty was searching for it."

The others looked to Rupert, but he merely shook his head. "I have no recollection of this, nor do I know of any fortress. We take leave of you sir."

Again, they turned away and headed towards their campsite. Drego was left by his fire, a pained and sorrowful expression on his countenance. But the others did not care to see it, and hastened to put distance between this sinister fellow and themselves.

As if to punctuate their need for haste, it abruptly began to snow; not a light flurry, but a blinding curtain. The companions might have experienced difficulty finding their way back, but Raja and Majesty kept them on course. It was not long before they located their campsite. The fire was almost burnt down, and the other horses appeared restless.

"This snow is certainly unwelcome," declared Daniel. "Yet we must head towards Martan without delay. Each moment will make the road the more impassable. And I now am suddenly filled with desire to leave Zurland in our wake."

"Yes, we can all agree upon that," said Rupert. He was profoundly unsettled by the night's events... the sleepwalking, Drego and his strange tale; he felt dangerously exposed.

"Let us not pause even to eat, though it is several hours till dawn. We must take our chances with the weather and perhaps the snow won't last long."

Even as he expressed this hope, the storm grew into a true blizzard. Another time, the comrades might have been entranced, for only Daniel had experienced such an event, and it proved strangely, hypnotically beautiful. But this was not the moment to appreciate nature. They loaded their horses and swiftly departed. Again, they blessed the fact they had trustworthy steeds. For had they been on foot, as in former days, this would indeed have proven an impossible circumstance.

Ghost-like, they moved along the vanishing road as steadily as worsening conditions would allow. Riding high on horseback exposed them to the elements, as wind and snow whipped at their faces. The hoods from their cloaks did little to protect them. All were hungry, and ate from individual stores of dried fruit and nuts as they went. But how they wished to indulge in cups of steaming tea and bowls of hot porridge!

The border to Martan was likely two days distant. But if the snows refused to lessen, there was no telling what hazards might be encountered. From examining Rupert's map, they knew a village or two lay along their route, where shelter from the elements might be sought. But without discussion, they agreed this must not be attempted. For Drego knew or guessed their identity. Others were likely suspicious. They feared being challenged by King Ryker's soldiers or spies. For the moment, their only goal was to leave this uncertain land in their wake.

It might have been wiser to avoid the trail and attempt a border crossing somewhere in the sparse woods; but Rupert thought better of it. Had they done so and encountered guards, they'd be hard-pressed to offer an innocent explanation. Moreover, travel, even by road, was growing more arduous by the moment, and to venture overland in such hazardous conditions seemed foolish indeed.

The party passed a lone farmhouse, a blazing fire visible within. How they longed to pause and warm themselves! They were by now thoroughly numb with cold. Liam realized the wish to travel nonstop might not be father to the deed itself. They had already gone many hours, and relief was required by all. Finally, he rode alongside Rupert and pointed this out. The boy was hesitant but consented, silently urging Majesty and Raja to seek out shelter. And it was not very long before Raja spotted an outcropping of rock offering a measure of respite from the falling snow, though none from the frigid atmosphere.

The travelers quickly gathered beneath the overhanging cliff. At least they might now shake the layers of heavy, soggy snow from their garments. Morley lit a fire from the small supply of wood they carried. A welcome, if inadequate, blaze greeted them, and warm food and drink was prepared. They wolfed down their repast, and the horses fed on some of their precious oats, as there was no grass anywhere to be found.

At first, none ventured to speak, for they were greatly fatigued, and as yet unsettled by their encounter with Drego. There were eventually a few comments delivered on his fantastic tale, but the further from him they went, the more at odds they grew on the subject. Upon reflection, some wondered if he might have been truthful after all. Or at least, what he *believed* to be truthful.

"How were we to know for certain?" demanded Rupert. "We could hardly afford to take the risk."

"Agreed," said Morley. "Could any imagine him sitting amongst us now, yet still being able to express ourselves freely? He would have to be accepted *absolutely* or not at all."

Still, there lingered nagging doubts, especially from Lira. Suddenly, she glanced up from her steaming porridge.

"*But what about Raja?!* We've quite forgotten *him!*" The others regarded her in puzzlement. After all, Raja was there, safely at Rupert's side, devouring his share of the food. The hound, too, turned in her direction upon hearing his name.

"What do you mean, sweetheart?" inquired her father. "Clearly, we haven't forgotten Raja. Here is he."

Lira shook her head, causing her thick flaxen braid to fly. "No, silly, I meant *Raja and Drego!* When we came upon them, Drego had hold of Rupert, but Raja didn't attack! We know Raja would *never* let anyone harm Rupert…or any of us for that matter. So why did he permit a stranger to lay hands upon his master? It makes no sense - unless Raja could *trust* Drego…knew he meant Rupert no harm. That, indeed, he was trying to *help* Rupert!"

They all looked to the girl, speechless. For what she said was the absolute truth…none could think of a convincing argument against it. Finally Morley spoke, but without great conviction.

"Perhaps Drego put a spell on Raja, as he may have upon Rupert?" he ventured. And indeed, anything was possible. By why was no one convinced?

Rupert himself felt abashed and more than a bit ashamed of his hasty conclusions. "What if Lira speaks true? Perhaps our fears led us to disdainfully dismiss the poor fellow without considering the possible verity of his words. It is disagreeable to think I've done him an injustice."

"If you have, we are equally guilty," admitted Liam. "All but Lira. But what's done is done. Perhaps he's trustworthy, perhaps not. Now is not the moment for guessing games. We must press on without delay. I fear the storm shows no sign of diminishing."

With no further regret or reflection, they prepared to mount their horses. Then, without warning, the steeds began to shy and Raja to growl fiercely. The mastiff dashed in front of Rupert, baring his teeth. At that moment, the others saw.

Atop the outcropping of rock loomed some sort of mountain wildcat, formidable in size, poised to leap at Rupert. The boy stood unmoving, rapt and fascinated. All weapons were strapped to their steeds. The men had a moment of dire indecision - whether to freeze in place or back away towards their horses. Morley grabbed Rupert and forced the boy behind him as Daniel did the same for Lira. Raja commenced to howl, and the eerie sound tore through the otherwise silent, snowy landscape.

Yet Rupert knew no fear. If the beast pounced, it would prove impossible to impede his attack since they were unarmed. Rupert, however, decisively took charge. He boldly stepped again in front of Morley, staring up at the snarling phantom looming above. He regarded the marvelous creature directly in the eye. At the same time, he whispered to Raja, urging him to hush, and the frantic hound reluctantly obeyed.

Rupert moved forward yet again, making himself ever more the ready target. Stunned, his friends hissed at him to halt where he stood, but the young prince shook his head. Then Rupert commenced to make a strange, soothing, guttural sound, one they'd never heard before, all the while never removing his golden eyes from the muscular, razor-fanged beast.

The encounter continued for several heart-stopping moments. But at last, the menacing carnivore backed from the ledge and vanished into the blinding veil of snow. As his friends gathered round, daring to breathe once more, Rupert felt a radiant warmth rise within. He had experienced a true measure of communion with the creature, never fearing for an instant. It had been so magnificent, beautiful, powerful. Rupert had never seen a species such as this, and was filled with exaltation.

He was drawn back to reality by the congratulations of his comrades. "You will never cease to amaze us, dearest boy," declared an awed Liam.

Lira was also quick to offer praise, as did the others. But it took another moment for the horses and Raja to regain calm, and for their human companions' heartbeats to reclaim their normal rhythm.

At length, they set out once more into the challenging storm. But the encounter with great peril had renewed their confidence. For Rupert was their extraordinary young king, and they'd somehow overcome their next obstacle; to cross the border and leave Zurland behind. And whatever attempted to intervene - from nature's wrath to King's Guards - surely they would find a way to triumph over them.

Reality did not allow them to savor their joy for long. The snows continued to pelt their bodies, and their horses' steps grew labored. Rupert sensed Raja was beginning to struggle. Rupert drew Majesty to a halt, requesting Daniel to lift the dog up to ride with his prince. Raja objected, until Rupert explained that his body heat was required to keep his master warm. And indeed, the sight of boy and dog riding together could not help but bring weary smiles to his friends.

Onward they struggled all through the day and night. They did not know precisely the distance to the border, but it must be drawing very near. They feared being conspicuous, for there were no other travelers to be seen. Clearly, all sensible citizens were taking shelter until the blizzard passed. And then, without warning, the border crossing was upon them. The howling storm had concealed it from their sight.

Rupert, who had been in a trance of fatigue, realized too late that Raja had been whining for the past moments; for the wild winds had prevented the sound from reaching his ears. Then suddenly, apparition-like in the pelting veil of white, a large party of armed guards materialized before them. Were they simply soldiers of Zurland, or allies of King Ryker, on the lookout for desperate fugitives?

It was too late now to wonder. The comrades had no course but to proceed boldly forward - and hope whatever stratagems they might instantly concoct would permit them to survive another day.

Chapter Eleven

The companions tallied their adversaries as they held their breath. They'd hoped to devise a likely tale to present to the guards, but had delayed too long. Now, a dozen soldiers stood before them, their figures ghostly in the swirling white. Behind the barricade stood a fair-sized wooden structure, perhaps barracks where the men slept. Likely more guards were within. Rupert and his friends were heavily outnumbered.

"What ho, who goes there?" called out the leader. He and several of his men stepped forward to view the fools who journeyed in such barbarous conditions.

Liam directed his mount forward while Lira and Rupert knew enough to draw to the rear. "We are a party of travelers, as you see," Liam began, his brain scrambling for a plausible fiction to present. "We must cross to Martan without delay, for our kinswoman lies ill there."

"It must indeed be grave to call you out on such a night," observed the rough-hewn captain with a false amiability. "I shall require further details."

"It is my own dear wife who has been stricken with fever. She was visiting her sister when word came of her plight. We must hasten to her side." His tone conveyed a dire urgency.

"And precisely where is your destination?"

Liam hastily conjured up Rupert's map in his mind's eye. The name of several settlements in Martan came to memory, and he breathed a sigh of relief. "Why, we are headed for the village of Normary," he stated, hoping for the best.

"Normary, is it? Why, my grandmother hails from that very spot. I know it well. State the name of the family where your wife is to be found. I'm certain to know them."

Liam felt his comrades' tension rise. It would be a lucky guess indeed to provide a suitable reply. His mind scrambled for inspiration, lest he be well and truly caught.

"Do speak up," growled the captain. "Else, I'll tend to think I've been conversing with a liar!"

Most alarmingly, a deep, clear voice rang out from somewhere behind the companions; one that they, with frozen fear, instantly recognized.

"Why, the man *is* a bold-faced liar, and not a very skillful one at that!" And the voice that made this ghastly declaration belonged to none other than Drego. Some way or other, he had been following them. Now, all their suspicions were proving true. Drego *was* a spy, and about to turn them over to the troops. Morley, Daniel, and Liam reached under their cloaks for their concealed weapons. But outnumbered, they stood little chance in an all-out fight, and they knew it. However, the response to Drego's ominous words was hardly what the comrades might have anticipated. The captain broke into raucous laughter.

"Drego, you old rascal, the last fellow I thought to see on a night such as this! But you're welcome indeed. And what have you to say about these rag-tag vagabonds armed with suspicious fables? You've labeled them liars, and I quite agree."

Drego chuckled as he dismounted and moved to the captain's side. They clasped forearms in greeting. "Yes, at least *I'll* be truthful. These fellows are with me. I've recruited them to join my troupe, and we've been performing in Zurland. We're heading into Martan to flee this blasted winter tempest."

The guard frowned doubtfully. "If that be so, why the sorry tale of a sick wife?"

Drego gave a roguish grin. "That was my doing. I was tarrying with a pretty local lass. I instructed them not to wait; and I urged them to practice their acting skills on you, old friend. Seems they're not very convincing, however. But trust me, they do better with comedic tales and singing."

"Well, you rogue, since you vouch for them, I'll take your word. For you've entertained us many a time and we consider you one of us! But before you depart, do give us a melody or two. We're numb with cold, and in dire need of cheering."

Drego turned to Rupert and his friends, his eyes silently urging them to go along with his tale. They needed no further encouragement, and Daniel, reaching into his knapsack, produced his flute.

"I have the very song to entertain you gentlemen," Lira's father proclaimed in a merry voice. "Come, let us sing 'The Cheerful Maiden' for these fine fellows."

Daniel began the lively tune, as he had done before their evening campfires on a number of nights past. Rupert, Lira, Morley, and Liam began a heartfelt rendition. All had pleasant, if not exceptional voices, but their performance was immensely improved when Drego joined in; for he had an extraordinary voice, tuneful and powerful, giving the others a polish they did not truly own. They managed to complete the song in perfect harmony.

The weary guards were delighted, and begged for an encore. Daniel moved to comply while Drego produced a small harp-like instrument from his own knapsack. Daniel hastily suggested a traditional melody called 'Pale Moonlight' since the others knew it well. The rendition, this time accompanied by harp and flute, brought tears to the eyes of the lonely troops. The players were rewarded by hearty applause muffled by heavily gloved hands.

"Well, I'm certain you'll prove popular wherever you appear," the captain declared. "Now best be on your way, for the snows are growing deeper by the instant. I'll look forward to our next encounter, Drego."

"I trust that will not be far in the future, old friend," Drego replied. "For these feet seem designed for eternal wandering." And with that, he again clasped arms with the captain, remounted his horse, and led the way across the border into the land of Martan. Without bothering to look back, he was certain Rupert and the others would follow without protest...and they did.

The party proceeded through the swirling snows, none daring utter a word. Drego had not betrayed them; indeed, he had come to their rescue, and without a moment to spare! Their silence began to grow awkward. Finally the nomad from Gitano, who continued to lead the way, pulled his horse to a halt. He regarded his companions with an ironic smile.

"I know this land well enough, as I've passed through countless times since childhood. There is a village not far off. Do you wish to pause for a meal? Or to pass the night?"

The comrades did not know how to reply. Morley took a deep breath. "Clearly, we owe you an apology. We are in your debt for coming to our aid."

"Yet you still can't bring yourselves to trust me, is that it?" Drego ventured with a twisted grin. "Need I hurl myself off the nearest cliff to convince you of my loyalty?"

"I say we indeed share a meal and properly convey our gratitude," declared Liam. Perhaps after further discussion, the companions might come to an understanding about this enigmatic fellow.

They continued through the pelting whiteness. Happily, before they reached the settlement, the storm greatly abated. Moreover, Rupert felt a growing euphoria. Not only had they overcome the blizzard, succeeded in yet another hazardous border crossing, faced down a mountain cat - but best of all, he grew aware of his own mysterious 'inner voice' returning.

Nothing could fill him with more joy or confidence. That very inherent guidance conveyed that Drego *was* to be trusted after all. Whether his companions were now equally convinced, he was not certain. For it demanded a huge leap of faith to entrust an interloper with their secrets.

They welcomed the sight of the village and the inn. The companions did not speak the language of Martan; though Drego did. They advised him to order a meatless repast. Even the tea served was different from any they'd encountered; not strong and dark in color, but rather pale green and strangely fragrant.

"This is jasmine tea," explained Drego. "You will find, as you continue eastward, that it grows common. I myself enjoy it more than the heavy brews you're aware of."

They found even the bread to be different - not huge, round loaves, but small and flat in shape, sprinkled with seeds - yet tasty nonetheless.

"Well, I don't suppose you wish to discuss the local cuisine. Nor do I. I merely wish to convey that I am at your service, and trust I may prove to be useful. Yet I comprehend your business must be of the most pressing sort, and do not wish to impose myself upon you."

"What made you follow us?" demanded Rupert with a half-smile. For now that he'd opened his heart, he'd taken a sudden liking to the strapping, flamboyant fellow.

"Some instinct told you'd certainly have difficulty with the border crossing. I knew I might be of some help in that direction. After that, I was prepared to withdraw, if you so desired. But it was my mother's greatest wish, as well as now my own, to serve you with all my heart. I can speak multiple languages, am trusty with a sword, and can entertain you in the bargain! Not many can promise as much, I'll warrant you."

The companions now found themselves of one mind. This decision was punctuated by Raja, as if comprehending his approval was of some import, moved from Rupert's side to lick Drego's hand. Lira grew wide-eyed at the sight. She'd always liked this man and knew to trust him. She was well satisfied the others had agreed with her intuition.

Rupert's friends turned to the boy-prince. All wore looks of consent. There appeared no need for discussion. The lad fastened his gaze on the man who had, such a brief time before, been an object of vast suspicion.

"Drego, you are most welcome to join us. When we leave this inn and may claim a measure of privacy, we shall reveal the nature of our journey and answer any queries you may have. For there can now be no concealment between us."

Joy, as never heretofore experienced, blazed through Drego's heart. The man without a home now at long last felt he had one. For his true place was wherever young King Rupert and his friends might be found. And he vowed to remain steadfast forever.

Chapter Twelve

The companions decided against remaining the night at the inn, determined to find a place where they might converse openly. Drego reportedly knew of an abandoned barn not many miles distant. They departed soon after completing their meal, and indeed, Drego was able to lead them to their sanctuary as promised.

"I'm relieved to find it intact," confessed Drego, "for I have not passed this way for a year or more. It is hardly a castle fit for my prince, but may please you nonetheless."

Rupert smiled. "It should serve very well. Whatever offers shelter from the elements is agreeable."

Very soon humans, horses, and Raja were settled around a welcome blaze. The effects of the frigid temperatures could still be felt, but none minded, at least for this night. Drego was burning to hear the saga of Rupert and his miraculous survival, and how he had come into his present circumstances.

The young prince lost no time in unfolding his narration, of course commencing with his singular upbringing in the forest, his inscrutable grandparents, his eventual unearthing of the royal treasure, followed by his family's untoward disappearance – in turn leading to his venture into the wider world. The tale took some while to complete, for Drego had many questions and urged no detail be omitted. Of course, Liam, Daniel, Morley, and Lira added their own commentary, but when the telling was complete, Drego regarded them in awe.

"Quite the most amazing thing I have ever heard - very like the great narratives of ancient legend; hardly something that could be occurring *now*, to people I know. And to think that I, too, am now part of this remarkable saga."

"Yes, indeed," agreed Liam. He nodded towards Rupert, who understood. The boy rose and moved to Majesty's side. "You will be provided further proof of the truth, if such were needed," Liam continued. A moment later, Rupert had retrieved the royal treasure, which was, as usual, wrapped in a well-worn blanket among the burdens Majesty carried. Rupert bore it to Drego, then slowly unrolled the faded coverlet. What was revealed made their newest companion gasp and utter an involuntary cry.

"Why, this is a royal treasure, no doubt of that! I believe I've seen this very ruby ring on the hand of King

Marco! Of course, I was but a tot, and so cannot vouch for my memory. Yet it does look passing familiar!"

He turned to Rupert. "May I be permitted to examine them? Unless you'd prefer I did not. I am not worthy of laying my common hands upon them."

Rupert smiled. "Nonsense, you are one of us now. Please do not hesitate."

Gingerly and reverently, Drego took each of the treasures; firstly, the gloriously carved and bejeweled sword, then the ruby ring, the gilded looking-glass, and finally the fabulous necklace belonging to Queen Khar-shar-leen. He was at a loss for words, but the tears in his eyes and awe in his aspect revealed plainly what was in his heart.

"I too, felt unworthy of handling these treasures," recalled Morley, his warm green eyes dancing. "However, I quickly got over that, considering I am risking my neck day and night to protect them and their true owner!"

The others could enjoy Morley's jest, but Drego could not. He held up the ruby and gold ring again towards the firelight, allowing its brilliance to dazzle his eyes. He finally made to set it down on the blanket with the other treasures. But it was at that moment that Rupert saw something in his new friend's expression that caused his heart to freeze. The look had blazed in Drego's eyes for only an instant, but Rupert was certain of what he'd perceived. For awe had been replaced by something else…*blatant greed!*

To Rupert, it was as if he'd received a blow to his belly. The air went out of his lungs in a gasp. The others turned to the boy.

"Rupert, what is wrong?" asked Daniel, giving him a penetrating look. But Rupert quickly recovered, comprehending it would not do to give Drego any inkling of his true feelings.

"Why, I am fine," replied the youthful prince with enforced calm. "I merely recalled the moment I discovered that ring in the basket."

"I'll never forget how Grandfather Liam and I found you near death after you secretly tried it on!" declared Lira, going on to retell that part of the tale.

Rupert silently thanked her for distracting the others. He had already done Drego a disservice by doubting him, and did not wish to repeat the error. After all, that look of avarice had existed for but the briefest instant. Might Rupert have somehow imagined it? Should he tell his friends of his fears, or instead bide his time? Perhaps it was wiser to observe Drego with an eagle eye. But the euphoria of gaining a new and trusted comrade was gone from Rupert's heart, like a light brutishly smothered.

The young prince took up his treasures. He would not place them on Majesty's back until the morrow, determining to guard them well this night.

Meanwhile, the others hardly realized anything was amiss. Lira gleefully suggested they take full advantage of having a fluent speaker of Veshti in their midst. Drego was delighted to initiate a simple conversation in their newly acquired tongue, and was full of praise at how much progress had been made in a brief time. He corrected their pronunciation when warranted, and led his students in a lively, if simple, chat.

Rupert found himself joining in; also insisting upon being taught basic phrases in the tongue of Martan. Again, Drego happily obliged. Yet, feigning nothing was amiss was not an easy game for Rupert. He was long accustomed to holding nothing back from his friends. Even had he been so inclined, it was impossible to state his newly born suspicions in Drego's presence. He must await an opportune moment.

They finally slept, but Rupert could not take rest. He was distressed to imagine his instinct to trust Drego had been misguided, placing them all in peril. Rupert relied upon that inner voice. Now, what if it was no longer to be trusted? He must keep ever vigilant and observe what Drego might unwittingly reveal.

The party prepared to set off at dawn. Rupert was unnerved and depressed. Drego, not knowing Rupert well, noticed nothing, but his friends did. Liam called the boy to his side and meant to question him. Before he could do so, Rupert was overcome by a massively powerful intuition. It seemed to come from nowhere; akin to being knocked over by a gargantuan wave. He had received a directive that must be immediately heeded!

All eyes had been drawn to the young sovereign, who had fallen to his knees, his magnificent eyes growing enormous. Liam knelt beside him.

"What has happened, Rupert? You are ghostly pale. Are you unwell?"

Rupert shook his head, but there was a pause before he could utter a word. In the meanwhile, his friends had gathered round. Daniel, also much concerned, knelt so he might look directly into the boy's haunted visage.

"Please do tell us what has occurred," Daniel pleaded.

Rupert regarded them all. "I believe I've been given a 'command'...or an 'intuition'...that we travel through Martan *avoiding all settlements!* We must shun *every* contact with the populace!" He looked his friends in the eye. "I know this means our journey will prove trying indeed. I'm sorry for that, please believe me. But it *must* be this way!"

Morley spoke after a stunned silence, realizing what Rupert was asking of them. "But *why*, Rupert? What is the cause that we isolate ourselves? Do you sense the presence of King Ryker's men?"

Rupert shrugged and slowly took to his feet with Daniel's aid. "I wish I knew. Perhaps King Ryker's army *is* here; perhaps it is unrelated to that. But this 'decree' cannot be ignored. *That* alone I am certain of!"

Liam turned to Drego. "You know Martan. What will be the consequence should we travel off roads?"

Drego shook his head. "True, I've spent not a small amount of time here. But I confess I've always welcomed the sight of towns and villages. Should we do as Rupert demands, we will encounter untold trials. It is winter, do not forget, and food is scarce. We cannot hope to traverse this vast kingdom without obtaining supplies."

The others looked to Rupert for comment. For Drego only spoke true.

"How much food do we carry with us?"

"It might prove sufficient for a week," responded Morley. "What say we put ourselves on short rations and travel as Rupert desires. Perhaps later he might receive another message permitting us to mix with the locals. For things are always in flux, isn't that so?"

Rupert could only nod. What other course did they have? Drego, however, did not seem so easily convinced.

"I must repeat that I'm quite familiar with Martan and its peoples. They are open and trustworthy, and likely no friend of King Ryker. Why make the journey so much the more trying?"

Rupert did not welcome the challenge. He again suspected Drego. The fellow clearly preferred to come in contact with the citizens. Perhaps he hoped to pass on information to local spies.

"You are new to our number, Drego," Liam began shortly, "so you are not familiar with the fact that Rupert's intuitions have preserved us time and again. We are not about to question his authority at this late date. I promise he has good reason for his declaration, and we would be wise to heed it." Liam gave the newcomer a sharp look. Drego was not slow to comprehend his protests were causing consternation.

"By heaven, do not believe for an instant that I question my liege! I merely wish to offer my experience of Martan. I would never dream of challenging my rightful sovereign."

Rupert was not soothed by these fine words, and observed that Liam, too, was regarding their latest addition with clouded eyes. But there was nothing to be gained by continuing the debate.

"Let us be on our way, then, and avoid connection with the populace. We shall head due east and make our supplies last," declared Daniel in his most sensible tone. And thus, they completed their preparations and began the trek through the mountains. Snow was piled high. Their map revealed several more towering peaks to cross before the terrain might become less daunting.

They proceeded in silence. Lira, still charmed and trusting of Drego, pulled her prancing black horse beside his, and began to converse in the language of Raja-Sharan. She beckoned Rupert to join them, and hoping to conceal his dark thoughts from the others, ambled alongside on Majesty. Come what may, they would need to speak the local tongue when they reached that far-off destination. Rupert would be practical and take advantage of their tutor.

However, his troubled mind continued to plague him. Traveling off-road was not what he'd envisioned for this part of the journey. They had nowhere near enough supplies to sustain them. Examining his surroundings, he recognized there was little hope of finding edibles along the way. Winter had set in with a vengeance. They must rely upon their very meager, inadequate reserves.

Rupert's heart grew cold, comprehending he was likely dooming his companions to vast suffering and a terrible fate. And the responsibility would rest entirely upon his shoulders. For he feared that by heeding his words, his comrades would before very long begin to starve.

Chapter Thirteen

The party traveled as swiftly as possible that day, not pausing till almost sunset. Though snow did not fall, a piercing wind blew, making them experience the cold most bitterly. They'd wrapped scarves about their faces, leaving only eyes unshielded. Luckily, just as Liam was about to suggest a halt, they came upon a series of caves, which would offer a measure of shelter. One was discovered to be large enough to accommodate the horses as well as their riders.

Aware of the urgency of preserving short rations, nothing had been consumed during their long day's ride, and none voiced complaint. But before they might partake of a longed-for supper, there was business to see to. Morley had determined they unload their supply of foodstuffs from their steeds and take an accurate inventory. Soon the party stood staring at their scanty stockpile.

"Well, it's not much, and that's a fact," stated Morley. "But we'll just have to figure out how to stretch it without turning the lot of us into skin and bones."

Rupert could not smile at Morley's jest...for reducing them to 'skin and bones' was just what he feared.

"We mustn't forget the horses," their young prince reminded them. "There will be no grass to graze upon for a long while, I believe. They'll have to share our stash of oats, which means no porridge for us."

Liam counted out what they had...two sacks of oats, another of dried fruits and nuts, another of dried beans, and a half-empty sack of tea. That was all. Of course, they'd meant to stop in many a village and town along their route, and so had not thought to carry much with them. Their possessions were few - blankets, warm clothing, and concealed weapons - as well as the royal treasure, and a number of books.

"This is meager indeed," observed Liam, stating the obvious. "I fear we cannot make do. We must find *some* way to supplement our stockpile, or our situation will rapidly turn untenable."

Rupert recognized that Liam spoke true. Yet his 'vision' to avoid the people of Martan was also absolute truth. "I cannot resolve our dilemma," Rupert declared with regret, "though surely, we shall think of something."

Drego spoke up with caution. He was well aware he'd somehow drawn the ire of his young liege. However, someone had to be practical. "Rupert, if you'll forgive me, I do have a suggestion. You say we must avoid the towns, and perhaps that would be the case for *you*...for King Ryker may have spies about. And should someone observe your eyes to be their true golden color instead of their dark brown disguise, that would be potential disaster, I agree."

Rupert sought to display no amazement. For he was certain, in telling his tale to Drego, that he had *not* mentioned the uninitiated believed his eyes were dark brown. Rupert only recalled he had been shocked to learn that Liam, Lira, and others could not apprehend his eyes were golden. Why did Drego now say his eyes appeared *dark brown* to the world at large? The boy longed to question him with sharp words.

The man continued, noticing nothing amiss. "Remember, I am no stranger to these parts. It would attract no undue notice if I, alone, were to appear in a settlement to purchase necessities. I could also gain intelligence; to discover if there is talk of foreign soldiers hereabouts. We could obtain what we require, and be none the worse for it." Drego looked for approval from his companions, thinking he'd formed an excellent plan.

The others exchanged glances. It *did* seem a feasible solution to their dilemma. Now Rupert must give the final blessing. Daniel turned to the youthful prince.

"What say you, Rupert? Would you think it hazardous if Drego ventured out alone? For certainly, none are searching for *him*."

Rupert wanted to shake his head 'no'. Simply the fact that *Drego* had made the suggestion was enough to arouse suspicion. What if their newest member *was* some sort of spy? Entering a town would permit opportunity to pass on a message. On the other hand, how could Rupert call himself a worthy leader if he let his people perish from hunger?

"I am not convinced it would be safe for even Drego to venture among the populace. Yet any tactic enabling us to obtain what we desperately need should hardly be dismissed out of hand."

Rupert was giving tacit approval, though his belly churned with anxiety at the thought of leaving Drego to his own devices. At least Rupert could prevent *that*. "It would be advisable if Morley accompanied you. You could also take an extra mount and return with food sufficient to get us through Martan without pausing again."

Daniel concurred. "I know your instincts dictate we should not approach settlements at all. But you're right in permitting Drego and Morley to make the attempt. Indeed, it may be the only hope if we are to make it through."

Rupert nodded, but his friends comprehended he was far from satisfied with this turn of events. After further discussion, it was agreed that Drego and Morley would set out the next morning, while the others remained where they were. They calculated the nearest road was seven or eight miles off, and the nearest town less than ten miles further on. With luck, the men would return before darkness fell.

Anticipating ample provisions upon the morrow, they allowed themselves to consume their fill of porridge mixed with dried fruit. The horses, too, were given their portion of raw oats. Rupert prayed that Drego could bring his plan to fruition, for it seemed very simple and practical. But black thoughts filled Rupert's being. Because a warning shouted that *no* towns were to be approached no matter *what* the circumstance!

Yet since he could not name the source of this apprehension, he felt compelled to permit the plan to go forward. With Morley to accompany him, Drego would have little opportunity to engage with any 'enemies' they might encounter.

The cave did not provide much warmth, despite the fire that burned within. Another blaze was built by the opening. The second served to keep wildlife at bay. The evening passed with songs played upon Daniel's flute and Drego's harp, as well as more practice in the language of Raja-Sharan. Rupert, although he attempted to appear as if nothing was amiss, was not in high spirits, and the others took note. However, his friends were themselves concerned at their plight, and attributed Rupert's mood to that and nothing more.

After another largely sleepless night, the companions arose before dawn. Drego and Morley prepared to depart after their scanty morning meal. Rupert wished to warn Morley concerning his suspicions, but had no opportunity to do so. He instead requested they exhibit extreme caution, and at any sign of danger to return at once, with or without supplies. Both vowed to obey Rupert's command. And then they were off, taking Daniel's horse along as well.

When the two men had departed, Rupert faced a dilemma. Should he speak his doubts to Liam and Daniel? And what of Lira? His young friend held a soft spot for the seemingly charming interloper. Was he judging Drego fairly, or was his imagination running away with him?

Rupert at last determined to approach Liam and his son. They would confer, and inform Lira if necessary. The opportunity presented itself when the girl, growing weary of the damp cave, asked if she might gather much-needed firewood. Her father agreed, and Rupert sent Raja to accompany her; for there was a likelihood of wildlife about.

"I'll join her in a moment," said her father, finishing up a tune. He treasured the wooden flute his daughter had presented him upon his recent birthday. It had been so many years since being permitted to enjoy something as innocent as music.

"Before you do, I have a matter most urgent to put before you," declared Rupert, nodding also in Liam's direction. "I wish you to be completely honest when I'm done; for my concerns may be of great import...or signify nothing at all."

"I have observed you have been troubled, my boy," stated Liam. "I presumed the cause was your latest revelation. You know you can always speak of whatever is in your heart."

Daniel and his father sat crossed legged on the frosty ground next to Rupert. The boy took a breath and began. He recounted his observations; the flash of greed on Drego's face when examining the royal treasure, the seeming challenge to Rupert's authority, and the slip of tongue concerning the color of Rupert's eyes. After making his case, Rupert felt a blush creep onto his cheeks. Once stated baldly and aloud, the boy realized his case against Drego was feeble indeed.

"Is that all you have against the fellow?" questioned Daniel doubtfully. "Surely, the fact that your eyes appear brown to the world in general must have been mentioned during the retelling of your saga. Perhaps we can cross that suspicion from your list of grievances?"

"Just a moment," interrupted Daniel's father. "I do not recall that Rupert's eyes had been described to be dark brown initially. I wager it was stated that only you, my son, had seen their true color from the first."

"Well, perhaps he'd assumed Rupert's eyes would appear almost black, since his hair is ebony, and his complexion darker than most hereabouts," observed Daniel.

"But, *why?*" challenged Rupert. "After all, Drego's own hair is black, but his eyes are gray. I begin to fear something quite dreadful. What if he cannot see my golden eyes at all? What if they actually *do* appear brown to his sight?" Rupert spoke in growing agitation.

"Do calm yourself," soothed Liam. "Are you seriously declaring you now believe Drego to be a *spy?!* The evidence is weak indeed. You *thought* you observed a flash of greed in his countenance…he *may or may not* have heard about your eyes during the telling of your saga. He *did* challenge your authority a bit…but we've *all* been guilty of that upon occasion."

"Yet I believe I've beheld doubt about Drego in *your* eyes," Rupert protested to Liam. And then he shrugged impatiently. "Ah, I have created a terrible dilemma with my hasty decision to bring him into our fold. For if we cannot trust him, we should send him away. Yet if we *do*, we know not what mischief he may create. After all, he knows our true identity. That could prove our downfall."

"I believe if Morley were here, he'd point out the obvious; we must either trust him and keep him with us – or not permit Drego to leave alive." Daniel spoke with a pained resolution.

"I concur," stated Liam, his expression cold. "However, we require far more proof than this. We shall observe Drego like a hawk. If he is truly our foe, we will catch him out eventually. There is a wise saying concerning keeping friends close and enemies closer. I'm now very glad you suggested Morley go on the mission. He can be trusted to keep a sharp eye out, even without being forewarned."

"Should we share our thoughts with Lira?" Rupert wanted to know. "I know she's rather charmed by the fellow, as we once were."

"Perhaps her instincts may yet prove true. And never forget, Raja seems to approve of him to the hilt. So again, we'll observe the fellow, but not jump to conclusions. And for the moment, Lira must remain in ignorance. The more normal we appear with Drego, the better."

Liam and Rupert agreed. There seemed nothing more to be said. The three left the cave to join Lira in her search for firewood. They would need to carry the largest possible supply, not knowing if it too would grow scarce. Rupert also spent time communing with Majesty, and then, feeling foolish, unloaded the royal treasure to make certain nothing was missing. He found it still intact.

The companions did not take a noon repast, though hoping Morley and Drego would soon be with them. It was only upon their return, rich with replenishments, that they might satisfy their growing appetites. And they hoped for word before evening.

News came, but far earlier than expected. Morley and Drego had departed with the dawn, and it was not many hours past noon when the party heard hoof beats approaching. Daniel, his father, and Rupert exchanged puzzled looks. Could the town have been closer than anticipated? But when Morley and Drego appeared, their horses were not burdened with fresh supplies. They were returning as empty-handed as they'd left.

Lira had run to greet them, a radiant smile lighting her face. It faded quickly at what she perceived.

"Why, what has happened? We were not expecting you till much later - and you haven't brought us any food."

Morley and Drego quickly dismounted, their expressions dark and tense.

"No, and we're not likely to any time soon, sweetheart," Drego advised the bewildered girl.

"Speak plainly. What has occurred?" demanded Rupert to Morley.

"Then, here it is. We reached the road without incident, but approaching the nearest town, we came upon a barricade, manned by a dozen jittery soldiers. They ordered us to return from whence we'd come, and spoke in no friendly manner. It was made clear that a plague has struck Martan, starting in the east and heading this way. All travel has been forbidden, borders closed, and citizens ordered to keep to their homes."

His listeners regarded Morley in horror. This explained everything - why Rupert had been so adamant that they visit no towns or mix with the populace. *There was pestilence in the land!*

"I believe the guards were tempted to lock us up in case we'd already been exposed. But they likely dreaded contact with strangers, so they instead forced us to turn back. I sought to obtain information about the disease, but they did not disclose much. A rash, headache, and very high fever are among the symptoms; that is all I could gather." Morley was grim and his mood spread at once to the others.

"Well, Rupert, it appears I owe you another apology," declared Drego. "For your inner warning certainly proved accurate beyond a doubt. But that gives me no pleasure, for it leaves us in a ghastly dilemma - one from which there is no escape that I can fathom. Unless *you* perceive some hopeful outcome."

However, Rupert could only regard Drego in despair. *Plague! Quarantine!* Their peril was greater even than imagined. Perhaps they could escape exposure to the dread disease. Yet, how were they to survive without food? Rupert might have sunk to the ground in anguish, but could ill-afford to exhibit weakness at this critical juncture.

Liam, sensing his mood, moved to Rupert's side and placed his arm around the boy-king's shoulder. Rupert leaned against him gratefully. He looked up into the tall man's calm yet grave blue eyes. His mentor attempted to convey fortitude to his prince, and Rupert responded with a feeble smile.

But Rupert's heart was filled with turmoil and terrible darkness. It appeared he had led his precious companions into a death trap. The burden of keeping them alive was truly his alone, and he vowed to somehow find a way out for them all. But for this moment, no inspiration came.

Chapter Fourteen

Grim faced, the companions sat about their flickering fire. Every alternative seemed bleak indeed. It took all of Rupert's self-command not to break down in front of the others. An ominous idea was born in his heart, and he wished to flee from his own thoughts. But that was fruitless. *He* had the responsibility of rescuing his friends from their predicament, and must not permit personal feelings to cloud the issue.

The silence was broken by Liam. "Well, it appears we must be practical and ration what we have to the utmost. But there is no escaping the bald fact that we cannot survive long. A week or two at most, I would hazard to guess."

"No doubt," his son concurred. "Yet it appears we have at least one month's travel before we can cross out of Martan…that is *if* we can hope to cross the frontier in stealth."

Drego spoke next. "One month's journey would be lucky indeed, even if we could make use of the roads. Since we cannot, we must predict twice that estimate…at the very least."

No one spoke after that. Lira sat upon her father Daniel's lap, hugging him close. She looked into his eyes, then her grandfather's, and next turned to Rupert. For surely one of them would find a solution to their dilemma. She hoped to discover inspiration herself.

"How unfortunate it is now winter," the girl sighed, "for we can hardly count on finding much in the way of growing things."

Rupert knew now was the time to speak. He supposed his friends must have come to the very conclusion so cruelly tormenting his thoughts. Yet they'd likely hold back out of respect for their young leader. Gritting his teeth, Rupert took to his feet, addressing his comrades with a look of wild but steely determination.

"You *know well* what you must do! I will not cause you to suffer on my behalf. You are here because of me, my cause. You must…we *all* must…survive. Therefore, you shall begin hunting for game - begin this very day! That is the only rational choice."

Rupert's companions exchanged looks, and then turned eyes to the ground. All comprehended, with the possible exception of their newest member Drego, what revulsion and horror this declaration had cost their prince. Rupert revered animals, communed with them…

indeed they had been his only childhood companions other than his inscrutable grandparents. None could forget the terrible moment when Rupert discovered his fox friend Kara, slain by King Ryker's guards. His howls of grief and fury had nearly brought about their downfall.

At last, Morley spoke. "Rupert, I wish with all my being I could conjure another way. But I fear there *is* none. We must always recall our mission - to reach Raja-Sharan, secure aid from your royal relations, and raise an army to liberate our homeland. If we perish here of hunger, all will have been for naught."

Liam stood to embrace the boy. "I apprehend the ghastly burden this decision entails. But I, too, cannot envision another way." He turned to the rest of the companions, attempting to avoid the appalled look of disbelief on his granddaughter's tear-stained face. "Rupert, will you partake of meat yourself?"

Rupert could not speak, for a lump had arisen in his throat, and it seemed as if a ball of fire was searing his belly. But he shook his head 'no', with great vehemence. He could not, would not, eat the flesh of any living creature. Yet his companions had done so all their lives until joining him. It was only right they do so again.

Lira rushed to Rupert's side, embracing him fiercely. "Don't worry, Rupert. I won't eat meat either. I don't want to anymore."

But Rupert took her by the shoulders and pushed her back until able to stare into her wide, sapphire eyes, which continued to flood with tears.

"No, Lira, you *must* resolve to eat what we catch. Raja will too. After we are safe, you may refrain again if you wish. But for now, you will obey me in this."

Daniel spoke, partly to comfort his daughter, in part for Rupert's sake. "Yes, Lira, you must partake with the rest of us, because we must leave our other food for Rupert. He will not have enough to eat if he must share with you."

Rupert began to protest, but Liam interrupted. He pointed out that the oats had to go to the horses, leaving only one small sack of beans and one of dried fruit and nuts. If they divided that, it would be gone in a few days. But if left to Rupert, he could hopefully survive a number of weeks if reduced to extremely short rations. The others, including Raja, would be sustained by the fruits of their hunt. That plan alone made sense.

Rupert was forced to acquiesce. Daniel moved purposefully to his horse to retrieve his bow and arrow. He was by far the best marksman among the men, and took the grim task upon himself to provide food for his family and friends. He turned wordlessly and headed from the cave.

Rupert knew he must not go alone. He turned to Raja, called him to his side, and gave an order he had never uttered before.

"Raja, hunt! Go with Daniel and hunt!" Raja looked into his master's eyes to determine if he'd understood correctly. Seeing that he did, he raced to Daniel's side, and together they headed out and towards the barren trees. In another moment, they were out of sight.

There seemed nothing more to be said. Rupert, feeling the compelling need to remove himself from the others, strode from the cave, stumbling to the top of the nearest hill. His heart was breaking. He was sending one set of comrades to slay another. Yet what was the alternative? At this moment, the weight of his burdens almost crushed him.

Then, a sudden unwelcome thought crossed his mind. This was just the beginning! If his hopes to free his homeland ever came to fruition, it would require *many* battles, death, a war. And who could predict what perils need be faced before that far-off day? He must be firm in his resolve. Men would die because of his orders - willing to lay down their lives, abandon their families - to serve their liege. He had not the luxury to shrink from difficult, heart-breaking decisions. Not if he were to prove worthy of his heritage...not if he were truly a *Golden-Eyed King.*

Daniel did not return until darkness was upon them. By then, Rupert had rejoined his friends. Raja pranced to his master, as if demanding his accolades. Daniel carried a sack over his shoulder, and with a look of apology to Rupert, the hunter emptied the contents by the fire. It contained two rabbits, each bearing the mark of an arrow upon it. Rupert sensed the distress in Daniel's heart. He went to his friend, embraced him, and kissed his cheek.

"Thank you, Daniel. I know it cannot have been easy for you."

Daniel wanted to beg pardon from his prince for slaying these creatures and to the others for providing such meager fare. "I fear there is not much game about; hardly enough to sustain us. Perhaps we may hope for better on the morrow."

The thought of the next day, with the necessity of more death for innocent creatures of the forest, made Rupert wish to wail in grief. But such an exhibition was a luxury he could no longer afford.

"We all share your hopes. And now I think of it, is it not high time that *I* learn to wield a bow and arrow? I shall not hunt, but I can learn to strike a target. Will you not teach me, brother?"

Daniel was struck by Rupert's graceful gesture. It assuaged any lingering fears that Rupert thought ill of him for the necessity of his dark task. Furthermore, Rupert was right. Daniel and Morley had long planned to teach him the uses of weaponry. If they waited for a time of tranquility to do so, they might wait forever.

"Yes, I shall be honored, my lord, to instruct you as best I can. And Morley or my father should train you with the sword."

"A fine idea," agreed Liam. "Come, we can begin this very night." He moved to his horse, which bore weapons found in the cottage of Rupert's grandparents, as well as those confiscated from fallen soldiers. He found suitable bow, arrows, and blade, handing them to Rupert, who received them with a look of determination.

"I'll content myself with cooking dinner," murmured Drego. He continued to sense Rupert's displeasure, and did not wish to burden the others with the gruesome task of preparing the slaughtered game.

Rupert glanced his way. "Thank you, Drego," he said shortly. "I do appreciate that." He strode off, weapons in hand, towards a clearing where he might practice. Daniel, Morley, and Liam accompanied him. Lira remained with Drego to aid in preparing the meager evening repast.

Less than an hour passed, one in which Rupert focused with all his being on the instruction given; for he must become highly skilled in the art of defense - the art of death. He felt abruptly so much older, as if he had truly left childhood behind. Now grim realities were the order of the day. But he could hardly avoid the odor of roasting rabbit flesh not far from where his arrows flew. It took all his will to fight off the churning that writhed through his belly.

And then it was time to eat. As they gathered round the campfire, Rupert steeled himself against the revulsion at what was to occur. He must not make his friends experience remorse, because they were forced to do what was required to stay alive. What troubled him even more was that, divided up among his companions, the meat was absurdly insufficient for their needs. Raja, too, had to be included. They would inescapably face starvation if their situation did not miraculously improve.

Rupert, overcome with despair and guilt, reached into the sack of dried fruit and nuts and produced the merest handful. That would serve as his dinner. He had not eaten since morning, but had no appetite. He was grateful, for in coming days, his desire for food was bound to return with a ravenous vengeance. And his friends, four-legged and human, would be endlessly suffering also. Yet surely, *surely*, they would find a way to endure.

Chapter Fifteen

The following weeks proved a nightmare of anxiety and torment. The companions, including their animal friends, felt themselves grow weaker by the day - even by the moment. The combined skills of Daniel and Raja could not provide game that did not seem to exist in the barren terrain. On some terrible days, Daniel rode off at dawn, Raja by his side, and did not rejoin his friends until darkness had long fallen. Yet despite his desperate efforts, he'd return empty-handed. Even when more luck was with them, there was never enough for all. And when they did not eat, Rupert himself refrained. He had unsuccessfully begged them to share his meager rations of beans, dried fruit, and nuts. But his comrades were aware he was eating barely enough to sustain life as it was.

Having no alternative, struggle on they did. Rupert was in a state of constant anguish over their dire predicament. Their dwindling supply of oats was in no way adequate for the hardworking steeds. Before his eyes, Rupert could witness the stallions growing thinner, their stamina rapidly dwindling. Should they falter, or even die, there was no hope for the companions to continue their trek. By now, the travelers had been reduced to such a feeble state, they would be hard pressed to walk a single mile; and their journey had countless miles to go.

Sometimes it seemed that Kashkara, which lay beyond Martan's eastern limits, might as well have been on the moon, such an impossible distance did it appear to Rupert. He supposed his friends felt likewise, but dared not broach the topic. For he feared once negative thoughts were permitted to be blatantly expressed, their spirits would take an even greater plunge. The brutal cold and frequent snowfalls did nothing to lessen their sufferings.

Rupert's admiration for his companions grew greater with each horrendous day. None uttered a word of complaint...with the exception of Morley, who apologized with a twisted smile if his growling stomach should keep his friends from their sleep. They did their utmost, one and all, to appear as if nothing was greatly amiss; that these were simply a few difficult days on a journey that had known many such.

Rupert recalled those days past with a strange longing and affection. Their desperate flight through the forest after the escape from prison seemed almost effortless in retrospect. True, they had hardly slept or eaten. Then they had faced an adversary - the King's Guards, led by the relentless Ned - whom they'd outraced and outwitted by their own efforts. Yet now, they faced an enemy - hunger and plague - they had no power to overcome. And Rupert, beyond all things, despised the feeling of helplessness that overwhelmed him.

Little time was spent in converse during their grim progress, hoping to conserve what flagging energy they possessed. Evenings, after the most meager of repasts, were passed in now-desultory practice in the language of Veshti, or music played half-heartedly upon Daniel's flute or Drego's harp. But merry singing or raucous banter were things of the past, it seemed.

Every evening, before dinner, Rupert insisted on proceeding with lessons in archery and sword. The weapons proved unwieldy for Rupert, but steely determination made him carry on. Daniel and his father alternated the instruction, finding their prince an apt pupil despite dire conditions. But as time went on, Rupert's body trembled helplessly under the struggle required to draw back his bow or lift up his sword.

It broke Rupert's agonized heart to see his beloved comrades grow pale and thin. Even Drego, new to their number, was clearly showing signs of deprivation. He had been strapping and robust just a few weeks past. Now, his face was gaunt and gray. But the greatest torment was to see Lira grow hollow-cheeked and ashen. She, who always sparkled like a star, bloomed like the most beautiful of blossoms, was sallow and sick. Rupert witnessed Daniel observing his child with despair. The youthful prince could *never* fail to acknowledge their predicament was his creation, and his alone. There *must* be something to be done to rescue them from this nightmare!

Nightly, he strained heart and mind for consolation or inspiration, but none came. He felt abandoned and heartsick. His friends looked to him with mute faces, hoping for some sign of a change in their fortune. Though none blamed him with words, Rupert saw blame in their looks; even if it was his own burdened soul that imagined it.

One evening, Rupert was feebly attempting to practice archery, Daniel by his side. The young pupil seemed frustrated that he could not hit the target, hung upon a nearby tree, as precisely as he wished. Daniel, his voice hardly more than a whisper, counseled patience, but Rupert felt only impotence at his own shortcomings.

The lackluster lesson was interrupted by a rustle in the nearby barren bushes. Teacher and pupil turned to look, when suddenly from out of the brush raced an animal, strongly resembling a deer, but obviously a breed new to their experience. The graceful creature was perhaps not fully grown, with long, spindly legs, a slender body, and beautiful, huge dark eyes. Raja instantly was on the alert, and looked to Rupert for leave to chase down the prey. Rupert glanced swiftly at Daniel…realizing this encounter was the opportunity to provide, at last, a hearty meal or two for their friends.

Rupert had never witnessed Daniel make his kill, and he did not desire to now. The woodland inhabitant was so young, perfect, vulnerable. They both knew what had to be done. Daniel, gesturing for Rupert to turn away, slowly raised his weapon. But Rupert vehemently shook his head, stepping purposely in front of his friend. Swiftly raising his own bow, the Golden-Eyed Prince, willing himself not to think, let his arrow fly. Rupert witnessed the innocent being collapse to the earth. It had been a clean shot and a swift death.

Rupert, avoiding the look of compassion, gratitude, and astonishment upon Daniel's drawn features, swiftly turned away, racing behind a nearby rock. There he quietly wretched up a bitter bile from his hollow belly. Hot tears fell down his face. Yet if he were to be a worthy leader, Rupert would be required to participate in what was necessary, and not merely delegate unpleasant tasks to others. They were starving, and for once, he could provide them with sustenance. He could not always place the burden upon his brother Daniel.

And so, this night, his friends might eat their fill. They were mute with admiration upon hearing of how their meal had been procured. All embraced Rupert, knowing the agonizing sacrifice his actions had required. Liam kissed him on both cheeks and knelt before him on bended knee. Rupert had been moved by the expression of esteem, but absolutely despised the act that had brought it about.

However, in the following days, game proved again scarce, and their physical decline brutally resumed. The only thing serving to brighten their spirits was that, at last, they had emerged from the mountains. The bitter cold was behind them, at least for the moment. They found themselves on a somewhat flattened plain, with jagged cliffs on either side. The party was indeed grateful as temperatures grew less frigid, and their horses would welcome the more friendly terrain.

Three days later, Rupert again had an episode of sleep-walking. Luckily, Raja immediately alerted the others, and the boy had not been allowed to wander off as a result. He remained in his strange half-sleep for several hours, however, and again uttered something about 'a fortress' and nothing more. Upon fully awakening at dawn, Rupert had no recollection of what had occurred.

"I wish I knew *what* 'fortress' meant...or where it might be found," he weakly whispered in frustration. However, at least it served to clear one matter in the mind of Rupert and his friends. Drego claimed Rupert had spoken of a fortress when he'd first encountered the boy. Now they could believe the report. Rupert had always doubted the veracity of the tale.

"Well, let's do keep a sharp look-out," said Lira. "For shelter would prove welcome indeed." The others looked about their barren surroundings without much hope, however.

Nonetheless, it was the very next day, when the companions had hardly the strength to continue another step, that the startling sight did indeed present itself. It was Rupert who spotted it high atop a distant cliff. The sizeable structure appeared run-down, perhaps deserted, but it was the first sign of civilization encountered since abandoning the roads.

"Rupert, that surely must be it! The fortress!" gasped Morley, his voice feeble and hoarse. "What do you think?" His long auburn hair was now lank and blew about his face untidily in the heavy breeze. But a faint light of hope returned to his tired green eyes.

Rupert hardly knew what to believe…yet this must be no mere coincidence. "I cannot know for certain, but let us waste no time in putting the theory to the test!"

"Just a moment," cautioned Liam. "Presumably, we shall be forbidden entrance since there is plague about. We are strangers, and may be rightly feared to be carriers."

"Whoever dwells within could be sick, and we could catch it, do not forget," added Drego, now suddenly cautious.

"We have no choice," spoke Rupert with weary resolve. "We'll hardly last another hour in our state. Let us approach and see what we encounter."

"Shall I scout ahead and discover if our greeting be friendly?" Drego wanted to know. But Rupert did not like that idea.

"No, we shall proceed together." And with that, they turned their fading, half-starved horses towards the high cliff. It would be a challenging task for their steeds, but their faltering riders could no longer hope to make the ascent on foot.

It required almost an hour to reach the stone structure. The comrades' approach had been obvious. But none called out to challenge them as they halted before the entrance. Indeed, only an eerie silence surrounded them.

"Looks like the place has been abandoned for who knows how long," ventured Morley. Indeed, only the moan of the wind against the rocky walls greeted their ears. Something did not seem right. But all wished to explore further.

With a gesture from Rupert, the party dismounted and stood hesitating outside the archway marking the opening to the inner courtyard. Leading their stumbling mounts, their riders cautiously made their way forward, their own steps unsteady.

"What-ho, anybody here?" called out Drego, raising his voice with effort. But no answer came. The footfalls of their boots and the horses' hooves upon the cobblestones made a lonely echo. Where had the inhabitants gone?

The party proceeded with trepidation while crossing a drawbridge leading into the interior. Soon they came upon stone rooms, one to the right, another to the left. The first chamber presented them with such a sight that Rupert and his friends believed they must be dreaming.

For what they beheld was food…sacks upon sacks of supplies! They raced towards the mirage, to find it indeed real. Tearing open a number of the bags with drawn daggers, they discovered beans, rice, dried fruit, and nuts. Not pausing even for a moment, they reached in, one and all, snatching handfuls of nuts or fruit and commenced to devour it like hungry wolves. None was immune, and Rupert, his mouth still salivating from the dream-like deliciousness, stumbled to every member of his party and feebly embraced them, an embrace all managed somehow to return.

It took only a moment for Rupert to remember Raja, and gave him his share...more than his share... of rations. A rasping shout of joy reached the boy's ears when Daniel discovered sacks of raw oats among the booty. Three were immediately torn open, and the horses were allowed their fill. Their steeds whinnied in delight.

Rupert was certain he'd never felt such rapture. It moved him to tears to observe Lira, her father, and grandfather clasp arms. For the family had been so very close to perishing, and now might, phenomenally, hope to survive!

The celebration continued. Stacks of firewood were arrayed against the wall. It did not take long to build a roaring blaze, and soon teeming bowls of porridge, sweetened with nuts, dried fruit, and even honey were prepared, and instantly consumed. Tea, something they'd long been denied, was also here in plenty, and they partook of cup after steaming cup. The comrades continued to laugh, cry, embrace, and exchange looks of awed joy - euphoria providing their depleted bodies with counterfeit energy. And at last, they were able to speak of the miracle that had occurred.

"Well, Rupert, it appears you've done it again! You told us of a fortress, and here it is to save the day," proclaimed Morley, a tiny measure of color now returning to his gaunt visage. He was filled with admiration anew for his astonishing prince.

"Yes, I do believe this is the most beautiful structure on earth," cried Lira, sitting on her grandfather's knee. Seeing a radiant smile return to her wan face made Rupert's heart glad.

"I do not mean to appear ungrateful, but to what do we owe this good fortune?" Rupert wondered aloud. "Where have the inhabitants gone? And why did they not take their supplies with them?"

"Perhaps they were ordered to depart in haste, and bring only what they might easily carry," ventured Daniel. "But I agree it is all very peculiar. However, let us investigate upon the morrow - and enjoy the fact we may truly hope to see it dawn."

With that, Daniel broke out his flute, and led his companions in a merry tune, with Drego quick to join in with his harp. Their profound moment of celebration had renewed their energy sufficiently to sing their way through the song - though in truth, their condition remained feeble indeed. But even Raja was inspired to howl out his own accompaniment, to the raucous cheers of his human friends.

"It was all worth it," Rupert thought to himself. "We have somehow survived." He regarded his companions with endless admiration. How could he be so fortunate as to have such people to share his fate? For surely, there were no finer, braver, more gallant beings on earth!

The revelry went on for some time before profound exhaustion claimed them into sleep. The sorely debilitated friends were at last secure with plentiful food, and thus, the belief that life, and their journey, would go on. But the very next morning this happy belief was to be horribly overthrown.

Chapter Sixteen

They arose after a restless, discomfort-ridden night, the result of unwise indulgence after long weeks of starvation. Yet Rupert and his friends still found themselves eager for breakfast. Liam sternly warned that they partake of their new-found bounty sparingly this day, else they'd continue to pay the price. But it was difficult to exercise restraint after enduring endless distress and want.

"I somehow never realized how delicious porridge is!" exclaimed Lira with glee, laughing as she willingly shared her portion with a happy Raja. Rupert and Daniel had seen to feeding the horses, and all their party, animal and human, appeared in revived spirits.

"Let us explore as soon as we may," urged Morley. "For who knows what other delights await within?"

"Yet, we best proceed with caution," urged Rupert, as an unwelcome quiver of fear chilled him.

The inspection would commence as soon as they completed the morning repast. It was also decided the comrades would remain within sheltering walls for several days at least, so they might regain a measure of badly depleted strength. The horses, too, required rest. But Rupert was growing uneasy.

Finally they set off, none wishing to be left behind. For many of the party, it would be their first experience in such a dwelling, and they were indeed curious. Beyond that, was the mystery of why the place had been abandoned.

The very first room they came up provided great reward. It was located directly opposite from where the food had been stored; but this chamber was filled with weapons - so many of every type; swords, daggers, bows and arrows, even suits of armor. Morley gave a look of disgust when spotting the heavy metal uniform. He turned to one and spat upon it.

"Bah," Morley exclaimed. "How I despised being encased in those torture suits! It was akin to being imprisoned, and I already felt as if King Ryker's slave."

"I am certain that's true," said Liam, attempting to calm his friend after his outburst. "But let us be grateful for these fine weapons. I can assure you, we'll not take armor with us; but as for the rest, they're welcome indeed."

"Especially the arrows," observed Rupert with a grim satisfaction. The young prince felt they could never carry enough; knowing they'd face untold enemies as time went on. "The dilemma is that we cannot possibly transport all the food and weapons we have uncovered - though it troubles me to leave anything so precious behind."

"No help for that," said Drego.

After a few satisfied moments examining their booty, the party proceeded to the structure's upper floors. There, a disturbing sight awaited them. Most of the furnishings seemed intact. But here and there, chairs, tables, and other objects were overturned, giving the appearance of a departure made in confusion. Proceeding cautiously to the highest level of the dwelling, they encountered an unsettling silence; the echoes of their footfalls could not diminish the feeling of coming upon a dead world.

The first of the chambers proved empty, but as they approached what seemed to be a large hall, Raja let out a chilling howl and stood stock still. Daniel, Morley, and Drego drew their blades, motioning the others back. The three men proceeded to push the great wooden doors open wide. What they observed sent them reeling backwards.

They raced towards the others, motioning them to flee. And before Liam, Rupert, or Lira could satisfy their curiosity, they obeyed, none pausing until they had returned to the lower floor, where the food and weapons had been stored.

Rupert regarded the foreboding aspect of the trio. "Do tell us what you have seen," he begged. "For you appear as pale as ghosts."

"That is because we *have* seen ghosts, or at least their remains," declared Daniel, aghast. "The hall was filled with bodies…perhaps a dozen, perhaps more. Some were slain by arrow, but most appeared to have perished of illness."

His companions regarded Daniel in horror. So, there was plague within the fortress walls! The very place that had preserved their lives might now seal their doom.

"That explains much," whispered a haggard, shaken Liam. "Clearly, when sickness broke out, most of the inhabitants fled, carrying with them what they could. Some who had already fallen ill might have sought to escape as well, and were slain by the others." The dark image of events penetrated the mind's eye of his listeners.

Rupert expressed the thought that none could bear to speak aloud. "Then, *we* may have been exposed as well. Is that not so?"

"We cannot know for certain," cautioned Daniel. "Let us depart with all haste."

"Would we then not spread the disease to others?" asked the always compassionate Lira.

"We have not yet crossed paths with any of Martan's citizens…at least none living," reminded her father. "We must hope this luck will continue. But remaining here would prove far too perilous."

There was a terrible silence. The longed-for wish to recuperate from their last agonizing weeks was not to be granted. Instead, they must flee without delay, and pray they had not brought contamination upon themselves.

In a very short time, their horses were packed with all they could possibly carry in the way of food and weapons. The travelers loaded their knapsacks as well, and once again found themselves bound towards the eastern border of Martan, and the land of Kashkara. They could not bear to contemplate that cruel sickness might be added to their countless trials. Surely, they could escape that fate!

Rupert and his friends moved purposefully, putting distance between themselves and an invisible foe. The horses, far from recovered, could not travel as rapidly as their riders might have wished. But still, they were able to make decent progress, and day's end found them a good fifteen miles from the fortress of death.

"We owe Raja a vote of thanks," declared Morley, "for his warning prevented us from blundering into that hellish hall. Since Daniel, Drego, and I observed caution, we likely did not approach close enough to the victims to do ourselves harm."

"We can only hope that is true," sighed Liam.

"Do not forget, we carry many healing herbs with us, so we could treat anyone who *did* fall ill," Lira reminded them.

"May we have no need of them," Rupert prayed. But he *was* grateful to possess a large supply of medicines obtained from Liam's farm and his grandparents' cottage. Yet he could hardly be certain they'd stave off some dreadful foreign pestilence.

However, the comrades soon had reason to be hopeful. The next three days passed without incident. All had good appetites, and felt stronger for the nourishment now theirs in plenty. Even the horses regained a measure of stamina and made good time. Drego guessed, after once more perusing Rupert's map, that they might need only one further week to reach Kashkara. Since the borders had been closed, at least the last they'd heard, it was decided the only course was to cross in stealth. They would only hope that kingdom was plague-free and they might travel there without hazard.

However, just as optimism began to reign, Lira fell sick. She had awakened one morning, five days after they fled the fortress, complaining of a pounding headache, and refused breakfast. Her companions were immediately alarmed, and upon examining his granddaughter, Liam found she was burning with fever, and that a blistering red rash covered much of her frail body. A wave of horror washed over the group as he announced his findings.

"Daniel and I will be responsible for her care," declared Liam firmly, directing his piercing blue-eyed gaze in Rupert's direction. "Rupert, Morley, and Drego, you *must* keep back. Do not approach for any reason. We must seek to contain this before *all* are in peril."

Rupert immediately made protest. "No, we are *already* exposed! I must help Lira, as she did when I was ill."

Daniel shook his head. "No, Rupert, it's not the same. Your illness was not contagious. I know my father would order me from Lira's side if he could. But she is my daughter. Remember Rupert, all is lost if you become ill. Your life is not merely your own. *You must not perish, come what may!*"

Despite the truth of Daniel's words, Rupert could hardly value his life above Lira's. But father and son proved firm. They also had Drego and Morley on their side, though all were stricken at the thought of the beauteous, vivid lass coming to harm.

Thus, there was nothing for Rupert and the others to do but witness her suffering from afar. Liam and Daniel utilized the many healing remedies in their arsenal, but none seemed to touch the demon raging through her fragile body. She moaned and cried out in pain, but did not seem conscious from almost the first.

Within another day, matters grew even worse. First, Daniel fell victim to the dark disease, and in another hour, Liam, too, collapsed in an agony of pain and fever. Blistering red blotches covered their bodies, clearly adding to their sufferings. Rupert could no longer be restrained. All three, father, son, and granddaughter, now lay helpless.

Rupert would not permit them to succumb! Drego urged caution, reminding the boy-prince of his duties. Morley, however, sided with Rupert.

"We can hardly consider ourselves friends, or even human beings, if we witness our comrades dying in torment while thinking only of our own precious hides! I cannot comprehend you, Drego,"

With that, Rupert and Morley crossed the invisible line separating them from their fallen comrades. Rupert, who had knowledge of healing, continued to brew concoctions to ease their pain, Morley offering what assistance he could. They built a huge fire and covered the sick with layers of blankets. At least their patients were kept warm, but attempts to make them drink the herbal concoctions proved less successful.

Rupert regarded his cherished adopted kin in horrified despair. If any perished, he could not go on. Liam was Rupert's soul, his conscience. Daniel was his treasured elder brother, and Lira, his precious, loving sister. All three had suffered so much during their separation. They had been joyfully reunited these past months. To think it might all have led to nothing; nothing but death in a lonely, forbidding landscape in the midst of an alien land.

Another torturous day passed. The three seemed no better to Rupert's terrified eyes. Morley could only concur. Drego had finally joined them, but still clearly disapproved of Rupert's decision to put himself at risk. But Rupert could hardly keep a clear thought, so overwrought was he. Combined with this was the fact that he had neither eaten nor taken rest since Lira had fallen ill, several days since. But all urging to sleep or take nourishment fell on deaf ears.

Upon mopping the sweat-streaked brows of his friends yet again, Rupert longed to wail in despair. No response did he receive, no matter how intensely he called out their names. There was no doubt in his mind; they were growing weaker. They could not survive much longer…perhaps not even through the night.

In greatest, darkest anguish, Rupert took to his feet, and commenced to stride back and forth like one possessed. He shouted aloud, without being aware of the fact.

"Surely, there is *something* I can do!" he repeated again and again. "Here I am, a Golden-Eyed King! Have I no power to command death to depart from those I love…from those whom I cannot live without? Whatever you are that guides me…*how dare you remain silent!?*"

Morley and Drego, who also suffered greatly in their distress, feared for Rupert's sanity if the victims failed to recover. Rupert would not merely suffer a ghastly loss, he would take the blame solely upon himself.

Drego had a desperate intuition. He came to Rupert's side, causing him to cease his pacing…forcing the distraught lad to hear his words.

"Rupert, perhaps there *is* something you might do."

"Then tell me at once!" cried Rupert harshly to the man he could not trust. "For healing remedies have come to naught, and I despair, I truly despair."

"You forget that you have the blood of Raja-Sharan in your veins. There are many healers in that land, and it is said the royals carry that gift. You must save your friends, not with herbs and teas, but with your own strength, *your own will!* You must *try*, Rupert. It is our only hope."

Rupert regarded Drego with skeptical and bewildered eyes. "Of what do you speak? I know of no such power or ability. Surely, this is no time for riddles."

Drego regarded him, his gray eyes determined and direct. "I *do* speak plain. You are a Prince of Raja-Sharan, and there is a power that likely lies within you. I cannot tell you how to proceed. You must address your own heart."

Rupert glared at the man, perplexed. Yet then, he *did* begin to hear a distinct voice from within. It told him to withdraw, to become silent and still. As if in a trace, Rupert proceeded to a nearby tree, one with spreading, sheltering branches that seemed to give off a serene, welcoming energy.

Rupert sat beneath it, listening to his own breath. And somehow, amidst the terrors that assailed his spirit, he found himself growing calm, growing quiet. It was as if a hand of peace had descended upon him. He remained motionless for many moments. Morley and Drego watched as the boy-prince then slowly took to his feet and made towards Daniel, Lira, and Liam, as if in a dream.

Rupert knelt beside his dying comrades. His drawn but radiant face wore a look of tender detachment. He held out his hands towards Lira, who had become shrunken and wretched with the tortures of her ordeal. He gently placed his fingers upon her head and abdomen. In a few moments, he followed suit with her father and grandfather. He spent no more than an hour at his task, then withdrew towards the tree and sat silent again. At length, Raja and Majesty went to his side, and their presence appeared to draw the boy from his trance-like state.

Rupert blinked and looked up. He gave a puzzled look to Morley and Drego, who gazed at him mutely. He spoke, his voice hardly above a whisper.

"I do remember all that has transpired, and feel most…peculiar - as if I'm not quite here. But I now believe that, despite everything, all will be well."

The boy rose, somewhat unsteadily, then without haste made his way to where his loved ones slept. Drego and Morley accompanied him, as did Raja and even Majesty. The three stricken comrades lay pale and still, but their sunken faces no longer burned red with fever.

Gingerly, Rupert knelt beside them, as the others followed suit. Rupert gently touched Lira's forehead. He glanced up in puzzlement. "Why, I do believe her fever has broken," he whispered, not quite daring to believe. Morley and Drego announced that the same held true for Liam and Daniel.

Rupert, Drego, and Morley exchanged looks of bewildered but profound elation. *Something* extraordinary and inexplicable had occurred. Something none quite comprehended. Something that, without Drego's presence, might never have come to pass. Thus Rupert felt, at that moment, he understood everything and nothing. And that all existence was even a greater mystery than before.

Chapter Seventeen

L iam, Daniel, and Lira lay drowned in sleep for many hours. Rupert continued to experience concern, hardly grasping what had occurred the previous night. Drego and Morley offered smiles and congratulations, but Rupert, though feeling a measure of relief, was yet profoundly perplexed.

It was only when the sun again commenced to set that Liam began to stir. Rupert gasped in joy, immediately at his side. The patient was weak, yet managed to inquire, in a faint whisper, about his son and granddaughter. Rupert could reassure that his family now appeared out of danger. As if to confirm this report, within a very few moments, Daniel and Lira opened their eyes as well.

Drego had prepared rice gruel for the sick ones. None but Drego had ever taken of rice, but he vowed it was just the thing to aid them in regaining strength. "My mother told me it was the sovereign remedy for those recovering from illness." Rupert, Drego, and Morley each fed one of their friends, and happily, they were able to keep it down with no complaint.

By the next morning, the trio showed marked improvement. They could sit up and feed themselves from the continual supply of gruel, this time also containing garlic, which Drego assured would add stamina to the mix. They were now able to speak with a measure of strength, and indeed, were full of questions as to what had taken place.

"I do remember caring for Lira, then saw Daniel fall victim as well," said Liam with effort. "Yet, I'm quite unable to recall anything after that."

"That's because you fell ill yourself, and though Rupert thrust upon you all the healing herbs available, none responded as we'd hoped. I must confess, we were in despair," reported Morley, throwing a glance in Rupert's direction. For he, too, was still attempting to fathom the perplexing circumstance of these miraculous healings.

"I believe Rupert will have something of interest to report concerning your recovery," said Drego. But Rupert proved reluctant to speak.

"Do tell us," chimed in Lira. "For you all look rather strange and secretive."

"Indeed, that's true," added Daniel. "Do we owe our recovery to some remarkable event? Did one of those mysterious, disappearing ladies arrive with a magical potion?" He spoke with a smile, but was growing curious.

Evidently, *something* had taken place that caused Rupert to blush.

Drego and Morley nodded encouragement to their prince, and taking a deep breath Rupert finally described the marvelous, if yet imperfectly understood events leading to their restoration.

"It was a truly unfamiliar, powerful, and peaceful feeling," Rupert concluded. "Yet, I remain bewildered as to what did, in fact, occur."

There was a pause as his listeners attempted to comprehend Rupert's report. "Well, whatever the truth of the tale, you are clearly responsible for our being alive at this moment," declared Liam with a fascinated gaze into his prince's golden eyes. "I, too, cannot claim to understand, but sometimes in life, comprehension only comes well after the event."

"Perhaps it is not as mysterious as all that," exclaimed Drego. "In the land of Raja-Sharan, as well as my father's country of Gitano, it is widely believed all things contain the energy of life...whether trees, animals, people, it matters not. When you fell ill, your energies were dangerously disturbed. Rupert was able to harness his own energies to balance them again, allowing you to heal."

Drego's audience regarded him with perplexity. The explanation was perhaps too simple, yet in part made sense to Rupert. Since earliest childhood, he had been able to *feel* the forest and its creatures. It did not seem too great a leap to call what he felt 'their energies' - and if one *could* truly feel such a thing, would it not conceivably be possible to interact with it?

Rupert expressed some of these thoughts, and the others listened in respectful silence. "It may be feasible, Rupert," said Daniel. "Yet I wonder if you could truly interfere with death itself?"

Drego again had something to add. "Of course, I cannot answer such a query. Yet I was taught that each of us has our own fate. Our actions can influence it to some degree, but likely we are never completely masters of our destiny. So perhaps, if you had *truly* been destined to die, Rupert could not have intervened. The possibility existed of your being healed, thus, Rupert was able to hasten that event."

None knew what to make of such a theory. Rupert hardly found it agreeable.

"If all is fated, then our lives are set out for us already. I find that notion most unsatisfying. I reject the very idea. I *must* believe I am master of my fate...that we *all* are! I cannot find solace in any other possibility."

Liam smiled. "I, too, share your views on the subject. The unexpected is always happening to us, wouldn't you agree? Yet plainly we cannot be in control of *all* that occurs. Perhaps it is a combination of fate and our actions that determines our path?"

It seemed the subject was impossible to settle with ideas or logic. None could know where the truth lay. But they were pleased to debate the topic, happy beyond measure in the essential fact that Lira, Daniel, and Liam, by whatever fate or miracle, were on the road to recovery. All else seemed secondary.

The companions remained where they were for several days, for all, not only the formerly sick, needed to replenish their strength. The past weeks had been an agonizing ordeal. Yet before very long, they felt well enough to grow restless. The border to Kashkara could not be many days' journey. Without doubt that land, too, was filled with the unknown and possible peril. But that did not cause the comrades to be less eager to be on their way.

As soon as the travelers could sit upon their horses once more, they set off. The weather was favoring them, as it was somewhat mild for this time of year. The companions shed several layers of clothing they had been forced to don earlier. All were cautiously optimistic they might soon cross the frontier of Martan without interference.

The comrades met with no impediments in the following days, and spirits rose. None could forget that myriad disasters had assailed them so recently, yet they somehow triumphed over them. Rupert felt boundless joy when reminded of that fact. Perhaps there *was* a mysterious force guiding him - one that kept him and his friends safeguarded through darkest encounters.

This pleasant thought was now interrupted. The travelers were about to pass through a thick grove when Raja, who had been trotting several yards ahead, commenced to bark and howl. Majesty, too, reared up on hind legs, almost throwing the daydreaming Rupert. The entire party came to an immediate halt.

"Rupert, get back," warned Morley, drawing his sword, and Rupert obeyed by pulling Majesty to the rear of the group. It was done for safety's sake, but also to keep Rupert's golden eyes hidden from any who might draw near.

Liam and Drego also drew weapons, and Daniel had bow and arrow in hand. Rupert reached for his bow, attempting to give Lira a reassuring look in the process. After all, it might simply be an animal on the prowl; nothing to be greatly alarmed about.

Such soothing ideas were overturned when a voice harshly called from behind the trees. "Throw down your weapons, for you are surrounded." Only Drego could comprehend the words, however, since the intruder spoke in the language of Martan. The tone of voice, however, hardly required translation.

Drego whispered to his friends what had been said, and Liam nodded for him to respond. Drego called out that they meant no harm, but had no intention of lowering their weapons.

After a confused silent standoff, a handful of men stepped from behind the trees. All were armed with either sword or bow, and their weapons were raised. These fellows were clearly not soldiers, which the comrades observed with immediate relief. But they had a desperate look. And frightened men might prove capable of anything.

The companions were again ordered to disarm, and again, refused. Drego demanded to know the reason they interfered with honest travelers. But no response was forthcoming. It appeared something of a stalemate, since neither group wished to approach the other. All feared the plague. Liam was not at all convinced that catching it once made it impossible to catch it twice.

"Tell them we have been sick. And inquire again what they want of us," instructed Liam.

Drego obeyed, and saw fear in the eyes of the strangers upon hearing the news. Their leader spoke, reporting that many of their number had succumbed to the fever, only this handful having survived. They'd fled their village weeks before, and had depleted their meager supply of food. They charged the companions to give over their own rations. The reckless men aimed arrows in the comrades' direction, as if to drive their point home.

"They can hardly expect us to comply," murmured Drego to his friends. "We cannot starve to save their lot."

"No, but we can help," whispered Rupert. "May we not give what we can spare? And direct them to the castle? There is plentiful food still to be found. If they avoid the upper floor where the plague victims lay, perhaps it would be safe enough."

Daniel agreed, and told Drego to make the offer. But evidently it proved unsatisfactory, for an arrow unexpectedly flew, piercing Drego's left arm, while another whizzed over Daniel's head. Drego cried out in surprise as well as pain. Raja, howling, raced in the direction of the archer who had wounded his friend. Urgently, Rupert commanded Raja back, and reluctantly the mastiff returned to his master's side.

"Drego, are you badly hurt?" cried Morley, alarmed at this turn of events.

"Be assured, 'tis not much as these things go." Wincing, he yanked the arrow from his arm, causing the wound to bleed freely. Both groups kept their eyes locked upon the other, but no more arrows were unleashed. It seemed none wished for a bloodbath.

The leader of the would-be bandits signaled his men to lower their weapons. "We are not robbers," he explained, "but we cannot permit our families to starve. We have women and children with us."

Drego translated, and the leader spoke again. "Did I not just hear your name? Was it not 'Drego'? I have heard it before, though it is one foreign to us." He gave the wounded man a swift once-over. "Are you not a performer who wanders this land?"

Drego managed a wry smile, despite the blood dripping from his arm.

"Yes. Did my last performance displease so much you desired my death?"

While the leader spoke in whispers to his friends, Drego translated for the companions. Daniel had cautiously ridden to his side, and producing a cloth from his knapsack, attempted to bind the wound. The blood refused to be stemmed, however. Drego winked in Daniel's direction. "Do not concern yourself. I've been hurt far worse than this in my wicked past!"

Suddenly, their opponents approached with their weapons lowered. In response, the companions followed suit.

"We are not murderers," their leader assured the party. "We search for food. We did not mean you harm, but our sorrows have made us desperate. Please go your way, and leave us to our fate."

Drego again translated. The suffering and distress of the strangers seemed palpable.

"Tell them we can help," said Liam. "We can follow Rupert's inspiration to give what we can spare, and direct them to the castle, with proper warnings."

Drego again made the offer. This time the attackers agreed, stepping back as Morley unloaded a sack of rice, one of oats, and one of dried fruit. After Morley remounted, the comrades backed off so the men on foot might take up their supplies. Both parties regarded the other with compassion but also trepidation.

"I again make apology for your injury, Drego," said their leader. "My name is Yakim. My family and I saw you perform more than once. My wife and two of my three children now lay dead of the fever, and what is to become of those who have survived, I cannot guess."

After hearing Drego's translation, Rupert's heart was torn with empathy. The other would-be robbers had surely suffered similar fates. How could Rupert have persevered if Liam, Daniel, or Lira had perished? Perhaps unwisely, Rupert urged Majesty forward until he neared the beleaguered group.

"It is with great sorrow that I hear of your loss. All here have suffered much. Yet one thing I know – *we must never give up!* No matter what lies ahead, we must draw courage from the deepest part of our being and somehow endure. For life is *always* precious, though we sometimes cannot, through our pain, perceive its value. Yet be assured, someday you will once more."

Rupert spoke with such vision and clarity that a translation was almost unnecessary, but Drego carried out his task nonetheless. The strangers regarded this youth, his face largely concealed by the hood of his cloak, sitting astride a magnificent horse, speaking in a manner ringing with authority. They all wondered at him. Then, before they might inquire as to his identity, Rupert nodded to his party and they set off, circling a wide arc around their ambushers.

"We wish you well. Go in peace," called Rupert over his shoulder, as Drego transmitted his words.

Finally, the comrades continued on until they felt safely away. It was then that Drego toppled from his horse in a faint.

Chapter Eighteen

They swiftly dismounted and raced to Drego's side. It was only a brief moment before the wounded man regained consciousness, immediately apologizing for his show of weakness.

"Do allow me a short bit of rest," he assured them, "and I shall be fit to continue."

Liam brushed his remarks aside, while carefully removing Drego's outer garment so he might more closely examine the injury. The arrow had struck deeply and bleeding was profuse. All the while, Drego continued to protest that he required nothing more than a brief respite.

Liam, however, moved into action; calling for various herbs, ordering a fire to be built, and unrolling several blankets so Drego would not be required to lie upon the cold earth. After a more thorough evaluation, with Rupert eagerly offering assistance, it was concluded that Drego indeed required rest for a day or two to make certain no infection set in.

The wound was rapidly cleaned and bandaged after healing ointments were spread upon it. Since it was by then mid-afternoon, Drego reluctantly agreed to recuperate till the morrow. After being obliged to consume healing teas, the patient was soon sound asleep.

"This incident recalls our first meeting in prison," mused Daniel, glancing at his prince with a smile. "For I had received a similar wound to my shoulder, and your healing skills, plus the medicines smuggled to you from my father with Morley's aid, served to save my life. Drego spoke of the role of 'fate' earlier. What a matchless mystery that is…as is life itself!"

Rupert, too, recalled those days. Being unjustly imprisoned along with a dying stranger had indeed been an unforgettable experience. One, in fact, that had forever altered his existence. He had no way of knowing that the anonymous soldier he'd labored to keep alive was none other than Lira's father, Liam's son.

"I too, frequently contemplate the strange occurrences that have shaped our path since destiny brought us together. It is likely something we may never *truly* comprehend, at least till *all* the pieces of this perplexing puzzle fall into place."

Meanwhile, Lira was more concerned with the here and now, inquiring again and again as to Drego's condition. She was reassured, however, that if complications did not arise, all should be well.

However, that evening Drego broke out in a fever. The wound showed signs of festering. Liam and Rupert acted quickly to stave it off, administering healing unguents and teas. For a few hours, their patient became delirious. He cried out in the language of Raja-Sharan. Most of his mutterings were unclear, but Rupert comprehended the words *'ta-kumi'* - meaning *'I will obey'* repeated several times.

Lira was beside herself with concern, as the soft spot she carried for the dashing and charismatic fellow had not dimmed. Even Rupert, who could not overcome distrust for Drego, was relieved when dawn brought undeniable improvement. His fever broke, and the wounded man came to himself not long afterwards.

"This is but a scratch, though it has proven troublesome enough," he whispered when forced to drink more healing brews. Drego insisted he was fit for travel, but the tea contained a strong dose of an herb which produced drowsiness. He soon slept again, and did not awaken until sunset.

"How is it that I've dozed all through this day? I do believe some mischief is afoot."

Liam laughed. "I must plead guilty, for your tea was derived from *'noctura,'* which gained you the rest required, whether you wished it or not!"

Drego, now strong enough to sit up, had the good grace to grin ruefully. "Guess only such devious means would have accomplished that," he admitted. "But I hope you find me fit enough for dinner. I find myself mighty hungry."

All took this as a good sign, and Lira noted that the pallor had begun to recede from his cheeks. She prepared rice gruel, though he muttered a protest when catching sight of it.

"Bah, I was hoping for something more substantial. But since my pretty miss made it herself, I'll be pleased to partake." Lira blushed with pleasure.

"Do you suppose you can travel on the morrow?" inquired Daniel. "I confess being eager to depart Martan."

Rupert could not help but be amused. "It seems we find ourselves anxious to flee every territory we cross. Shall we encounter hospitable soil before reaching Raja-Sharan?"

Drego shrugged, but proclaimed he would be fit to travel by morning. Liam had a wait-and-see attitude.

However, with the dawn, Drego's condition had further improved. His arm had ceased bleeding, though clearly still caused pain. It would take several weeks to completely heal, and there was nothing to be done for that. The comrades determined to continue on, and after the morning meal, made ready to depart.

As they commenced through the uneven terrain, Rupert determined to satisfy his curiosity on one point. Drawing Majesty along side Drego's mount, the boy inquired if he recalled any dreams while his fever was high. He gave Rupert a sideways glance, claiming he remembered nothing.

"Why do you ask, Rupert?"

Rupert hesitated. Reluctantly, he described overhearing Drego incoherently raving in the language of Veshti. "I did not understand all of what you spoke, but I believe you repeated the phrase '*ta-kumi*.'"

Drego regarded the boy blankly and then forced a smile. "Do you expect me to be held responsible for my mad mutterings?"

Rupert felt convinced Drego *was* withholding something, and the boy did not like that fact...he did not like it at all. For the moment, it would simply be another black mark against the person who so frequently aroused Rupert's displeasure.

That evening passed pleasantly enough. Drego insisted on preparing their repast, in thanks for the fine nursing he'd received. The bean and rice dish was judged to be quite palatable, along with the jasmine tea he brewed. There were language studies, and a few songs accompanied by Daniel's precious flute. A perusal of Rupert's map gave reason to believe their party might cross into Kashkara within three or four days.

Perhaps due to recent events, the companions found themselves ready for sleep earlier than the norm. And sleep so soundly they did, that it was an extraordinarily groggy Rupert that struggled to force his eyes open the following morning. His head ached abominably, and for a moment he could not move. Might *he* now be stricken with the fever that had almost taken his friends?

Yet the boy did not feel precisely ill, but instead, heavily drained of energy. He momentarily wondered if he had not suffered another of his bizarre disappearances. But open his eyes he finally did, and was instantly reassured that his companions lay nearby. However, *something* was clearly amiss. The day was cloudy, but the hour was advanced - likely half the morning was gone!

Rupert struggled to sit and felt a wave of dizziness. He did succeed in gaining his feet. Gazing down at his recumbent friends, his heart hammered sickeningly. He had one thought…where was Raja? Where were Majesty and the other horses? They could neither be seen nor heard.

The frantic youth dashed clumsily toward where the horses had been tethered. "Majesty, Majesty! Raja, Raja, come to me!" he cried…but there was no response.

Battling panic, he raced to his companions. They were all beginning to awaken, and Rupert knelt, shaking them and calling each name to hasten return to their senses. Next, Rupert became aware of something dreadful and sinister – *Drego was gone!*

"I knew it!!" he cried aloud. Drego must have run off in the night! Taken everything with him! Another horrific realization assailed Rupert like a blow. *"The treasure!"* he moaned. It had been lashed to Majesty's pack. Now both were gone.

By then, Rupert's friends had gained their footing, and understood the meaning of their sovereign's cries. "Tell me what has occurred, Rupert," Liam begged with urgency. "Speak plainly."

"It is obvious. We have been drugged. Perhaps the noctura. Drego insisted on preparing dinner, also our tea. We have slept far too long, and awaken to find everything gone; your horses, my Majesty, Raja, even the treasure." Rupert's words caused the others to look about desperately. The news became yet more dire.

"Most of our food has vanished as well...*and* all our weapons," declared Morley. "The filthy scoundrel!"

"This cannot be true," cried Lira in tears. "Drego was our *friend!* He would never have acted so."

However, the facts spoke for themselves. "I'm sorry, darling," said her father. "I know how you liked him. But it does appear we were betrayed in a most dishonorable fashion. Rupert, I fear your suspicions were only too legitimate. Had we but heeded your warnings, we would have dispatched the villain before he could leave us in this state!"

Liam sought to keep fear from overwhelming his spirit. "But what of Raja and Majesty? Would *they* have willingly left your side? It seems unthinkable."

Rupert replied in an agony of bitterness. "Never! Drego must have drugged Raja as well. He was likely bound and put atop one of the horses. Majesty, too, must have been given something to make him docile. He'd have to be able to walk, while unable to resist. But *why*?! What are his motives for leaving us to perish?"

"Who can guess?" replied a furious Morley. "Perhaps he means to sell our food, our treasure, our horses, and most valuable of all – the fact that a Golden-Eyed Prince is vulnerable to any villain wishing to take advantage of the opportunity. Perhaps King Ryker's spies are hereabouts, awaiting Drego's intelligence. That filthy turncoat has likely been their agent from the first."

"This cannot be so!" protested a stubbornly unconvinced Lira. "Raja and Majesty trusted him from the first. How could that be if he were truly bad?"

"There are those with power over the minds of animals as well as the hearts of men," ventured Liam. "We cannot know the answer as yet, but we must acknowledge the reality of our plight. Almost everything we possess is gone, and Drego gone with them."

Rupert gave another gasp of horror and reached into his tunic. His hand returned empty. "The map, the map, too, is lost," the boy whispered in utter defeat. This calamity was *his* responsibility, and his alone. *He* had made the decision that Drego should enter their circle - and now catastrophe had been brought upon them.

"This is the *very worst* that could have happened! We are left with barely enough food for three days...no horses or weapons. The border is an endless journey if we must proceed on foot. No doubt Drego has alerted his *true* friends as to our whereabouts. This is the worst," repeated the heartsick young king.

Liam came to his side, kneeling beside Rupert, so he might gaze directly into the eyes of the broken-spirited liege.

"Do not believe that, dearest boy. It is certainly *not* the worst for us! Do you not recall only a few days since, Daniel, Lira, and I might have perished with fever? Or that you yourself might have succumbed to it, thus ending hope for our homeland? We are yet alive and still together. Fate has indeed dealt us a mighty blow, but we are not yet defeated!"

Rupert managed a wan smile at the wise man he honored so much. Liam was, at the same time, right and wrong. The boy could not easily overlook his dreadful errors in judgment that had brought them to such a pass. But yes, it *was* true he had most of his loved ones with him, more precious than any riches.

"Indeed, Grandfather Liam, I *am* grateful. But we *must* get back Raja, Majesty, and the treasure. And the map, the other horses, our weapons and food! We must get them all back!"

"A fine idea, Rupert, but how?" inquired Morley. "We're now on foot, and that blasted Drego probably has traveled all through the night and half the day."

Before any might consider practical matters, an even more ghastly event overtook them. With their animals gone and none to give alarm, the companions, without warning, found themselves surrounded by a gang of ten men, emerging ominously through the trees surrounding their camp. Rupert and his friends, distracted by their many woes, failed to take heed until it was far too late. The comrades saw the intruders - and what they observed sent terror through their veins.

These were no hungry farmers or villagers, desperate for food or a way to flee the plague. No, these were clearly brigands, hard men with cold eyes. Not an ounce of humanity or pity played upon their expressions. Perhaps they were the very men Drego had summoned to destroy his now forsaken former comrades.

Daniel drew Lira behind him, but since they were surrounded, all were equally vulnerable. Morley and Liam attempted to block Rupert from view, but these attempts were also in vain. They were truly cornered, truly helpless.

Knowing the prey was in their trap, several of the ruffians stepped forward, while the others remained with arrows pointed at the defenseless party. The intruders had long, unkempt, dark hair, while some had beards. All wore an odd assortment of garments; some rudely made, others appearing to have, at one time, belonged to the rich - but there were no uniforms to be seen. They had an ominous, brutal aspect to their countenance.

Their leader, a tall, menacing fellow perhaps in his thirties, approached with two accomplices. Rupert and his friends dared not move. One false step and the archers would not hesitate to shoot; they sensed this fact at once.

The men pushed Liam, Morley, and Daniel roughly to the ground. The ruffians then commenced to scour the camp, but found, to their disgust, only the most meager of supplies.

"Bah," exclaimed the leader, "you're a poor lot, and that's a fact." He spoke in a language new to their ears, but Rupert immediately recognized it as something akin to the tongue of Raja-Sharan. He therefore could comprehend a small degree of what was being said, supposing his friends could do likewise.

Dread filled Rupert's heart, as he wondered what these brigands intended to do with them. If thievery was their aim, there was little of value here. Would they move quickly on in search of more promising prey? Or did they have something else in mind? Perhaps these were Drego's cohorts, sent to kill or capture them, to be sold to their enemies?

The man in charge and his accomplices one-by-one forced each of the adult captives to their feet. They were then subjected to a rude search, their clothing being inspected for hidden treasure. Rupert's friends felt a grim satisfaction that Drego had left nothing of value behind.

This bleakly comforting thought did not linger, for at the next instant, Rupert and Lira were also forced to their feet and harshly searched. A medallion and a ring that Rupert wore about his neck...gifts from Liam and Morley...were torn from him, almost knocking the boy to his knees in the process. Rupert's cloak fell back, enabling the enemy to observe Rupert's countenance for the first time. The villain grabbed his chin, rudely turning the captive's head from side to side, as if examining an animal at the village market. His eyes gleamed.

Next, Lira was yanked to her feet. The girl carried nothing of value. The odious fellow's eyes narrowed at the sight of another beautiful child. He turned to his comrades.

"Well, this is a poor lot, to be sure, but these pretty children will fetch a pretty price," he reported with a jolly laugh.

The comrades comprehended, and terror grew in their hearts. Clearly, the man had not seen Rupert's golden eyes, but the boy's extraordinary looks as well as Lira's stunning beauty would be enough to seal their doom.

Daniel grabbed his daughter up into his arms, and Liam and Morley each put protective arms around Rupert. "You have taken all we own," said Liam hoarsely in the Veshti language. "You must go your way and leave our children untouched."

The man stared for a moment, surprised that Liam could communicate in this foreign babble. But then, the evil fellow simply laughed. "Be glad we merely take your children. Or would you prefer we take your lives as well? I wouldn't want you to suffer hereafter longing for your little brats!"

With a nod from their leader, his men moved forward to tear Rupert and Lira from their kindred. While the young ones battled and screamed out in protest, Liam, Daniel, and Morley, though unarmed, came to their defense, paying no heed to the archers surrounding them.

"Put an end to this nonsense," the leader muttered and his men moved in to obey. The children beheld the horrifying sight of their family being savagely kicked and beaten by the brigands. And despite their struggles, Rupert and Lira were roughly bound hand and foot and hurled atop separate horses, their riders holding the hostages helpless. They could not even turn back to see what had become of their loved ones. Had they been left alive? Or slaughtered where they lay?

Lira and Rupert managed to exchange terrified glances before the horses took off. The boy longed to convey courage to his little friend, but his own heart was frozen with terror. How strange that at this moment, the words of Grandfather Liam…words uttered just moments ago, but now seemingly from another life, came to his ears - that the trials they had endured were by no means the worst that could have happened.

How prophetic that seemed now! For Rupert comprehended that nothing could be worse than the reality he now shared with Lira; and the inescapable fact that his other comrades likely lay dead upon the bloody ground.

Chapter Nineteen

The band of brigands raced their captives through the rough terrain. Rupert attempted to estimate the distance traveled since being ripped away from his friends, but could not be certain. However, he concluded they were heading due east, in the direction of Kashkara. How ironic, the prisoner-prince thought, if he and Lira were carried to the very destination they'd so longed to reach these past weeks.

The situation grew more and more dim. Several miles from their campsite, another group of bandits, numbering a dozen or more, joined the original troop. There were now twenty-five in all, filling Rupert with even greater desperation. For even if his friends had managed to survive, how could they possibly fight when so outnumbered? Adding to that, they must proceed on foot, their horses being taken, along with their weapons, by the villainous Drego. In large measure, he despised Drego even more than his captors. They must be common criminals, but Drego had been one of their own!

There was no pause in their punishing journey till night fell. The victims were yanked rudely from their horses and tossed upon the cold ground. They were still bound hand and foot, but there was some comfort in the fact they might sit together and were at last free to speak.

"These men do not understand our native language," Rupert assured Lira. "Let us still be cautious, however."

Lira immediately understood that no reference be made to his golden eyes or likewise sensitive subjects. The girl looked to her young prince, fear clearly written on her features, but it was an emotion she attempted to surmount for Rupert's sake.

"Did you see what happened to Grandfather Liam, my father, or Morley? I know they were attacked, but do you know if they were...badly harmed?" She could not bring herself to utter the question that haunted her - whether they were dead or alive.

"They were certainly alive, Lira, when we were carried off. And we *must* believe they still are. We know *nothing* will prevent them from coming after us!"

"I know," she replied stoutly. "This does remind me of when you were taken away and imprisoned, Rupert. Remember, Grandfather Liam and Morley came to your rescue, and father was reunited with us as well! So perhaps this time there will be another such outcome. We must have faith and not fear."

Rupert looked at his adopted sister with admiration. How was it possible to be so young and yet so very brave? It was a reminder that he must endeavor not to give way to despair. He was responsible for Lira's safety. Her family would never forgive him if he failed in this regard. Whether they were now living or had perished, he must not fail them.

"You speak true, Lira. We must ever have cause to hope. And let us not forget Majesty and Raja. They were disabled somehow by Drego, but that cannot continue for long. As soon as they recover, they will certainly find a way to us, no matter how long the journey!" Rupert spoke to comfort the girl, but also to reassure his own battered heart. For surely, there was simple truth in his words.

Before long, one of the ruffians approached and cut the bonds tying their hands. Their feet, however, remained bound. Two wooden bowls of food were shoved in their direction. "Better eat, for you'll do us no good sad and scrawny." He snorted at their blank expressions and moved off.

The meal consisted of some sort of meat, along with a flat, round object that appeared to be bread. "Here, Rupert, I'll give you my bread. I know you won't partake of meat." Rupert nodded and they ate quickly, though neither had appetite. They had no wish to draw the ire of their captors and also knew they must keep up their strength.

"Perhaps we will find opportunity to escape," whispered the girl.

"If such a moment arises, we shall surely seize it. Did you understand what the men said in our camp?"

"I could tell they spoke in a language not unlike Veshti. I believe they said something about 'pretty children' and 'pretty price.' I suppose they mean to get money for us somehow."

Rupert had hardly heard of the concept of the buying and selling of people. In his own homeland, there indeed existed slavery under the tyranny of King Ryker, but that involved compelling unwilling youths into the army, while forcing young girls into unwanted marriages. This seemed different. He could readily conceive of someone paying money to get control of the true heir to the Golden-Eyed Throne. Yet if he was thought to be an ordinary child, who would pay good money for him…or for Lira?

Questions ceased, for several of the odious guards drew near. They did nothing more than snatch the bowls from the children's hands, then bind them tightly once more. They were again quite helpless.

The captives were pushed down near the huge campfire and each given a blanket. In a vile way, they were being well-treated. Those men must believe them truly valuable; else Rupert feared these blackguards would as soon kill them as not. Never had he seen beings of such cruel aspect, until he recalled the cold and relentless Ned, King Ryker's guard, who had pursued Rupert and his friends with such brutal single-mindedness. But Rupert and Daniel had escaped from Ned's prison, so he had motive for his cold revenge. These brigands, however, knew nothing of Rupert or his circumstance. Their despicable actions were alien to Rupert's experience.

How could these men give no thought to the plague? How was it they approached the comrades' camp without hesitation? Perhaps many of their number had already perished from the fever and the others felt unlikely to catch it now? Rupert, with another chill in his heart, recognized these ruffians seemed to fear nothing.

Lira and Rupert hardly slept. Wild thoughts raced through their minds. Rupert remembered the mysterious woman who caused him to disappear for several days. Certainly, she could readily come to their rescue. Why did she leave Rupert and his precious friend to endure such hardship?

His reflections could not but return again and again to the traitorous Drego. The boy had half-expected to find him here, in this den of thieves. Perhaps knowing Rupert and his party carried money and treasure, he had merely been awaiting opportunity to strip them of all their possessions. Well, if these brigands were not his mates, likely he was instead one of King Ryker's spies. Or simply wished to keep the stolen property himself. Rupert would now never discover the truth.

Of course, his thoughts returned relentlessly to his comrades. Thinking of his friends created such terrible anxiety that Rupert dared not dwell on them. But he did not possess sufficient control to keep dark dread at bay.

The next morning, they were again fed in a hasty manner, forced upon horseback and continued east. Rupert's mind was constantly racing, longing for rescue or escape. Logically, there was no chance of deliverance any time soon. Rupert was therefore determined to get away, but though wild schemes circled his brain, he had no cause to believe success might be possible.

Their melancholy trek continued for a number of days. The men seemed in no haste to reach whatever destination they had in mind. In fact, they stopped more than once, their scouts having spotted fresh prey. On those occasions, Rupert and Lira were left behind with a small number to guard them, while the others went off upon their grim task.

On those occasions, the main group of brigands had returned after an hour or two, bearing stolen food, money, or horses. Each time, there were signs that a battle had taken place, their victims having sought to defend themselves and their belongings. The brutish devils always displayed blood-spattered clothing, along with dreadful smiles upon their dark faces.

"Those fools thought they could get the better of us," one of them reported as he dropped a sack of rice to the ground. The others laughed harshly. No more need be said. Rupert immediately understood those predators had cold-heartedly dispatched their quarry.

More endless days passed and the young captives struggled against giving way to despair. They conferred whenever possible and the bandits did not seem to care. The two were treated with no more feeling than if they were sacks of grain. They were kept bound, fed, placed before the fire by night, and constantly watched. But they hardly seemed human to their guards. They were something else...something more like merchandise.

In a way, Rupert was grateful for this disregard. Those men could have beaten or abused Lira or himself and there would have been nothing to be done. But in the main, their captors apparently gave no thought to their existence. They were a minor nuisance and nothing more.

After a week of this terrible journey, things began to change. The band moved away from the back country and headed for civilized parts. Rupert and Lira found themselves traveling along an actual road; the first seen in almost two months' time. Even more startling, they came upon other people, people that were clearly not of the land of Martan. They must have crossed the frontier into Kashkara!

Rupert studied everything with eager eyes. Certainly the citizens would comprehend their plight. Somebody must surely come to the aid of two bound children! Yet while the villagers tossed the prisoners casual glances, expressions of pity were rare indeed.

The language they heard spoken was the same their captors used. Therefore it must be that of Kashkara. Rupert was thankful that at least he would understand some portion of what went on about him.

The prisoners were taken through a string of villages and towns. The populace was quite different in appearance from the citizens of Zurland, Martan, or their home country. Most were dark of hair, men often wore beards, and many women wore veils to cover the lower portion of their faces. The men donned tunics to their knees, with fitted trousers beneath and wide leather belts with swords and daggers strapped to them.

The women wore flowing, belted tunics and billowing pantaloons or long skirts. Some favored brightly colored vestments, others wore only black. The effect was strange and sinister, but even more so was the cool indifference with which the townspeople regarded the two helpless youngsters.

Rupert wondered why the men did not stop long in any settlement. Once or twice they had paused at marketplaces, but the leader had shrugged, ordering his men to move on. Finally, after another week, the brigands came to their apparent destination. It was a city with mighty walls surrounding it. Rupert's mind raced to his precious map. He had memorized much of it and so believed he knew well where they'd come. It was a place called Talbaz, one of Kashkara's major settlements.

As the party entered the town gates the sight was indeed impressive, with towering structures and a bustling populace. But Rupert could intuit Lira's fear, while he himself faced terrifying thoughts. For if the brigands indeed planned to sell them, this would be the likely opportunity. A large population center would mean a thriving marketplace. Who knew what horrors might await them? Again, Rupert forced himself to recollect that his friends would never cease searching for them. Their duty now was to remain alive and strong - no matter what occurred.

It would have been difficult for the young prisoners to imagine the sight their eyes soon beheld. They were taken to a teeming bazaar. Goods of every imaginable type were on lavish display. Nothing in Rupert's previous experience could have prepared for this. There seemed to be thousands of people milling about. Exotic aromas assaulted his senses, as spices from distant eastern lands permeated the air. Loud voices speaking myriad tongues filled his ears, while his eyes beheld signs of many nationalities. Without doubt, this was some major trading site. Rupert and Lira were also astonished to find animals never before beheld - among them camels, some with one hump, others with two.

In different circumstances, Rupert would have been captivated by these sights; transported to another world. But that feeling only served to make the young liege feel the more isolated, more distant from his kindred.

The brigands halted, dismounted, and Lira and Rupert were rudely pulled down. The brigand leader looked them over coldly.

"The two of you are a filthy mess, that's certain. You'll have to sparkle if we want a goodly price." Several of his henchmen dragged them off to a nearby inn, where the thieves were evidently well known. There, Rupert and Lira were provided with hot water and ordered to wash themselves, a feat they found challenging with bound hands. After that, they were given cleaner clothing in the local style. Lira's curls, long unkempt, were brushed with no great gentleness by a female employee. When finished, she tackled Rupert's matted black hair. Rupert sought to whisper pleas for aid to the woman, but she merely looked bored.

Very soon, the brigand chieftain returned to claim his prize. "There, you both look almost presentable," he smirked. He grabbed each with a rough hand, pulling them into the street. They were about to be sold in the marketplace and there was nothing Rupert could do to prevent this catastrophe. He had failed to protect Lira. In doing so, he had failed his dearest companions. And the bitterness in his heart made him almost wish he were dead.

Chapter Twenty

Rupert struggled with every fiber of his being to keep his wits about him. He was a prince, with generations of bold warrior blood flowing through his veins. How could he have come to this; so utterly powerless to determine his fate, to save his precious friend?

He searched for one ray of light in this dark disaster. It penetrated his frantic mind that none had yet uncovered his true identity. If the brigand leader had been aware royalty lay within his grasp, he would have without hesitation sold him to King Ryker or his allies. However, for this moment, the terrible reality of being reduced to an article for public sale blackened his heart.

He must remain with Lira! By no means could she be torn from him. Exactly how this might be accomplished,

Rupert's frenzied thoughts could not fathom. But he could not fail her!

The brigand leader and several cohorts dragged the helpless captives through the teeming marketplace. Never had Rupert witnessed such masses of people...the throng thick with buyers and sellers and sightseers. Much pushing and shoving occurred, and Rupert desperately hoped for any chance to grab Lira and run. Run anywhere, for he could not know in what direction safety or aid might be found. Yet bound and helpless, the boy-prince could only admit their plight appeared hopeless.

Nonetheless, Rupert whispered words of encouragement to Lira. He swore again and again that they would survive this calamity, finding freedom and family once more. Rupert recognized that, once sold, they would be left unbound...or else be useless to whoever might acquire them. Being unbound meant a measure of freedom - and freedom would mean opportunity to escape.

The bazaar was huge, and it took some time before reaching the location where slaves were auctioned. A large platform formed a stage on which the desolate victims would be paraded before the mob. Several hundred citizens had gathered to witness the horrible spectacle. Rupert and Lira were yanked to a halt before a callous-looking fellow. A turban covered his dark hair and he was clad in a long, white robe. The brigand chief shoved the children in his direction while the auctioneer eyed them with scant interest.

For a brief time, the men haggled. Rupert could comprehend something of what was spoken. He surmised the brigand demanded a large percentage for his prize, while the slave trader offered a good deal less. The debate grew heated, but at last a bargain was struck. Their captor left his booty in the hands of the slave master.

The bewildered prisoners were unceremoniously pushed into a crowd of other unfortunates, also about to meet their fate. Rupert stared in disbelief - men, women, children, even infants, of varying appearance, all bound and in some cases gagged, had been herded into a fenced-in area, surrounded by armed men. Many wept, as families clung to one another. The brutality of the scene tore at the young prince How could human beings treat their fellows in this ghastly manner?

In this forlorn predicament, Rupert had an uncanny thought. Hitherto, he had only dreamed of freeing his *own* people, his *own* homeland. But since fleeing his native country, his eyes had been opened to the realities of this world. How he now longed to fight injustice *wherever* it might raise its ugly head! He vowed to oppose cruelty whenever it was to be found; heady thoughts for a boy about to be sold at auction.

Then once more, he recalled the words so sincerely addressed to those terrified villagers-turned-bandits fleeing the plague…that no matter *what* the tribulation, life was always precious and worth living. He knew, even in this darkest of junctures, that somehow it remained true. He leaned down to whisper those very thoughts to Lira. She looked up at him with a petrified expression, yet managed to nod in agreement.

Regarding Lira's lovely countenance gave Rupert another reason to fear. He had seen none resembling her among the victims to be sold. Rupert's dark hair, eyes, and tanned complexion had aroused comment in his homeland, a land of very fair citizens. But here in Kashkara, his appearance was no rarity, and it was *Lira*, with her silver-gilt curls, fair skin, rosy lips, and dazzling dark-blue eyes which would single her out. That fact, along with her exquisite beauty, would make her a desirable commodity and himself less so. The hope of being purchased together dimmed as his heart filled with dread.

Rupert was forced to witness tragedy after tragedy as one by one, the prisoners were herded upon the platform to face the horror and humiliation of their fate. It mattered to no one, it appeared, if families were forced asunder and children torn from parents' arms. It seemed as if he had been transported to some hellish netherworld. Perhaps the young prince was dreaming? Could he have caught the fever and this was but a dreadful delirium?

Yet, real it was. The prince and his adopted sister searched the vast crowd with frantic eyes. How they longed to see a familiar face, though logic told them it could not possibly be. How could Liam, Daniel, or Morley have found their way here, even if they yet survived? It would take weeks or even months on foot to reach Talbaz. But hope was reluctant to die in the human heart. Every desperate wish raced through their thoughts. Rupert even attempted to believe the lady who had caused his disappearance before would do so again...along with

Lira, of course. But nothing of the sort occurred. And after many nightmarish moments, Lira was pushed to the platform, seized from Rupert's grasp.

There was an immediate hum of interest from the loathsome citizens. Just as Rupert had feared, her exotic beauty drew immediate notice. Much of the bidding had been desultory, but the atmosphere now became charged.

Abruptly Rupert, without conscious thought, cried out. "She is my sister! We must remain together!"

There was a moment of disbelief from the throng, followed by a scattering of amused laughter. No slave had dared speak out. His words had been understood by the majority of those gathered, causing rude responses to spring up here and there.

"Not much family resemblance is there?" called one fellow with a smirk. "Any idea who your fathers might be?" sneered another, to further crude snickering. Rupert was growing desperate. He would not permit Lira to go into this terrible unknown alone.

"We will work hard if kept together," the captive prince declared boldly, "but not at all if you separate us." That drew another general laugh, as well as a sharp cuff across the mouth by the auctioneer, sending Rupert staggering backwards. Yet he would not be silenced.

"She belongs with me!" he repeated, his voice suddenly dark and cold and unafraid.

"Who's the little prince?" yelled out another of the mocking townspeople. But there was less laughter this time. There *was* something extraordinary about this boy that set the crowd buzzing.

"If he wants to stay with his pretty sis, let him," shouted a nasty-looking fellow. "My wife says she fancies the pair, so let the brat have his wish!" Another buyer concurred. Miraculously, Rupert was dragged upon the platform to find himself beside a trembling Lira. She could not take his hand, bound as they were, but leaned against him to display her relief and gratitude. Rupert knew he had won a small victory against overwhelming odds. No matter what occurred, the two would share the same fate.

The bidding commenced. Not all were tempted to purchase both brats, but those who were found themselves in avid competition. The two were undeniably comely, while complete opposites in appearance. That fact alone gave them distinction.

The odious fellow who had called out earlier was among the most interested bidders. He was very tall and wore a white turban covering most of his black hair. A jagged scar ran across one side of his face, from brow to chin, and a patch covered his right eye. He had a prominent, hawk-shaped nose and a long, oily beard and moustache. He was not alone, for a woman, only partially veiled, stood by his side. She seemed determined to acquire the children and had no reticence demanding her fearsome husband continue the quest.

Another interested party seemed no less in earnest. The man was short, plump, and middle-aged, but had a much younger female companion. Rupert could not guess if she were his wife or daughter. But she too seemed greedy for the attractive young ones, desiring them for her own household.

After a heated competition, the other bidders dropped out when the price for the two reached the enormous sum of ten pieces of silver. Other slaves had sold for far less. The two remaining bidders appeared ready to retire from the fray, but their wives insisted they get what they wanted. Thus the men were obliged to continue, at least while they hoped to keep their ladies in good humor. At last, the second couple gave in, refusing to top the price of fourteen silver pieces. And so, the Golden-Eyed Prince and his friend found themselves the property of the tall man with the scarred face and his strong-willed wife.

The rest of the mob cheered, jeered, and applauded to see the bidding rise to such unexpected heights. They had been royally entertained, while thinking the victors indeed foolish - for the foreign urchins were likely spoiled and useless. Yet as it was not their money wasted, the citizens could afford to be amused.

The large sum was duly paid and two young ones handed over to their new masters. The couple gave them looks of cold appraisal, as if already regretting their extravagance, then led them off. The last sight Rupert and Lira had of their brigand captor was that of the auctioneer pouring pieces of silver into his hands. The fellow looked happy enough with his share. He turned without a backward glance and melted away into the throng.

The prisoners were dragged without ceremony through the still-teeming bazaar until reaching a horse-drawn cart. Several servants on horseback stood guarding it. The captives were tossed into the back, half-filled with other purchases...none of them human. Without ceremony, the man and wife climbed onto the front of the cart and took off.

Rupert knew there was no escape. He was bound. The servants riding behind the cart were watching every move. Nevertheless, he and Lira remained together! Against all odds, the prisoner-prince had managed to achieve that miraculous feat. He closed his eyes and in his heart of hearts, addressed Liam, Daniel, and Morley.

"I will never betray you, I swear," he vowed. "I will stay with Lira and protect her with every breath my life allows. We will find means to escape and come to you. Even if you should no longer live, I will be strong and pledge to fulfill my destiny - my own and Lira's!"

Making that vow filled him with new resolve. Though logic might declare all was lost, that he and Lira had been reduced to mere chattel - the lowest of the low - he felt strength stirring within. Prisoner or not, his own heart, his own true self, was forever free. Nothing would make him lose hope now.

The cart made its way through the throngs with difficulty, their pace being absurdly slow at times. Rupert felt he could easily walk more swiftly than the cart was traveling. However, he was in no particular hurry to reach his unknown destination. For whatever awaited could not be good. He whispered words of encouragement to Lira. Yet courage already glimmered in her sparkling eyes. Her Rupert had honored his pledge to remain together and she was grateful beyond measure for that.

Finally they were leaving the walled confines of Talbaz in their wake. The cart continued for some distance. This area, too, appeared well-populated. Farms and dwellings dotted the roadside upon which many a traveler made their way.

At length, they turned off the main route onto a dirt path. Directly before them was a house of pleasant yet modest proportions. Rupert had imagined those who had bought them must be rich indeed to afford such a high price. But upon approaching, the dwelling seemed to gain in consequence. It had two stories and a handsome courtyard. A barn and one other building stood to one side. Two corrals were visible as well.

Rupert had a welcome thought; perhaps he would be allowed to care for the animals here. No matter how harsh their confinement, there would be a degree of pleasure in that...unless the creatures were raised for slaughter! Then he attempted to wipe that thought from his brain. Their circumstances were dire enough without conjuring more sorrows.

The cart drew to a halt and Lira and Rupert were taken down. The husband and wife made towards the entrance as their captives were forced to follow. Then the large double-door was swung open to reveal an entrance chamber. It was tiled with colorful mosaics depicting lively scenes of festivities and harvests. Somehow the place had a comforting air. A ray of hope swept through Rupert. Without knowing why, his heart began to pound wildly in his chest. Abruptly, he grew faint and could barely breathe.

The towering, scar-faced fellow drew his dagger and severed the bindings from their hands and feet. He turned and marched away. His wife led them towards a room with a closed door. Gently, she pushed it open and spoke her first words.

"Do not fear, young ones. Go see who purchased your freedom."

Entering within, Rupert and Lira beheld a sight they could barely comprehend. Surely, they were delirious or in a dream! For standing before them - beaten, bruised, terribly injured, but absolutely alive - were Liam, Daniel, and Morley.

Chapter Twenty~One

For a timeless time, none uttered a word. The three battered men remained frozen where they stood. Rupert himself felt incapable of moving a single muscle. At last, Daniel uttered an incoherent cry and his daughter found herself gathered in his arms. Then Rupert managed to stagger towards Liam. His strength gave way. The boy fell to his knees, pressing his head against his mentor's broken body. Rupert wrapped his arms about Liam's legs and held fast, never wishing to let go. His family was here! *Alive!* How could this be anything but dearest fantasy?

Lira and Rupert ultimately approached each of their loved ones, embracing them fiercely; fearful their reunion might somehow vanish into a dream. But real it was. Rupert discovered his frantic grip caused discomfort to his comrades. They must have suffered cracked or broken ribs, he surmised with alarm. Each man's face was dark with bruising, their eyes blackened and swollen, while Morley's nose appeared to have been broken. Liam was leaning upon a walking stick. Rupert's heart was torn to see their suffering. But they had survived!

None had yet uttered a single word. At length, Liam found his tongue, his voice husky and dark with emotion.

"There is another who wishes to greet you, dear Rupert." With that, another door opened and Raja raced into the room!

Rupert was able to articulate a cry of absolute, astonished joy before the delirious hound reached his side, pouncing upon him. The mastiff succeeded in knocking his young master completely off his feet. The boy lay helpless as the one hundred and thirty pound Raja slobbered his face with salutations. Rupert wrapped his arms about Raja's neck, commanding himself not to weep. For the young prince felt if he permitted himself that luxury, he might lose command entirely.

After Raja was finally reassured that Rupert was indeed with him once more, the pup released the boy, only to charge in Lira's direction. She was seated upon her father's lap. Not wishing the injured Daniel to be assaulted by the happy hound, she threw herself on her back so Raja could not knock her over. As Raja began his happy attack, the others could finally break into smiles and tentative laugher.

Rupert now uttered his first words to his friends. "Majesty?" was all he could whisper.

"Yes, Rupert," replied Liam, "he is outside in the paddock along with our other horses. The treasure, the map…everything has been restored to us."

Too many dramatic emotions had drained Rupert of strength. A thousand queries assaulted his mind. "But…how…why?" he stuttered.

"There is another who can answer your questions," advised Morley. "We owe our very lives, this joyful reunion, to him. Would you permit him to address you?"

"Of course!" cried Rupert, afire with curiosity. But when the door opened, Rupert was not prepared for the sight that greeted him. Entering the chamber was the scar-faced ruffian who had purchased Lira and himself. Who was this mysterious fellow who had so fortuitously come to their rescue?

The tall man took several steps in Rupert's direction. His hands rose to his white turban. Slowly he unwound it, allowing his long black hair to fall free. But his next actions were far more startling. He removed the scar cutting through one side of his face. It had been false, created with some sort of putty-like material. He next lifted off the eye-patch. The eye beneath was intact.

Rupert began to flush with fury as he comprehended what was occurring before his eyes. Continuing relentlessly, the fellow peeled off his long, oily beard and moustache. All had been merely pretence. For revealed beneath the remarkable disguise was none other than Drego, the despised traitor!

A multitude of wild thoughts assaulted the young sovereign. He longed to grab the dagger still strapped to the villain's belt; grab it and plunge it into the Drego's treacherous heart! He had betrayed them, caused his family to be brutally assaulted, he and Lira to be carried off as slaves! Yet the others claimed this was their savior. Rupert's face grew red with agitation and rage as words adequate to his emotions eluded his shattered mind.

Drego did not wait for Rupert's condemnation. He went before his king, prostrated his towering form before the boy, then kissed his feet. Rupert backed off… as if the man's merest touch was contamination. However, another in the room had a very different reaction.

"I *knew* you could not be so wicked!" exclaimed Lira, racing to his side. She tapped at his shoulder, hoping he would look her in the face. But he remained visage down before his retreating liege. "Rupert, you must listen to Drego. Clearly, he saved us all. How can you still doubt him?" the girl pleaded.

"Yes," spoke Rupert, his utterance strangled with choler. "I will hear his words. I am most eager to know how he dares to explain his despicable actions."

Cautiously Drego rose, but only to his knees, regarding his prince with impassioned eyes. "Thank you, my lord. I will tell you all. If, when I am done, you still condemn me, I will willingly take my dagger and plunge it into my heart, should that be your desire."

Lira gave a cry, but Rupert merely smirked coldly, unmoved. Drego was a consummate actor. His prince was by no means impressed with this melodramatic display.

Drego began his tale. Lira, now seated between her father and grandfather, attended with eagerness.

Liam, Daniel, and Morley seemed to silently urge Rupert to heed the telling with an open mind. But they knew Drego's fate would lie with their boy-king...and him alone.

"It began when I was shot by the arrow and taken with fever. As I lay in delirium, my mother appeared to me...yes, my mother who has been dead these several years. She spoke of a terrible fate awaiting us. A band of roving brigands, little more than cold-blooded murderers, was fast approaching. They would not only steal everything of value, they would slaughter us should we resist. Our only hope would be for me to take your possessions and flee to a place which was revealed to me."

Here, Rupert could not help but interrupt. "This is absurd! Even if your mother *did* inform you of the danger, why did you not simply *tell* us? We could have retreated to shelter ourselves. Why did you instead drug us, abscond with our possessions, and leave us to helplessly face death?"

"*Because you would not have believed me, my liege!*" exclaimed Drego, though reluctant to antagonize Rupert further. But the truth had to be told. "If any of the others had warned of coming catastrophe, you would have credited them in an instant! Yet I know you mistrusted me. I cannot claim to say why. Perhaps it is because I was new to your company. I had hoped that, upon joining you, I was truly accepted, my lord. It soon became clear such was not the case. I somehow lost your favor and could not win it back." Drego gazed up at Rupert with gray eyes that appealed for compassion.

Rupert remained skeptical. However, he nodded curtly for the man to continue.

"Knowing I could in no way convince you to flee, you would nonetheless have been on the alert for danger. Certainly, Raja and Majesty would have provided warning an attack was imminent. You all would have fought... fought to the death to defend one another and your treasure. But the brigands had us outnumbered. In no way could we have survived.

"My only hope was to abscond with everything of value and hide it away. You must have guessed that I drugged your food. I did the same to Raja and Majesty. But how my heart broke, knowing you would awaken to find everything gone, while you would rightfully blame me for what was to occur. I could only pray you would not oppose the robber brigade and as a result, they might allow you to live."

Rupert could not but acknowledge the truth of Drego's words. He recalled all too clearly that, while their prisoner, he had witnessed the robber gang carry out any number of raids. They had always returned with blood-stained clothing and derisive mockery for those who had offered up a fight. Their victims had been done to death, their valuables seized as booty. Perhaps it *was* because the comrades had been unarmed which caused Liam, Daniel, and Morley to be beaten, perhaps left for dead, but not run through with sword or arrow.

"Of course," Drego went on," I could not *know* if my mother's stratagem would succeed. But it was our only hope. She had instructed me to wait for two days and nights and those hours were agony. As soon as allowed, I raced back to the campsite. There, a horrible sight greeted me.

"You, my lord, and Lira, were nowhere to be seen. Liam and Daniel had been brutally beaten. Morley lay yet unconscious. Their poor faces were nearly unrecognizable. Had they been able, I'm certain they would have slain me on the spot. I explained in haste what I could of the matter, then attempted to come to their aid. Since I had returned with medicines, Liam could tend to his son and Morley, who at length returned to the living. They determined to follow after you but could barely stand, let alone travel on horse back.

"It took some persuading, but I convinced them I knew your likely destination and that, if they would heal for a day or two, we could certainly catch up with your abductors. I surmised you could have been taken for one purpose...to be sold to the highest bidder. I knew the most logical site - the marketplace of Talbaz. If that were true, I was already formulating a plan and finally, your kinsmen were forced to allow me to carry it out.

"Only late yesterday we arrived, having journeyed day and night upon our swift horses. I feared for the condition of my companions, but they refused rest. How they were able to complete the journey while so severely injured, I cannot guess. Nothing but their greatest affection for you and Lira could have made it possible.

"We proceeded to this very house. It is the dwelling of my cousin, Shabaz, who was for years a happy member of my band of performers. I enlisted her aid, as well as two old friends…they appeared as the other couple who entered the bidding. I feared it might draw unwelcome notice if I alone attempted to purchase you both.

"Then you, my valiant Rupert, solved that dilemma by insisting you be sold alongside your sister. Such courage is hardly to be seen! Thus, our task was simplified. We obtained you together and brought you here, to be reunited with your loved ones. I would not permit them to accompany me to the bazaar as they'd desired. They are yet feeble…I feared an outburst if they beheld you upon the auction block. To succeed, my plan needed to be carried out without undue drama or display.

"And that, my honored liege, is the entire tale. Believe it or not, as you will. My fate is in your hands." Drego concluded his telling with tears of pain and bitter regret in his fine gray eyes. He had freely acknowledged his actions deserved severest condemnation. He knew well he did not own Rupert's trust. Therefore, he could hardly predict his response.

Rupert was indeed embroiled in a cauldron of conflicting emotions. Rarely had he felt such confusion. Drego was responsible for so much suffering, yet he *had* undeniably come to their rescue. The boy was compelled to admit the truth of Drego's words. Rupert would have not given credence to the message from Drego's dead mother. They would have battled the brigands, thus losing their lives and possessions – along with their every hope and dream.

He turned to Liam, Daniel, and Morley. They returned the look with unreadable expressions. Only

Lira happily accepted the account, gratified to find her trust for the man from Gitano vindicated in the end. But Rupert could not be certain. How could he credit his own judgment when it had failed him before so dearly?

Rupert could decide nothing now. He was incapable of thought. There was only one thing he desired to do. The young sovereign took to his feet and raced from the room, from the house, and found his way to the courtyard. He whistled and a mighty whinny returned the greeting. He followed his ears to a paddock behind the house.

There, behind a tall fence, was his beloved Majesty. The magnificent golden-brown stallion with the silken white mane and tail rose up upon his hind legs in joyous welcome. Running back to the end of the paddock, the beautiful steed raced forward, clearing the barrier in an effortless leap. An instant later, he was at Rupert's side, nuzzling the boy's disheveled black hair. Rupert placed his arms about his cherished friend's neck and at long last, was able to weep. His sobs continued unbroken for several moments until he finally wiped at the tears with his tattered sleeve. He climbed upon the towering horse's back.

Rupert knew what he wished to do. Grabbing on to the flowing, wild mane, the determined prince urged Majesty towards the fence again. And once more, the steed leaped over the obstacle with amazing grace and ease. Rupert's cries turned to an exhilarated shout as he urged the horse forward until they reached the far side of the paddock. Again, Majesty carried his prince aloft as if the barrier were no more than a minor impediment, flying through the air with flawless agility.

Time and again, Rupert demanded to be taken over the jump, while each time Majesty responded avidly. Boy and horse were reunited; again were as one. Out of the corner of his eye, Rupert glimpsed that Morley, Daniel, Liam, and Lira had come to observe. The reality of their miraculous reunion again dazzled his spirit.

Yet, in that instant, none truly existed for the boy but Majesty…and Raja, who had come to race by their side, howling with delight. And these splendid moments, of triumphing over high impediments, spoke to Rupert's heart. Each jump seemed to call forth further celebration and strength. Thus, within his dark and wounded self, something began to see light again and to heal.

Chapter Twenty-Two

With much reluctance, Rupert concluded it was time to leave off his unforgettable ride. He drew Majesty to a halt, slid down from his back and stroked the stallion's neck as he whispered his thanks. Then, with a growing serenity, he rejoined his companions, who had stood observing their prince.

Without a word but with gladness in his heart, Rupert gingerly embraced Liam, Daniel, and Morley, taking care not to aggravate their injuries. He next picked up Lira and whirled her about, to her surprise and delight. He radiantly regarded his loved ones, hoping to convey how deeply he treasured them.

"Come, let us return indoors, for you are in great need of rest," he said to his elders. "Moreover, I myself am in great need of food, for I am ravenous indeed." He turned and led the way.

Shabaz, the lady of the house, was there to greet them. As if in anticipation of their wishes, she guided her guests to a handsomely appointed room, where they found a low table surrounded by bright cushions. Spread upon it was a veritable feast. The tempting aromas set their appetites afire.

"Please, do make yourselves to home," Shabaz urged graciously. "My cousin Drego tells me you do not wish to partake of meat. I can assure these dishes meet that requirement. I take my leave of you now."

As she turned to depart, Liam spoke. "Where *is* your cousin?" he inquired.

She regarded her visitors with a polite but puzzled expression. "He has withdrawn to another part of the house and will not appear unless duly summoned by you," she explained. But clearly to Shabaz, her cousin had saved the day for these people, yet they were treating him with a coldness she found difficult to comprehend. However, Shabaz would not intrude on what was clearly a private matter.

"Well, gracious lady, we thank you for this banquet," declared Morley. "I do believe these dishes are new to our experience, so we would be much obliged if you would describe them."

"Oh yes, please do," begged Lira, intoxicated with the marvelous smells.

Shabaz happily pointed out the various delicacies, including eggplant fried in sesame oil, couscous, hummus, as well as something called halvah for dessert. After she withdrew, Rupert immediately sought to serve his friends, feeling honored to do so.

"I urge we endeavor to eat heartily, for we've come to resemble scarecrows." The boy-prince smiled, though it was true all the comrades had grown alarmingly thin after their many trials, including starvation, plague, and assault.

They began to taste the new dishes with caution, but soon were eagerly devouring the delicious repast. Yet there remained serious matters to be broached. Finally, Liam turned to Rupert and Lira.

"We have not yet heard of your encounter with those dastardly brigands. As you might imagine, we endured the greatest trepidation for your welfare. Please tell us…did they abuse you? Harm you?"

Rupert and Lira could see fear written plainly upon the faces of the three men who loved them. They at once attempted to set their tortured minds at ease.

"No, Grandfather Liam," Lira replied immediately. "They did not hurt us. I mean, we were not beaten or starved or the like. I promise you, it's true!"

Rupert also strove to reassure them. "It may seem difficult to credit, yet in fact, those cut-throats largely ignored us! We were bound, but fed twice daily and slept by the fire. We were likely of no more import than any other stolen article. They barely glanced our way the entire time."

The three regarded their precious children with obvious relief. "Just imagine if they had seen your golden eyes!" exclaimed Daniel in a whisper, wary of servants lingering nearby.

"Yes, that thought had occurred," noted Rupert with a smile. "I endeavored to remind myself how much worse the situation could have been; not an easy task. Of course, Lira and I were continually concerned for *your* welfare. What have you to add to Drego's report?"

"He told most of the tale," admitted Liam. "Had he not come to our aid, we would certainly have perished on the spot. We owe him much, Rupert."

"I see you are determined to discuss the matter. I, myself, am less so, seeing it involves thoughts quite disagreeable to me. I am instead content to dwell on our miraculous reunion; that we are truly alive and together! How this can be, I cannot rightly comprehend."

"Yet none of these joyful developments would have occurred without Drego," Lira insisted.

"What Lira says is true, Rupert," Morley added. "However, I can certainly see why you'd be of two minds about the fellow."

"All I know is…when I'm here with you, I am at peace. I do not feel that with Drego? Do *you?*" Rupert challenged.

Lira, of course, nodded vigorously, but the men remained silent at first. "He does know all our secrets," Daniel reminded them. "But somehow I believe we can trust him with that, even should we bar him from rejoining our company."

Liam sighed. "Perhaps you are right, my son. We may harbor much resentment, but from Drego's point of view, he acted only for our benefit."

Rupert shrugged, cut everyone another chunk of the mouth-watering halvah and stood up. "My mind is so full, I can hardly think with clarity. I am overwhelmed with the bliss of our reunion. My only regret is that two precious possessions have been lost...the medallion belonging to your brother, Morley, and the ring belonging to King Marco's grandfather, King Jaden."

Rupert recalled that Morley had presented him with his slain brother's medallion on the occasion of Rupert's eleventh birthday. The ring had likewise been presented that day, a gift from King Jaden long ago to Liam's own grandfather. They had been precious to Rupert, but had been snatched away by the brigands. "I wonder why Drego neglected to remove those mementos from around my neck when he took everything else?"

"Perhaps it was because he did not know of their existence," Morley reminded him.

Rupert shrugged and changed the subject. "Are we expected to remain beneath this roof? If we are to keep her cousin in exile, it seems peculiar to require Shabaz to act as our hostess."

"Yes, that would be most inconsiderate," observed Liam. "However, we must remain in Talbaz while we recover. Therefore, let us search for an inn without delay."

Rupert examined his friends' faces. Clearly, they wished to remain where they were. He sighed, knowing a decision about Drego could not be much delayed.

"It is almost nightfall. Let us see what thoughts the morrow brings."

Before long, they were shown to a charming, spacious chamber. Soft mattresses were spread upon the floor, enough for them to pass the night in comfort. Shabaz pointed out a bell resting on a table, urging them to ring if they desired anything at all. Then, after a servant brought in tea, the companions found themselves alone. Rupert pulled back a curtain to reveal a fabulous, full moon, low in the sky, brilliant in the night. Raja, beside his master, wagged his tail in appreciation. Lira came to stand on the other side of her prince and took his hand.

Rupert sighed with contentment. "Only yester-night, how impossible to conceive such a joyful outcome to our dreadful circumstance. We have been honored with so many miracles - I fear we have used our allotment."

"Even if that be so, we must ever be grateful for those granted us," reminded Liam. "Though we can only hope whatever guides your path will continue to make things right in the end."

"At this moment, my wishes for a kingdom seem very distant."

"Well, it is always wise to appreciate what is most precious," observed Daniel. "Yet I believe you will soon focus anew on your destiny." And with that, Rupert's friend drew out his newly restored flute and began to play a wistful tune while his listeners sang softly along.

"I, for one, would miss Drego so very much," observed Lira, "especially for his glorious voice. None of us can begin to match it." Meanwhile, after another sweet melody, the companions, overcome with the emotional exertions of the day, fell fast asleep, well aware that this was the first night in many they had spent together.

However, before dawn, Rupert had a hazy dream. In the morning, he lost no time relating it to his companions. "It lacked detail, but convinced me I must go to the bazaar with Drego this very day. Not that I wish to return to where human beings are bought and sold."

"Do you wish us to accompany you?" wondered Morley. But Rupert refused, knowing the men very far from recovered. Nor did he wish for Lira to go, even ordering Raja to remain behind.

"Does this concern whether he should rejoin our ranks?" Liam inquired.

"I cannot say. However, Drego and I must go together...though I far from relish the notion."

After another tempting repast, Rupert asked Shabaz to summon her cousin. Drego soon appeared, an unreadable expression upon his countenance. He refrained from untoward words while Shabaz remained in their company. Rupert curtly requested Drego accompany him to town and Drego, though taken aback, agreed.

Without delay, they were off. As it was only a distance of a few miles, Rupert desired to proceed on foot. They began in silence, but finally Rupert spoke up.

"Please do not think I relish going where a slave market may be found. But my dream instructed to go to the bazaar with you and I shall obey it."

Drego, regarding the cold expression on his prince's countenance, replied as follows. "You are quick to condemn what you do not understand, my lord. As you know nothing of Kashkara or its history, you proceed from a state of ignorance. I would never approve of slavery, but you should learn how it came to be in this kingdom."

Rupert felt the sting of Drego's rebuke. He could not imagine *any* excuse for the odious practice of keeping slaves. Yet it *was* true he knew nothing of Kashkara.

"Well, do not hesitate to enlighten me," he invited Drego with dark sarcasm.

Disregarding Rupert's tone, he began recounting something of the land's history. Kashkara had been prosperous and peaceable for centuries. A line of benevolent kings had ruled. But when the old sovereign died, some thirty years before, leaving his eldest son to inherit, things took a sudden turn. The new king, Yokub, a man more inclined to poetry than politics, permitted the country to drift. Meanwhile, a warrior tribe to the south began to threaten Kashkara's borders. Yokub's younger brother, Talal, urged their army be made ready for the coming fight. King Yokub dismissed his warnings. Inevitably, invasion came, and many thousands of citizens were slain or carried off as slaves.

Kashkara was in turmoil. The people demanded action. Talal, with the backing of much of the army, first imprisoned, then slayed his elder brother. Many had remained loyal to Yokub and the country soon descended into civil war, while at the same time, fighting continued against the invaders.

The enemy laid waste to much of the country, while the enslaved populace was treated in a most inhumane manner. But after long years of bitter combat, King Talal regained the offensive, capturing large numbers of the foe. He sought to fight fire with fire, enslaving all he did not slay. The populace applauded, as they were very desirous of revenge.

The conflict ended and years passed. The former enemy remained in servitude and the populace grew accustomed to this. Eventually, other foreigners came to be bought and sold in the markets - a bitter inheritance from years of brutal invasion and civil war.

"I cannot but regret what has occurred here," Drego concluded. "For the soul of the people of Kashkara has been woefully scarred by permitting this blight to continue. However, that is what war and vengeance do to otherwise decent beings, Rupert. And sometimes, these wounds are very long to heal."

Rupert had listened in silence. His views on the institution of slavery remained unchanged. Yet he could now feel compassion for Kashkara. Moreover, he had learned a valuable lesson - he must ever endeavor to *comprehend* a situation before passing judgment upon it. That was true now - and would be even more so if he hoped to be the just and compassionate ruler he vowed to become.

The young sovereign quietly thanked Drego for the history lesson, but held his silence after that. By then, they had reached the walls of Talbaz and soon the two arrived at the teeming market place. Rupert was relieved to discover the sale of slaves was carried on but twice weekly. At least, none would be on display this day.

"What is it you wish to see?" inquired Drego, "for the bazaar, as you know, is vast."

Rupert shrugged. For a few moments, he wandered this way and that, Drego at his side. He again took delight at the presence of camels, though he could intuit they were not overly friendly creatures.

The boy-prince's senses were assaulted by so many strange sights and smells. He was grateful to feel anonymous in the teeming throngs. Finally, Rupert experienced a powerful pull toward a crowded alleyway overflowing with stalls. Various objects were for sale... everything from clothing to household wares to jewelry. Rupert noted expensive items were likely to be obtained at another corner of the market; what lay before him now were goods less than luxurious - items jumbled carelessly upon rickety tables or spread on soiled blankets upon the ground.

Rupert moved slowly forward, not knowing why he was drawn here. He turned his head left and right... nothing caught his interest. Attempting to sharpen his perception, he was hardly aware that Drego remained with him.

Abruptly, the boy felt as if a hand had firmly caught the back of his neck, causing him to slow his steps. He turned about to see if anyone was truly touching him...but none was behind him other than the throngs occupied with their own purchases.

Rupert continued on a few feet until that same unknown power drew him to a halt, forcing his head to turn to the left. He found himself staring down at a carelessly arranged display resting on a tattered cloth.

Rupert knelt. The teeming cacophony of the market faded from his hearing. There was nothing but a peculiar vibration surrounding him. He regarded the merchant, sitting cross-legged, holding up various items for Rupert to examine. There was everything from rusted daggers to old pottery, turbans to moth-eaten clothing. Then abruptly, Rupert's world came into sharp focus.

The boy leaned over and with deliberation, lifted up an odorous, well-worn piece of material. Lying beneath was a pile of jewelry in an untidy heap. Rupert's heart violently pounded as he commenced to examine it. There, among the jumble, was the medallion from Morley and the royal ring that had belonged to the Golden-Eyed King Jaden! The very ring that had been presented to Liam's grandfather and later, to Rupert! *How was this possible?*

Gingerly, Rupert extracted the precious objects from the worthless mound. He stifled his desire to cry out with joy. Feigning disinterest, he commenced to barter with the seller, who responded with indifference. Soon, Rupert was in possession of his treasures once again, purchased for the merest pittance.

Rupert led Drego away, his steps euphoric. Now *all* that was cherished, which had been lost, was restored to him once more. He felt whole and guided and tremendously humbled and grateful. Now, the Golden-Eyed Prince realized one thing more...that Drego was destined to again become one of their number and to share in whatever destiny awaited.

Chapter Twenty~Three

For the first time since that long-ago day when Rupert escaped from King Ryker's prison, the young prince knew a sense of peace. Gone, for this moment, was the impulse to be constantly in flight from his enemies. Instead, he gloried in the knowledge that the comrades had miraculously prevailed over staggering tribulation.

Every morning upon awakening and each evening before sleep, he reminded himself he and his loved ones were alive...together. The same marvelous thought would again cross his mind during the day as he beheld his family in the most commonplace of activities...partaking of a meal, sunning themselves in the courtyard, engaging in converse. Young Rupert was acutely aware of these moments and determined to revel in them.

Gone were his ambitions to regain his crown; yet a measure of guilt accompanied that fact. Rupert could not erase the boundless burdens resting upon his inexperienced shoulders. Yet for these precious moments in time, he was eager to put down his load before reluctantly taking it up again.

This time of refuge was a necessity. Liam, Daniel, and Morley still suffered from the savage beating inflicted upon them. Two weeks had passed since that dreadful day. Some of the black and purple bruises had begun to fade, but the three continued to suffer from their myriad injuries.

"I turned three-and-forty not long since," Liam remarked with a rueful look, "but after the encounter with those vile fellows, I feel more like three-and-sixty!" Though the remark had been made with humor, Rupert was concerned. He insisted upon attempting to heal Liam and all three of his battered friends. After all, his efforts had been of use when the deadly fever struck. Strangely, the men proved reluctant.

"We are not so sick as to die," Morley had reassured his prince. "We only require time to heal. You should save your efforts for when they're truly needed."

Yet Rupert would not be gainsaid. His friends endured daunting pain. Unfortunately, Rupert's efforts did not provide the hoped for miraculous improvement.

"Do not be by any means discouraged," Daniel advised the young healer. "Perhaps your efforts are not truly necessary in this case, for we are in no great danger." And with that, Rupert had to be content.

Drego's cousin Shabaz continued to be a charming hostess. Since a long period of rest was needed by all, including Drego, Lira, and Rupert...who also had suffered greatly in past months...the companions had announced their decision to seek shelter at an inn. Shabaz would hear none of that, insisting with a whole heart her guests remain under her roof. In truth the comrades were delighted to comply, comfortable in her gracious home. Before very long, thanks to her hospitality and tempting cuisine, they began to regain much-needed weight as well.

The decision concerning Drego's fate had also been reached. When Rupert and Drego had returned from the marketplace bearing the royal ring and Morley's medallion, the companions had regarded them in awed silence. It was a 'coincidence' beyond reckoning. Clearly, something or someone had guided Rupert to that very spot in the teeming bazaar, allowing the boy to recover his treasures.

"Well, Rupert, your fabled intuition or guidance is clearly unaffected by our tribulations," observed Daniel. "This is beyond mere logic. Miracles truly never cease when one is in your presence!"

Rupert smiled. "May that continue to be so. The feeling was akin to when we attempted to cross into Zurland. We were well and truly caught...until a similar force guided me to turn my head and behold the soldier with the crooked leg. I immediately *knew* he must be our friend Sarah's husband; and thus succeeded in passing ourselves off as fortune tellers. I only wish I could comprehend who or what was providing this information."

"That may be apparent in time. Hopefully we may continue to rely upon it," said Liam wistfully.

"Well, one thing I now intuit is that you are meant to remain with us, Drego," declared Rupert, turning to regard the man he still did not fully trust. "However, you must vow to never again withhold information...even if your mother should so command."

Drego regarded his prince with a level look. "Yes, I can fully assure you of that. For you might now pay heed to my warnings. However, may I be so bold as to demand the same assurance of *you*, my lord? For you have held back *your own* thoughts, much to my detriment."

Rupert took the rebuke to heart. It was undeniable that he had experienced doubts concerning Drego, yet refrained from broaching them with the fellow himself. Instead, he had whispered in secret to Liam and Daniel. Now, Rupert must acknowledge he had done him a disservice.

"You speak true, Drego, and I have wronged you. I had concerns from the start, yet concealed them."

"Will you *condescend* to do me the honor of relating them?" asked Drego with more than a touch of sarcasm.

"It is merely this. Upon telling my story, I displayed the royal treasure to you. At first, you seemed genuinely moved - but then I perceived a look of unmistakable avarice cross your features. It pierced my heart with doubt and dread. For our secrets had been revealed, but what if you were in truth a thief? Someone who might betray us?"

Drego returned Rupert's direct gaze. "Well, you are clever to have observed what you claim. For you speak true. I, my lord, am not a saint. I have never encountered such honest and blameless fellows as Liam, Daniel, and Morley. But I cannot include myself in their number. I am neither pure nor good; merely human.

"As you know, my family twice lost everything in war...their homes, property, all they had. All my life, since age three, was spent as a nomad. I relished the life of a roving player, but we had next to nothing to show for it. When my poor mother became ill, I lacked even the means to buy her a home in which to spend her last days. We made due with a room an old farmer allowed us. I was required to work at taverns and festivals, unable to remain by my mother's side.

"So yes, upon viewing the treasure, the thought *did* cross my mind of how much comfort and security could be obtained by selling even one of the articles. However, I would never have done so. You may believe me or not, as you will. I cannot vouch for my every thought. I can only demand to be judged by my *actions*."

There was silence when Drego concluded. Finally, it was Lira who spoke. "Of course, I believe your words. For you could have run off with the treasure had you wished. Instead, you came back and saved the day." She went to Drego's side, giving him a hearty hug. She had always trusted this remarkable outsider and would not be dissuaded from doing so now.

Now, Liam had one final question.

"What would you have done, Drego, had you returned to find us dead? Your mother's instructions, that you take the treasure, all we had, and flee, certainly did not *guarantee* the brigands would not slaughter us. Whether by luck or fate, we survived. *But what if we had not?"*

All turned to Drego, hardly imagining what his answer might be. But he spoke without hesitation, turning to Rupert.

"If such had been the case, I would have returned to your homeland to seek out your cousin Rajiv and his son Lalja. For you revealed they were fighting to protect the populace and inspire rebels to come to your aid when you someday returned. I would have told them of your fate and then turned over the treasure to your blood kinsmen. Perhaps, in time, they might use it to inspire an overthrow of King Ryker. In that way, your death would not have been in vain."

His listeners regarded the man in surprise. Rupert felt humbled by his past distrust. For clearly, honesty and fine instincts dwelled in Drego's heart.

Thus, Drego was again invited to rejoin their number, with promises of new openness and honesty amongst them all. Drego was both vindicated and satisfied.

Time moved on. Liam, Daniel, and Morley continued to heal. Rupert spent these happiest of days riding Majesty, often along with Lira, who rode her black stallion. Raja was always by their sides. They were required to exercise the other horses as well, since the three injured men could not yet exert themselves. However, that 'chore' proved a pleasure.

Rupert also took advantage of this rare respite to study archery. An as yet frail Daniel was his instructor, though refraining from drawing the bow himself. A target had been set up outside the horse paddock, allowing the young prince to practice diligently for hours at a time. He also continued with the sword, knowing he was as yet no match for any grown man. As for the bow, he felt equal to anyone.

In fact Rupert had grown a good deal taller, despite the many trials and privations that were his. His companions, now that they were at some leisure, commented on the fact, much to his satisfaction. He wished he might magically grow *much* taller; to be a man rather than a boy - although some wishes were not his to command. He privately hoped to someday become tall and imposing, as his grandfather, King Marco, had been.

His friends continued to recover, permitting them to take a number of trips into Talbaz; taking care never to go when slave-trading was to occur. The town was sizeable. Impressive buildings of sand-colored stone dominated the scene. The streets teemed with life. Very foreign sights and sounds fascinated the comrades and they drank it all in with interest and pleasure.

They readily comprehended the need to familiarize themselves with exotic settings. For anything setting them blatantly apart could only prove to their detriment. Their party lost no time purchasing clothing that would permit them to blend in with the residents. That did not satisfy Rupert, however.

"We must endeavor to learn as much of the local language as possible," he insisted. "It bears a resemblance to the one spoken in Raja-Sharan, so we should learn it with facility. Drego will teach us, if you please. Moreover, we'd be wise to disguise our appearance."

The companions agreed. It was determined that mornings would be spent speaking the tongue of Kashkara and afternoons in the study of Veshti. As to the matter of camouflage, Drego, along with the lively Shabaz, took to the challenge with mischievous delight. They possessed a multitude of wigs, costumes, and other props from their days as traveling players. They assessed the situation with amused solemnity.

"Well, Rupert, as we travel east, you will fit right in. You require only the right clothing to be taken for a local. As for the rest of my friends, I'm afraid that will require some little work, for fair-hair is as rare as snow in the desert hereabouts." He regarded Liam, with his light blue eyes and pale blond hair, his son Daniel, with darker blond hair and deep blue eyes, Morley with his waving auburn locks and eyes of warm green, and of course, little Lira, with wildly curling flaxen tresses and sapphire orbs. Drego shook his head in mock alarm.

"Well, should they wear wigs? Or dye their hair?" inquired Shabaz with a mischievous glint in her fine eyes.

"Oh, let us dye our hair, please!" begged Lira. "It would be most amusing...and practical as well. For wigs could fall off, perhaps at the most inconvenient moment."

After some discussion, it was concluded they should dye their fair locks and that darker make-up be applied to their light complexions. Morley, Daniel, and Liam were not cheered at the thought, but practicality had to be their standard. Drego himself needed no such aids. His black hair caused him to fit in, though his light eyes, while not unheard of in these parts, were considered unusual. However, none of Drego's or Shabaz's arts included a method of altering eye color.

The transformation was carried out. Each of the party could not help but laugh when regarding their companions.

Lira relished the masquerade, looking as lovely as ever with her dark brown tresses. She also cherished the time with Shabaz, having spent virtually all her life deprived of feminine company. The lady of the house, in turn, was delighted to entertain the glorious little girl.

Several weeks passed. They were yet to meet the husband of Shabaz. Her guests learned he was a wealthy merchant, who had fallen in love when seeing her perform in a nearby province. He traveled extensively, leading trading caravans throughout the area...mostly going south from Kashkara into desert regions. Shabaz hoped he might return within a month, but there was no way to be certain of that.

Rupert continued to savor every peaceful passing day. Thoughts of regaining his kingdom, thoughts of Raja-Sharan, remained remote. The reunion with his adopted kin was still all that mattered. It was finally Liam, who albeit reluctantly, brought reality to the table.

"As you see Rupert, we are well on the mend and may expect to resume our journey shortly. Any thoughts on the matter?"

"I have been so truly content these many weeks. I wished to think of nothing else. However, I acknowledge we have a mission demanding to be taken up again," he concluded with a sigh. He grudgingly produced the map ever carried with him, spreading it before his now dark-haired companions. Drego leaned over Rupert's shoulder to peer at it.

"The farthest east I've been is about two hundred miles from here. I have never ventured beyond the borders of Kashkara in that direction, so my use as a guide may be drawing to an end. I do know a mighty river, the Anga, flows directly in our path. However, there exists any number of sturdy bridges spanning it, so that should present no special obstacle."

Rupert heard the name of *Anga* spoken aloud for the first time. The word threw terror into his heart. He kept his resolve against withholding thoughts from Drego or the others.

"I know not why, but the Anga River bodes very ill indeed. In fact, I greatly desire to avoid it." He strained his golden eyes upon the map, but could see no alternative that would not require a detour of hundreds of miles.

Yet at the same time he felt yearning anew to resume their journey. Abruptly, time once more became of the essence. They must by no means delay their trek to Raja-Sharan, though he could not declare why.

Rupert lost no time in conveying these revelations. He regarded his friends with growing alarm. Once more, fearful events lay directly before them – there could be no doubt of that. How could he continue to believe they would eternally manage to miraculously survive?

With a powerful flash of anguish, he perceived these moments, when they were alive and together, were sacred. For unimaginable hardship and peril loomed. Yet with no other choice, he announced their odyssey would recommence within a very few days. Rupert beseeched whatever force that was guiding their path to continue to be merciful.

Chapter Twenty-Four

Thus, it was a mere two days later that the companions took their leave from the lovely home that had offered them shelter. They bid farewell to the charming Shabaz, though first presenting her with numerous gifts purchased in the Talbaz bazaar. Their hostess received them with pleasure yet appeared to genuinely regret their going, urging with all her heart they consider her home as their own.

Rupert and his friends headed down the eastern road with more than one backward glance. The young prince knew the sacrifice required to leave such an oasis of tranquility. He hoped safe haven would also await them in Raja-Sharan, but that kingdom seemed far-off indeed and something of a fantasy.

In fact, however, the party had made fine progress and might reasonably think to reach their goal in several months' time. Yet Rupert had learned never to take such matters for granted.

One subject ever on his mind was food! After the painful weeks of starvation, a memory from which Rupert could never quite escape, he desired to carry a mountain of supplies. His friends had to introduce caution.

"We should not needlessly burden our mounts," Liam reminded his liege, though mindful of his fears.

Drego also endeavored to reassure. "We are traveling through highly populated territory, my lord. We should lack for nothing."

Rupert was not easily persuaded. After all, Martan had supposedly offered sustenance, but the epidemic had left them to starve.

"I realize you speak true," Rupert had replied. "However, the unexpected tends to be our lot. We must be prepared for every eventuality." Thus did he urge them to purchase as much as they could carry.

The party traveled at a reasonable pace, but determined not to press their progress until certain that Liam, Daniel, and Morley could endure long days on horseback. Happily, it did not take long for the three to gather strength, appearing once again up to the demands of their travels.

Kashkara was indeed thickly populated. The main roads were crowded with all matter of people - obvious foreigners as well as citizens of the land. Some journeyed in sizeable groups. A multitude of languages could be detected, along with a great variety in dress and appearance. Traders seemed plentiful, going from market town to market town to buy or sell goods from far-away kingdoms. Most traveled by horse, but camels occasionally made an appearance.

Rupert and Lira were enthralled. What a pleasure to travel openly! They received few glances, their clothing and darker hair permitting their party to blend with the masses. They drank in the exotic sights, sounds, and smells with abundant satisfaction.

Drego, observing their wide-eyed wonder, smiled. "Yes, this world is a contrast indeed from your land of origin. I can promise you even more amazing sights when we reach Raja-Sharan. Though I have never been there, my mother told me endless tales of that kingdom...where not only camels, but elephants, are said to roam." His young listeners were wide-eyed at the thought.

That night, Rupert brought up one problem he had been wrestling with.

"Who shall we say we are? We have twice come upon border crossings unprepared. We must not allow that to again occur."

His friends agreed. It was Drego who proposed a ready solution. "Why, we should pose as a troupe of entertainers!" he exclaimed as if the answer was quite plain.

"Why, yes, that would explain why we carry wigs, make-up to darken our skin, all sorts of strange attire!" agreed Lira.

Rupert thought this over. He could see the obvious advantages. "True - we could further claim the royal treasures are worthless props for our plays," he added, growing enthused. "For who would believe such a rag-tag group would possess anything of value?"

Morley, Liam, and Daniel considered. "Well, I myself have no better alternative - though how if we're called upon to perform? Those two little songs we sang may have fooled those friends of yours, Drego, but what about a more discerning audience?"

Drego laughed. "You have read my thoughts, Morley. I agree we must make our tale convincing. I shall teach you two plays; one in the language of Raja-Sharan, the other in the tongue of Kashkara, plus more songs to add to our repertoire." Drego smiled devilishly at his audience.

Rupert and Lira were not displeased, but the adults were wary. "Ho, that sounds like a lot of unnecessary nonsense," grumbled Morley, suspicious of Drego's innocent-seeming suggestions.

Rupert disagreed. "I see much good sense in Drego's stratagem. Naturally, we need not expect to be required to perform. Our numbers are too small for that. We can claim others of our troupe died of the fever...and that we hope to recruit new members. Until then, we are unable to entertain."

The others admired the idea. "Yes, Rupert, that would be an ideal way to disguise our identity. However, we may be called upon to *prove* who we are. Therefore, I shall teach you plays and songs...just in case."

Lira was alight with enthusiasm, inquiring what the plays were about.

"One is perfect for us. It concerns a brother and sister who become lost and search for their family. It is a thoroughly dramatic tale, though all turns out right in the end. The other is a comedy concerning a foolish husband who distrusts his faithful wife." Drego gave an unsettling grin in Morley's direction, causing him to fear the worst.

"And just who among us would play the loving wife?" the now dark-haired Morley inquired.

"I'm afraid that task would fall to *you*, dear Morley, for all our supposed ladies have died of the plague. It is not unknown for men to portray lady's roles, as there is often a shortage of actresses in this part of the world. So my friend, since you are the smallest among us men, I fear the lot of playing a female falls to you!"

Morley had to stifle the impulse to punch the smirking Drego in the nose. The chortles from his friends did not help matters. *'Smallest' indeed!* Morley stood a shade less than six feet in height, yet it was true Liam and his son stood several inches higher, while Drego was taller still. Before he could make one of several sarcastic remarks that flew through his brain, Daniel intervened.

"Do not worry," he reassured his friend. "We will surely not be called upon to perform. Only some rehearsing should be required. I presume no costumes would be necessary for that."

"Yes, Morley, this is not so bad. Consider that we were disguised as ladies day and night while fleeing our homeland," Liam reminded him.

At length, Morley grumpily gave his consent. That very evening, Drego commenced to teach the comrades their parts, along with several new songs. The constant practice in two foreign tongues undeniably aided their fluency very much indeed.

Their days passed pleasantly enough. They stopped often in towns, always enjoying the exotic cuisine among other delights. Rupert recalled their repast in former days, consisting mainly of dark bread, cheese, and porridge. Now, those were a thing of the past. They instead feasted on chickpeas, lentils, couscous, and many other remarkable viands. Rupert's sweet tooth especially savored a treat thick with sesame seeds and honey. Cashew nuts also were now among his new favorites.

The party never felt more safely anonymous. Rupert knew these moments were a continuation of the glorious respite that Shabaz had offered. They were still safe, still together, and no danger seemed to press in upon them.

Yet Rupert knew this was not to last. Every evening, upon examining the map, he intuited the dark presence of the Anga River looming directly in their path. It seemed to lurk like a demon, waiting to claim them. Rupert spoke of his fears openly, determined not to hold anything back.

"If only we could avoid it somehow," he wished aloud, not for the first time. Only troubled gazes answered his brooding countenance.

"We have examined every option, Rupert," vowed Liam. "There is simply no way around that obstacle. However, you may yet be provided with enlightenment when the time comes."

"That may be true, of course," the prince was forced to respond…though Rupert was not, in his heart, reassured. If they wished to leave Kashkara behind and enter Ribakesh…and ultimately Raja-Sharan…there was no alternative but to cross the Anga.

"I wish we could swim," sighed Lira, concerned at the troubled expression upon Rupert's superb features.

"Do not forget, our horses are excellent swimmers," Daniel chimed in. "For that matter, I'm certain Raja is as well."

Rupert looked to Daniel and smiled. For it *was* true. Perhaps their steeds could carry them across come what may.

"According to our map, there exists any number of bridges spanning the Anga. We need not concern ourselves overmuch," Liam assured.

However, Rupert could in no way stifle the fear gripping his heart; a sharp dagger he could not remove. Would they indeed traverse the river upon a sturdy bridge? Would the young prince then blush at his own foolishness?

Unfortunately for Rupert, the travelers made their way without impediment for the next weeks. How he wished he could make their progress…time itself…stand still. The days were so leisurely and pleasant. Harmony reigned. The boy reveled in their perfect fellowship.

Yet, time would not stand still. Thus, it came to pass they did indeed arrive at the banks of the mighty Anga. Drego once more reassured that the bridges spanning it were well constructed; countless travelers made use of them daily.

Rupert remained far from convinced. He could hear the crashing waters even before the river came into sight. It was overwhelming and awesome, thunderous and rapid, with a will of its own. The dynamic Anga seemed alive to the boy-prince, always so sensitive to nature's glory. His friends were equally impressed. Indeed, the pounding of rushing waters made it necessary to shout their words of exclamation at the magnificence before them. None but Drego had ever seen anything to compare.

The companions had reached the riverbank not long after sunrise. Few travelers were about, but Rupert could witness a small group cross from the other side without incident. The boy remained uneasy, however. Rupert insisted they dismount. His friends could not help smiling, as Rupert's actions seemed overly dramatic. The scene was marvelous and the substantial wooden structure appeared to offer no problems as to safety. Yet the boy solemnly kissed each comrade on the cheek, only then allowing them to remount.

Rupert had been inspired to cross last…though he knew not why. Therefore Drego led the way as the others followed in single file. Of course, Raja remained alongside his master, seeming to sense nothing amiss. Neither did Majesty, for that matter, which served to reassure Rupert. The boy waited until his friends crossed the two hundred foot span in safety.

Only then did the amazing youth, his glorious steed, and gigantic hound, take their first tentative steps across the rushing river. Rupert, choosing not to ride Majesty, proceeded on foot. He was sharply aware of his surroundings, sensitive to every reverberation and nuance. Rupert perceived imminent danger, as if surrounded by enemy archers. Yet looking up, he merely observed his friends cheerfully awaiting him.

Approaching the mid-way point, disaster struck. Raja and Majesty reacted to something the others could not feel. The dog commenced to howl. Majesty reared upon hind legs while whinnying wildly. Rupert anxiously looked about, seeking frantically to determine the cause. Several travelers had begun to cross from the opposite side, though they appeared innocent enough. The boy looked to his friends, who experienced growing alarm at the actions of Rupert's animal companions.

And then it happened: a huge roar from out of the earth which drowned out even the rushing waters below. The bridge gave a violent sway. Rupert had experienced nothing remotely like it and was stunned and bewildered. In the distance his comrades gestured frantically that he should run towards them. As he began to do so, another violent motion sent the heavy structure rocking beneath his feet.

In that very instant, the portion of the bridge on which the boy stood cracked and shook violently. He shouted for Majesty and Raja to flee. As if in a dream, Rupert found himself falling, falling a vast distance towards the raging waters below. He could not know what had happened to his horse or dog...only that he was alone, plummeting to his death.

It was the crash of cold water assaulting him which told Rupert he was yet alive, though helpless to fight against the raging current. He was aware of many things at once; the screams of his friends from far above, the horrible whinnying of terrified horses...and from somewhere, horrific howls from Raja. With one last conscious thought, Rupert felt gratitude beyond measure that his comrades were safe. But he knew his life was over and accepted that fact.

Water filled his mouth as he struggled against swallowing it. He was being forced downstream with tremendous speed. The heavy load of food upon his back dragged him down; the very thing he hoped would be life-saving had instead aided in his doom.

Abruptly, the rushing water transformed into something else - a powerful whirlpool. Rupert was completely powerless against it. He was sucked beneath the wildly churning waters, his lungs about to burst. Darkness enveloped him. One last image...that of his beloved friends' faces...illuminated his heart. And then, all was blackness.

Chapter Twenty-Five

Rupert's friends beheld the scene before them in frozen incomprehension. Without warning, the earth had begun to tremble beneath their feet, the horses were screaming, the bridge had collapsed, and their cherished prince was plummeting into the raging river. Time had moved in slow motion, but now, reality hit like a cold, crushing wave.

Before any could react, the earth heaved yet again. Their mounts responded with panic, but it was Lira's black stallion that took off in a lightning gallop down the road leading away from the bridge. Lira screamed once, then clutched onto the frantic steed's flying black mane. She had always protested against using saddle or bridle and was now paying the price. The fragile girl had no way of controlling the suddenly fearsome beast.

Lira's plight broke the others from their horrified trance. Her father immediately took after her upon his own steed. His youthful liege had fallen to his doom; now his daughter's life hung in the balance. Her out-of-control stallion seemed to gallop away at supernatural speed. Daniel cried out to his girl while pressing his mount to race as never before.

Though focused on his Lira, Daniel could not but be aware of people pouring onto the road. Many had been traveling towards the bridge, others lived in nearby homes, but all fled outdoors when the quake struck. Daniel had a fleeting impression of damaged dwellings amidst scattered cries of panic. But he was largely blinded to what occurred around him, thinking only of his precious child.

Then, he beheld a terrifying sight...a fallen tree across their path. Lira's panicked horse might rear up, causing his girl to be thrown. However, her stallion instead sailed over the obstacle and one potential disaster was averted.

Daniel pursued his daughter for over a mile when the miracle occurred. Another rider, coming from the opposite direction, apparently assessed the situation. The stranger drew his horse to a halt, causing it to stand directly in the path of the charging black stallion. Lira's horse reacted in fright, rearing wildly upon his hind legs.

Now, Lira lost her grip, tumbling backwards off the frenzied beast. At that very instant, however, Daniel reached her side. Just as she would have fallen beneath iron hooves, he was able to snatch her up, almost in mid-flight, swinging her onto his own racing steed. Then finally, with one arm wrapped firmly around Lira's waist, he brought his mount to a stop.

For a moment, father and daughter could only engage in the fiercest of embraces. Daniel then regarded Lira's tear-stained face.

"I am uninjured," she managed to gasp. "But where is Rupert?!"

Before Daniel could respond, the stranger who had come to their aid was beside them. The fellow had managed to catch Lira's black horse. Now a rope was tied about his neck.

"I believe this beast belongs to you, my dear," said their savior with a look of relief. "Is your daughter unharmed?"

"Yes, largely thanks to you, good sir. Our gratitude is beyond measure."

"Do not thank me. It was fate that acted upon our lives this day. Do you come from the direction of the bridge? Has it been damaged?" the man wished to know. He looked about Liam's age, clad in a turban, a white tunic over white trousers, along with a dark blue cloak.

"Yes, the bridge has collapsed," responded Daniel, heart racing at the thought of Rupert's fate.

"It is as I suspected. Had I not a doting wife, I would have gone to my doom a few moments since. I was leaving when she insisted my brown cloak had a stain upon it, causing me to wait until she could fetch one that suited her better. I was peeved at the delay, but see....she has saved my life!"

"But my...our...friend fell in the river!" sobbed Lira. "We must go back to save him."

"I wish you luck, little one," the stranger said. But his eyes looked into Daniel's and his message was clear. None could be expected to survive the fall. "Whether you find him or no, you must accept what destiny brings. Now pardon me, for I must return to thank my wife for delivering me from death."

With that, the fellow handed the rope to Daniel. He smiled faintly at Lira, then turned back in the direction from whence he'd come. Yet there was no question in Daniel's mind...the man had appeared out of nowhere to save his daughter's life. His discerning wife had provided salvation for more than her own husband this day.

Still riding on her father's horse, Daniel and Lira headed back towards the bridge. Again, they perceived many people running along the roadside in fear-filled indecision, not knowing where safety lay. Most houses remained standing, apparently, and not many injured were to be seen. But father and daughter could hardly spare a thought for anyone but their Rupert. Perhaps the others had managed to rescue him?

However, upon reaching the quake-damaged bridge, the two beheld a startling sight. There, among a growing crowd of citizens milling to and fro, were Drego, Liam, and Morley. However, the latter two were upon the ground. Drego was standing over them with a sword pointed in their direction. Liam and Morley sported blacked eyes. Daniel slid down from his horse, taking Lira with him.

"What is the meaning of this, Drego? Have you gone mad?" Daniel's eyes were afire with fury at the fellow, who had clearly laid hands upon his father and his friend.

"Well, thanks be that the little one is safe," Drego exclaimed. "As for your dear father and Morley, do forgive me, but both determined to bring about their suicides. I chose to prevent them by any method possible. Perhaps their moment of madness has passed." With that, Drego returned his sword to its sheath and held out a hand to Liam, aiding him to his feet. He did the same to Morley. Both men seemed to be suffering pain in their ribs once again.

Lira ran to her grandfather while glaring at Drego. Liam embraced his grandchild, powerfully grateful she had escaped harm.

"What Drego means to convey is that Morley and I felt compelled to rescue Rupert and were about to dive into the river."

Daniel was appalled. "Neither of you can swim a stroke – and the fall alone would have certainly killed you!"

"I'm afraid logic had nothing to do with it," confessed Morley. "We could not do nothing, even though Rupert had been swept from sight."

"And since cool logic would not suffice, I had to punch them in the ribs, knowing that would at least slow them down. However, it failed to produce the desired effect, so I blackened each in the eye and finally drew my sword. It was fortunate that Lira's horse bolted, else I would have been hard-pressed to stop all *three* of you from leaping to your doom!"

Liam smiled darkly. "I know you acted for the best. But what are we to do now?"

"Why, we must find Rupert!" declared Lira. "Where is Raja?" For surely Raja could lead them to their prince.

"He either fell or jumped in after Rupert," reported her grandfather. "Both were swept swiftly away. We must head downriver; they could have been carried off a very long way."

Lira observed that Majesty had made it to safety. The anxious stallion was still snorting and rearing. The girl ran to him.

"Where is Rupert? Where is Raja?" she begged. She listened for a moment, as the horse finally grew under control. She stroked his mane as he lowered his head towards hers. However, the information received was not what she'd wished.

"Majesty does not know…he cannot sense Rupert's presence. Perhaps he is too far away?" She would not say what she feared…that Majesty could not sense Rupert's presence because he was no longer alive.

"No matter," retorted Drego sharply. "We must head down river. There are myriad rocks in the water's midst. Perhaps Rupert and Raja were able to climb aboard and are awaiting us this very instant."

The companions tried to hope, but panic seized control of their hearts. They mounted their still-testy beasts gingerly. Daniel would by no means allow Lira to ride alone, so she sat with her father, her own stallion alongside, the rope about his neck fastened to Daniel's saddle.

Grimly determined, they headed downriver. Each set of eyes strained to discover signs of life. They knew from Rupert's map that another bridge lay about twenty miles distant. If it still stood, some of their number could cross to the other side and ride back from whence they'd come...for perhaps Rupert had been swept in that direction.

However, with each step, their hopes grew darker. The rushing of the mighty Anga made their prince's survival appear impossible...or highly unlikely at best. They had watched helplessly as Rupert had been swept away. Yet perhaps Raja could have defied even these treacherous currents to save his master? So the comrades continued on, willing to cling to the smallest hope.

They rode all through the day. The party began to fear they'd crossed Rupert's path, but failed to catch sight of him. The banks of the Anga were so very steep. It proved impossible to see every rock and crevice clearly. But surely, Raja would have sensed their presence and howled to draw their attention.

All along the roadway, citizens and travelers were wandering about, not certain it was yet safe to seek shelter indoors. From time to time, Liam or Drego sought to question them, inquiring if they'd seen a youth and his extremely large dog. But none, apparently, had. The people were quick to warn of aftershocks...informing the foreigners that after earthquakes, smaller tremors were likely to follow. Oddly, most of the locals did not think this most recent quake was anything particularly fearsome; the destruction of one bridge and a few dwellings seemed a matter of no great import.

However, to Rupert's friends, the fallen bridge represented a possibly overwhelming tragedy. With each passing moment, their fears grew apace. Finally, with night approaching, they were forced to make camp alongside the villainous river. Each heart reached out to Rupert in the black night, sending their affection and steadfast resolve to recover their prince, come what may.

Chapter Twenty-Six

Rupert found himself in very peculiar surroundings. The young prince was walking down a long entrance hall, lined by young women clad in colorful garments foreign to his experience. All had beautiful dark complexions, black hair, and shining eyes. The ladies threw flower petals upon his path...but behind them loomed guardsmen, dressed entirely in black, formidable and sinister. Rupert knew this setting was a palace. The walls were pink and gold, elaborately embellished. Here was elegance and luxury such as the Golden-Eyed Prince had never before witnessed.

On he walked. In the distance appeared two thrones. Rupert's heart began to react in a sickening manner. The hall widened into a gorgeous room, each article of furniture a treasure, even to the boy's unschooled eyes. Pink and gold, red and turquoise, glowed everywhere. Beside one of the thrones was a very young maiden. Rupert struggled to quicken his pace, yet was unable to do so. He felt compelled to urgently address the girl, but no words came forth.

Then, as he continued to make his painfully slow progress towards the double throne, a male emerged to stand behind the royal lady. He was dressed in bright, festive garments, but Rupert knew at once he was malignant and devious. He must warn the princess before it was too late! Rupert made to rush towards her, but the black-clad guardsmen surrounded him in a menacing mass.

Again, Rupert sought to cry out, but instead, waves of water assaulted him from every side. Darkness again enveloped his being. He must warn the lady! He must!

Abruptly, Rupert experienced a forceful pounding on his back. He gasped as water came rushing from his mouth. He choked, coughing up ever more copious quantities of what had been flowing through the Anga. Gradually, the darkness whirling about him began to lift.

Rupert gagged again and again. He sought to achieve calm, to breathe once more. He grew aware he was laying face-down on a very hard surface. Whatever had landed on his back continued its assault. He attempted to sit up. Upon doing so, he realized two things...that tumbling water crashed within inches of where he lay, and that Raja, dearest Raja, was with him. For the hound was busily licking Rupert's face with his slobbering, wet tongue, whining with delight. Rupert embraced his hero.

Clearly Raja had rescued his master from the torrential currents. How he had accomplished this, Rupert could not rightly guess.

Blackness enveloped them. Attempting to assay his circumstance, Rupert concluded they must be in a rocky cavern alongside the river. They were sheltered on a jagged shelf, just a foot or so above the rushing waters. There seemed no way of escaping their tiny refuge...for rocky walls loomed about them, with barely enough room to stand. If they attempted to step off the ledge, they'd be swept into the river at once.

Rupert determined not to panic. He must wait till daylight to discover exactly how dismal his position might be. He had no way of knowing if night had just fallen or if dawn was about to break.

Reality again intruded forcefully. Rupert was cold...so very cold. His body began to shiver and tremble, his teeth to chatter uncontrollably. He had no possibility of warming himself before a fire, but knew to doff his drenched clothing. He accomplished that task with difficulty, as his numbed hands had begun to shake furiously. He managed to remove his knapsack. Feeling inside, he came upon what he sought. Wrapped in oilcloth purchased in the Talbaz bazaar, Rupert found other garments that were relatively dry, to his vast relief.

Unsteadily, he changed into a long tunic and snugly fitting trousers. Raja did his best to help, keeping close to his master, warming Rupert's body with his own. Rupert withdrew something else...food. At least that 'excess' supply would prove of use...he carried enough to survive for several days.

Swiftly, he began to devour handfuls of cashew nuts, giving Raja his share. They proved soggy, yet palatable enough. After that, he swallowed a portion of figs and dates, fruits he had lately discovered and come to enjoy. The act of gaining nourishment helped warm his frozen limbs just a bit.

Gradually, the dawn began to creep into the tiny cavern. Relief filled Rupert's being, for remaining in the dark under such conditions was something he did not relish. As soon as it was sufficiently light he looked about eagerly, but found nothing to encourage. Indeed, it was just as he'd feared; the shelter was of solid rock and led nowhere. The only opening was what lay before his eyes…directly back into the raging river. Had his hound been able to reach the riverbank with his master in tow, he would surely have done so. Unless they could find a way to escape, this asylum could become their tomb.

Despite their grim dilemma, Rupert would by no means give up hope. Somehow, his friends would discover them. It was likely this tiny hole in the rocks would not be visible from above. Rupert also realized his cries for help…even Raja's mighty howls…would certainly be drowned out by the crashing waters.

At last, inspiration struck. *Majesty!* Surely, *he* could lead the comrades here! His faithful stallion would somehow make his message known…to Lira at the very least. Majesty would not fail them!

Quickly, Rupert explained his plan to Raja; they both focused on calling the valiant steed to their rescue. However, other thoughts intruded. Even if Majesty *could* relate where Rupert and Raja were concealed, how could his comrades attempt a rescue? The banks of the river were incredibly steep…it would be almost certain death to whoever might climb down, defying the destructive currents below.

Rupert was anguished. He did not desire his loved ones to risk their lives in any wild attempt to save his. Yet, he knew such thoughts were fruitless. They would risk *anything* to save him, just as he would surely risk anything to save them.

As light overcame the darkness, Rupert again examined his pack. He could now make out teeth-marks upon it. Clearly, Raja had managed to latch onto it, dragging Rupert to this haven. Surely, had Raja not found this dank place of shelter, they would both have perished. He did not hesitate to embrace his hound again while expressing his deepest, heartfelt thanks.

He recalled now the strange lady who had presented Rupert with that basket so very long ago. The mysterious lady who could appear and disappear at will. That basket had contained King Marco's ruby ring and the mastiff pup. How many times had Raja come to his rescue? It was perhaps beyond counting! He had to acknowledge gratitude to that strange figure to whom he owed so much. He wondered yet again at her true identity.

Several hours passed. Rupert could hear nothing but the overpowering tumult of crashing waters. At frequent intervals, he and Raja called out to Majesty with their hearts and minds. Surely before darkness fell, their friends would discover them.

Then, without warning, the earth shook and violently trembled. Even in this dark, dank cavern, he could feel it. Rupert clung to Raja. Water from the river sloshed into their tiny cave, bringing it to the ledge where they sat. Boy and dog had to jump to their feet to keep from becoming drenched once more. When the earth finally grew still, there were several inches of water where they had formerly been able to rest. Now, they were forced to stand in the cramped space. The young prince thought ruefully that he had been delighted at lately growing taller. For at this moment, a smaller stature would have surely proved preferable.

Rupert passed the long hours. He spoke aloud in the language of Raja-Sharan, then of Kashkara. He was proud to realize he had, in recent days, become fluent in both. He determined to learn many more foreign tongues if given the chance. It added so much to his ability to comprehend his surroundings...understand the alien world. He then proceeded to rehearse, in his mind, the plays that Drego had taught, then sang tunes newly acquired over and over. He did anything to keep his mind from focusing upon his perilous dilemma. Yet he could not help but notice the waters had risen even further, now reaching his calves. Not only was he growing frightfully cold once more, but knew terror at the thought of how high the river might possibly rise. And what of Raja? The danger for him was even more immediate!

The day passed with incredible slowness, yet Rupert wished it could last forever. For at day's end, only the promise of renewed darkness remained. Then, just as light began to fade, Rupert heard an incredible sound; a voice he at once recognized, calling his name!

"What ho, Rupert! Are you there? Shout out if you hear me!" Those marvelous words reached his ears, and quite overcome, it was a moment before he could respond. Faithful Raja acted first, howling at the top of his lungs.

"We're here, Daniel, over here!" cried the astounded boy, at last finding his voice. Soon thereafter, an extraordinary sight - a pair of boots - came into view, then legs, then a body. Rupert observed a stout rope had been fastened about Daniel's slender waist. His comrade lowered himself into the cavern, hunching his tall frame to do so. Instantly Rupert was in his arms and Daniel had his prince in a powerful grip. Raja, too, bayed a joyful greeting.

"Are you unhurt?" demanded Daniel, his anxious face scanning Rupert's when they finally released one another. He could observe his prince was covered with bruises, scratches, and myriad bloody cuts. But his golden eyes glowed and that reassured his frantic friend.

"Yes, I am quite well, thanks to Raja. Are all of you safe?"

"Never fear. You'll soon see for yourself. But now, let us make haste before another blasted quake occurs. I was lowered on ropes. Majesty and the others will pull us to safety. Morley may be the shortest amongst us, but I am the lightest, so the task of rescue became mine."

"Take Raja first," insisted the golden-eyed Rupert, "but I fear your weight together may prove too much.

Do you think we ought to send him up alone?" For Raja weighed in the vicinity of one hundred and fifty pounds. Daniel, though very slender, must weigh close to one hundred and seventy. Rupert's mind filled with images of his loved ones crashing down into the river should the fastening give way.

"You are right. I'll truss up Raja and allow him to be hoisted away. Our friends can lower the rope again and we will go after."

And so, they did. Rupert explained the plan to his reluctant guardian and the hound protested. He did by no means wish to leave his master's side. At length, he was forced to obey. Daniel untied the rope from around his waist, lashing it about Raja's stocky body. He then gave it a violent tug and slowly it was lifted up. Raja flew from sight. It was a remarkable thing to see...as if the mastiff could truly fly!

Rupert began to shiver helplessly. Daniel drew off his cloak, wrapping it about his prince.

"Was it Majesty who found us?"

Daniel smiled. "Why, of course you have guessed it. Your faithful stallion and your faithful hound again saved the day. I'm certain you could do very well with only your animal companions. We humans certainly have our shortcomings."

Rupert could only regard Daniel with overwhelming gratitude. He knew for certain he had taken an enormous risk to be lowered towards the raging river. Yet Daniel had likely done it without thinking twice. They were truly a family...a band of brothers (with one little sister) who would make any sacrifice for the sake of any of their number. Once again, Rupert could barely comprehend his good fortune in having such people to guide him and to share his destiny.

With little delay, the rope was lowered once more. This time, a heavy rock was tied to the end to give it weight. Along with the rock, a note had been attached. Daniel pulled it out and unfolded it. He gave a hearty laugh, then handed it to his prince. Rupert read aloud:

"Make haste you fools, for you are delaying our dinner! Your irritated brother-in-arms, Drego."

Daniel quickly retied the rope to his body and Rupert climbed upon his back. Somehow, they both knew it would hold. Then, with one backward glance at the tiny cavern that had briefly been his sanctuary and his prison, Rupert gave a firm tug upon the rope. Along with his beloved friend, he felt himself lifted out of the darkness into the open air, to fly above the raging river and back to the life that had so nearly been lost.

Chapter Twenty-Seven

Rupert and his rescuer indeed landed safely upon firm ground high above the tumultuous waters. They were greeted not only by their loved ones, but by a throng of curious passers-by, aware a rescue was in progress. In fact, several strangers had helped pull on the ropes manned by Liam, Drego, and Morley. Majesty, too, had taken part, as the line had been fastened about his body, his strength vital to the happy outcome.

Rupert swiftly embraced his friends, who exclaimed at his miraculous condition. Cuts and bruises there were in plenty, but he had survived with no great injury and all were in awe of that fact. Several of the onlookers were equally impressed.

"It is a marvelous fate that saved the boy, no doubt. A glorious destiny must await him," commented one fellow with a flowing black beard. He reached out to pat Rupert firmly upon the shoulder, as if in congratulations, before going on his way. Several others echoed similar sentiments before taking their leave. More than one citizen invited the party to spend the night as honored guests, but all offers were gracefully declined. The companions had no wish to pass this night amongst strangers, however kind.

Rupert continued to suffer from convulsive shivering, which set his friends into action. They wrapped him in blankets, transporting him to an appropriate nearby site. Soon, a blazing fire burned and steaming mint tea was in Rupert's hands. By the time a hot meal and dry clothing had been provided, Rupert's body at last ceased to tremble and his teeth to chatter. His comrades did not press their prince to speak till then, but now they hungered to hear of his experience. Before they could begin their interrogation, Rupert began.

"As you see, I have escaped injury, but instead observe Grandfather Liam and Morley sporting black eyes. Moreover, your ribs again appear to be damaged. I somehow intuit your condition cannot be attributed to the shaking of the earth."

Liam and Morley turned to Drego somewhat shamefaced, but it was Lira who provided the answer.

"Drego hit them, because they sought to jump into the river to help you, Rupert. Father could not stop them because my horse ran wild and he had to rescue me. So do not be angry…Drego saved them, don't you see?"

Rupert looked to the others for confirmation of this vivid tale.

"Well, Lira, thanks be your father kept you from harm. As for you, Drego, this is not the first occasion I've been torn between thanking you and cursing you - for your methods of 'helping' often leave something to be desired!"

"That is the only reason I allowed Daniel to go upon your rescue mission," chimed in Morley. "I believe we are of the same weight, more or less, but he was the only one lacking damaged ribs, which would have certainly hindered the effort. Drego, clearly, outweighs us all, so he would have been a poor choice...though personally, I would not have minded seeing him plummet into that soggy abyss!" Morley concluded with a hearty laugh, but there was a measure of irony to his words.

"Well I, for one, am eternally grateful we again have been spared." As Rupert spoke, a warm glow of happiness and wonder spread through his heart.

"I suppose the map is lost," sighed Daniel. "Certainly it would not have survived the waters."

Again, Rupert had a surprise in store. "Since Majesty is safe, I assume the map is too. For some instinct told me to place it within Majesty's pack." As the others regarded him in puzzlement, Rupert took to his feet and went to his steed. Opening the pack, he withdrew the map, quite intact. Lira gave a cheer and moved to kiss her prince's cheek.

Rupert placed the parchment by the fire and unfolded it. Indeed, it was undamaged and his friends sighed in relief.

"Good job, dear boy," exclaimed Liam. "It has served us well thus far. I'd not wish to venture forward without it."

After further recounting their experience of the quake, Rupert, after much praise of Raja's heroics, had something else to report.

"I had some sort of dream or vision." With that, he disclosed what he'd seen before Raja brought him back to life. He omitted no detail of the mysterious palace and its inhabitants. Upon concluding, he looked to his listeners. The companions believed this to be no casual fantasy.

"Do you know the location of the palace? Do you suppose it to be in Raja-Sharan?" inquired Liam.

"I cannot say with certainty. However, I *do* recollect being told by my cousin Rajiv of a palace of pink stone. I did not behold the exterior, but within, the walls were covered in pink and gold...whatever that may indicate."

"Clearly, this vision can only have an ominous portent. That royal lady was in danger from that forbidding fellow; and *you* seemed threatened as well," declared Daniel with a frown. "It was certainly a warning."

"We have been forced to travel with little information concerning our various destinations," observed Rupert. "We must not allow this to continue, for it is to our detriment if we travel blind."

"Yes, on the morrow, let us make inquiries of our next destination, Ribakesh, and perhaps Raja-Sharan as well. Surely, the residents of Kashkara must have *some* knowledge of their neighbors. At least they'll know more than *we* do," observed Drego.

Liam concurred. "However, our first business must be to purchase saddle and bridle for Lira. For earthquakes are far from uncommon in these parts. So my darling girl, it is simply too dangerous to ride without means of controlling your mount."

Lira, despite her recent ordeal, was not about to easily surrender her freedom of riding bareback. Before she could voice her opinion, however, Rupert spoke again.

"Lira, I see you are about to protest, but this cannot be allowed. In fact, I myself will secure bridle and saddle for Majesty. For marvelous as our horses may be, we cannot expect them to be without fear when the earth shakes beneath them. We must have means to inhibit their actions, so they do not bring themselves - or others - to harm."

"Very well, if *you* will use them, how can I protest?"

The men were glad of Rupert's words, for they had hoped to convince their prince on that very matter, but thought to find him stubborn in refusal. It made Liam smile to think how the lad was learning to face realities and bend to necessity.

The comrades spent a comfortable night under the stars, together and grateful to be. Upon the morrow, they set off for the nearby town of Mahndar. There, they not only wished to make necessary purchases, but to gather whatever information was to be had.

Upon entering the town, located about ten miles beyond the damaged bridge, the companions observed business proceeding more or less as usual; the streets packed and little damage visible from the quake. Rupert again wondered that the seemingly sturdy bridge had collapsed, when so many more frail structures remained unscathed.

They soon located a thriving marketplace with many a food stall to tempt them. The companions chose one at random, ordering a breakfast of goat milk yogurt, figs, and a flat bread with a hollow center called 'pita'. A lively young woman served them. After exclaiming at the fine looking gathering, she inquired if they might be foreigners. The comrades had addressed her in the language of Kashkara with some fluency, yet imperfectly.

"Why yes," responded Daniel, "we are from the west, but heading east. We would welcome any intelligence you may offer, for we have never crossed these lands before."

The young lady blushed, for she thought Daniel so very handsome and proved eager to be helpful. "Do you mean you are for Badarahm? I do hope not, for that's one place *I* would prefer not to venture."

The party exchanged looks. "Of what do you refer?" asked Daniel. "We are quite in ignorance, I fear." They knew it only as the land that lay beyond Ribakesh, their next destination.

The pretty lass regarded Daniel intently and continued in a confidential whisper. "Well, *others* travel there often enough, I admit, but it's a strange place, let me tell you. At least, that's what I hear. Personally, I've never left Mahndar, nor do I wish to! Especially for the likes of Badarahm! For it is well known that the populace worships the dead! And the dead rule the affairs of the living!"

Rupert should have allowed Daniel to continue the interrogation of the smitten girl, but he spoke in astonishment.

"*The dead control the actions of the living!?* What could you possibly mean?"

She turned to the boy with a smile, then quickly shifted her gaze back to Daniel.

"It is true…or at least that's what they *say*. I cannot pretend to know exactly…but *some* people claim the dead speak to them and they deliver those messages to the living. Even their Raja believes it! His chief advisor tells the king what his dead father wants and the living king obeys! It's quite spooky and I wouldn't want any part of it!"

They questioned the girl further, but she seemed to have nothing concrete to offer other than bizarre rumors and gossip. After concluding their meal, they headed for the blacksmith to purchase saddle and bridle. On the way, they spoke of what they'd learned.

"Well, Drego says *his* dead mother gives him vital information. Thus far, it's proven true. So how can we deny the possibility?" declared Daniel.

"Yet you can see this would be much open to corruption," observed his father with a grim look. "For *anyone* could claim this ability and who could prove it untrue? Certainly, the dead can neither confirm nor deny their supposed 'messages' as interpreted by others."

Rupert was intrigued and disturbed.

"How wonderful if my grandfather, King Marco, could communicate with me! However, if someone brought me his message, how could I credit it to be true? It is very worrisome that the ruler of Badarahm allows himself to be led in this manner. However, we do not know the facts of the matter, so we should perhaps draw no hasty conclusions."

They had arrived at the blacksmith and began with the necessary purchases. The owner exclaimed at Majesty's massive proportions, wondering if he'd find saddle and bridle to fit. Luckily he did. Finding equipment for Lira's black stallion proved no challenge. Before taking their leave, the comrades endeavored to inquire again of Ribakesh and the lands beyond. This citizen's reaction proved somewhat different from that of the talkative young lady.

"Yes, I have traveled to Ribakesh more than once. If you have never ventured into the desert, I suggest you'd prepare yourselves. Quite the challenge," he concluded, giving the party and their horses a close once-over. "You'd best trade your mounts for camels and be advised to join up with a caravan. Traveling on your own would be foolishness itself. Raiders abound who pray upon the vulnerable. The larger the party the better…though even *that* cannot guarantee against attack."

The companions did not welcome this news by any means. However, the follow had not mentioned the strange customs of Badarahm and so they sought to inquire.

"We have heard that ghosts rule there," ventured Liam. "Can it be true that the dead advise even their king?"

The blacksmith glanced at Liam with a grin. "Ha, that's all nonsense. Let them waste their time with such foolishness. At any rate, set your mind upon dangers the *living* may cause. The Raiders of Ribakesh have a fearsome reputation. Despite that, nothing stops the caravans from their business and most are well-armed nowadays."

The party thanked the fellow and moved on. "We must attempt to inquire of everyone we meet," said Rupert with a touch of bewilderment. "Obviously, the more information we gather, the better...even when reports contradict each other."

"I do not concern myself with absurd tales of ghosts told by foolish young girls," observed Morley dryly. "However, the information about caravans and raiders is much to the point. Of that, we must certainly take heed."

The comrades continued on with their journey, Rupert and Lira, now making use of saddles and bridles. The young prince felt a great uneasiness grow within. Information was the key! They were forced to live by their wits, for they could hardly hope to triumph by force of arms. They must expect to be vastly outnumbered and would always be - until and unless they eventually had an army of their own to command. Clearly, that day remained far-off at best...as distant as a dream.

Yet along with deepest concern, Rupert experienced a rush of elation. It arrived unannounced, coursing through his being. He yearned suddenly for the desert lands! The young prince knew it would be a month at least before the party might hope to reach that elusive goal. But it now called out to him and his spirit reached towards it eagerly.

Not for the first time, he wondered at the concept of 'destiny' - something he had heard referred to time and again here in Kashkara. Somehow Rupert trusted that, whatever awaited in that burning, desolate wasteland, his spirit would rise boldly to encounter it.

Chapter Twenty-Eight

Rupert found himself truly enraptured by the desert. Never had he been aware of nature, the rhythm of life itself, with such intensity. Everything about it spoke to the deepest core of his being. He was spellbound.

Firstly, there was the vast emptiness spreading out in a limitless horizon - flat, sun-baked sands, broken only by occasional mountainous dunes. For days and days at a time, no leaf of grass, no trees with swaying shade, disturbed the monotones of his surroundings. Yet, Rupert found this world thrilling beyond measure.

The Golden-Eyed Prince also greeted riding upon camel-back with a sense of eager adventure. He found those creatures to be indeed aloof and not always in possession of the best of natures. Thus, he made certain to seek permission before burdening them with the weighty loads they were required to carry each day.

Swaying high atop the balky beast was a gratifying experience. As huge as Majesty was, camels were yet taller. The youthful prince relished the view from such grand heights. The swaying of the camel's gait was also alien, but Rupert quickly became accustomed; although the first time he mounted one, he was almost tossed over its head when the ungainly creature took to its feet, hind legs first.

Along with each spectacular sunrise, the blazing sun of the desert days was something Rupert also adored. The heat came in blasts and waves and the boy could feel it penetrate the heavy robes he wore, into his skin and through to his very bones. It gave a powerful sense of union to the distant sun burning so brilliantly overhead. This was undeniably a strikingly alien world from the dark, damp forest that had been his home.

And the nights! The desert nights spoke to his spirit like nothing else in his experience. The baking heat of the day gave way to frigid, crystal-clear air. Never had he witnessed the night sky displayed in such glory; for no obstacle blocked his vision of the heavens. Lying awake night after night, staring up at the dome of the universe, the Golden-Eyed Prince felt both infinitesimally small and part of something vast and glorious. He was awestruck to his very soul. Rupert felt more alive, more self-aware, than ever in his life.

The young liege observed his friends did not necessarily share his passion for their new surroundings.

At day's end, there were numerous good-natured complaints regarding the woes of traveling upon camel back; furthermore, not all were enamored with the blasting heat. Yet they were well aware that Rupert was of a different opinion.

Several weeks previously, the companions had crossed the border into Ribakesh. They had taken no chances of being caught unawares, having repeatedly rehearsed a tale for the guardsmen; that they were a band of traveling entertainers now heading to Raja-Sharan. However, to their chagrin, the border crossing occurred without drama; they had been waved through with hardly a glance. Travelers were numerous and only the most suspicious of characters were likely to face a challenge.

Later that night, they celebrated their first uneventful entrance into another land.

"Well, that just goes to show," said Morley with a laugh. "We only need prepare as we should to find ourselves totally ignored!"

"A likely formula," Liam observed. "Now that we have a clever story arranged, we should never encounter an obstacle again."

They laughed at the thought, only wishing such could be true. "At any rate, we must concern ourselves with Ribakesh and then Badarahm," Rupert reminded as they sat about a fire drinking tea and munching on flatbread, cashews, and fruit that served as their supper. "It's clear we must join a caravan."

"One more thing, if I may be so bold," chimed in Drego. "We would be wise to renew our disguise."

He gave his friends a penetrating onceover. "The hair we darkened is now fading. Moreover, should we attach ourselves to a caravan, it might appear mighty peculiar were we observed applying dark make-up to our skins each morning!"

Lira giggled at the image. "Oh, yes, that *would* cause comment, no doubt! Though how are we to avoid that necessity?"

Drego smiled at the lovely lass. "Easily done my sweet, if you'll agree. I've taken the liberty of purchasing a dye made of walnut shells in the bazaars of Kashkara. It will darken our complexions and should last a number of weeks." He returned the startled expressions of his companions with a beguiling smile.

Lira turned to Daniel. "Father, what do you think? It seems advisable."

"I suppose so," he responded slowly. It was one thing to apply camouflage on a daily basis, but quite another to make a semi-permanent change.

"We must agree to it," urged Rupert. "After all, we are required to blend in. Even Drego and I, who are darker than you, begin to pale compared to those we now meet." He turned to Liam for his thoughts.

"I don't suppose King Ryker's spies are likely about at this late date, but we cannot be too careful. We require privacy for the task. I suggest looking for a cottage. It will be a welcome opportunity to sleep indoors…and we'll likely have no such luxury for the foreseeable future."

Within a day the companions found a suitable dwelling on the edge of the town of Tazma. They had visited the bazaar to obtain suitable clothing for their journey, consisting of heavy-weight, light-colored robes, turbans, loose-fitting trousers, as well as new boots for all. Lira's wardrobe was not dissimilar, for shielding themselves from the blazing sun was imperative.

Next came their disguise. The cottage had ample water from a well in back. They thoroughly cleansed their hair and bodies, no easy task. Then the dye was administered to their wet locks and dried skin and left overnight. By the following dawn, Drego was able to gauge their transformation with approval. Now all were dark of hair and complexion

"We look as if we hail from these parts," Drego opined to the group. "Moreover, since we now speak several local languages, we should do nicely."

"Yes," agreed Morley. "We can tell the natives of Raja-Sharan we are from Kashkara and the people of Kashkara we hail from Raja-Sharan!"

Rupert was amused, but agreed in principle.

"We can always claim to be from my father's homeland of Gitano," added Drego. "Not likely we'd run into citizens of *that* far-off place hereabouts."

After donning new garments, they regarded one another in satisfaction. Lira was absolutely gleeful, since disguise added to her sense that each day was a matchless adventure.

The companions spent most of their time in town. Tazma, located just inside the border of Ribakesh, was thriving. Numerous caravans passed through on their way east, heading back to Kashkara, or points south. Rupert was fascinated. People of exotic appearance and dress continually crossed his path. He found himself eager to speak to each one, wishing to know from whence they'd come and what their home countries were like. There was so much for him to learn and know! The more he experienced the more ignorant he felt. However, the young prince acknowledged the necessity against drawing undue notice, so he struggled to keep curiosity at bay.

The party made multiple inquiries concerning travel to the east and opinion proved unanimous. They *must* journey by caravan. Thieves and raiders abounded. There was comparative safety in numbers.

The comrades had been directed to the eastern edge of town. It served as the gathering place for those departing for myriad destinations. They were informed that several caravans had left the previous week and they would be required to wait about ten days until the next one. It was rumored to be a small group, but if they were willing to wait another week after that, a more impressive gathering was to make for Badarahm.

The companions made no decision on the spot, but as they turned to go, they were stopped again.

"I believe you have not purchased camels as yet," the bearded and turbaned fellow observed. "I strongly advise against facing the desert on horseback. Not fair to you *or* your mounts. The camel bazaar is one mile south. Get the finest you can acquire, for you'll not regret it." He looked them over, concluding the motley group could likely not afford beasts of high quality. He wished them luck and sent them on their way.

As it was almost evening, the comrades treated themselves to a delicious dinner of couscous and a mountain of eggplant before heading back towards the privacy of their temporary home. Once there, they discussed the options before them.

"I believe it is clear. We plainly must travel by camel. Our horses...even Majesty...should not be expected to carry us and suffer the great desert heat as well."

"Oh, we must *not* leave our steeds behind!" cried Lira.

"Don't worry, darling," soothed her father. "We shall do as Rupert suggests and bring them along. We shall need them once reaching Raja-Sharan."

"Yes," agreed Liam. "So let us purchase camels first thing on the morrow. We'll require a good deal of practice before we set out."

"Which caravan should we join?" Morley wanted to know. "The smaller one leaves sooner, but the larger might gain us more protection."

"More protection...or possibly a bigger target!" ventured Drego. "If I were a thief...and I'm *not*," he reminded his sometimes skeptical friends, "would I rather attack a less well-defended caravan - or a larger one which promised more reward?"

"Excellent question," declared Liam. "for both would offer splendid opportunities."

"I wonder if the caravans provide armed escort?" Rupert asked. "The Raiders of Ribakesh are said to be fearsome."

It was decided to make further inquiries and only then determine as to which caravan might offer the best security.

Meanwhile, they saw to the purchase of camels. Lira was too small to control the unruly beasts and instead would ride with the companion of her choice each day. The men would have their own camel, of course, but Rupert, ever mindful of the starvation faced months before, decreed they should purchase several in reserve to carry extra supplies. Now, water would prove even more precious than food. Though the caravan's masters had assured there would be many an oasis along their route, Rupert would take no chances. Even the horses were made to carry modest amounts of water, though burdened with little else.

Rupert was required to explain to Majesty why he was not to carry his prince for the time being. Majesty agreed, though not without reluctance. The golden stallion was protective of his master's safety and the balky camels appeared to feel no such sense of mission. Still, they were known as 'the ships of the desert' and a vast ocean of sand stretched to the limitless horizon.

Raja, too, had to be cared for. He would naturally wish to run alongside the mangy camels that moved at a stately gait. However, Raja's paws might well be blistered by the burning sands. Rupert therefore decreed he would wear leather coverings to protect them. Raja appeared skeptical, but Rupert was insistent upon having the last word.

After a week of practice upon camelback, under the instruction of a local fellow they had hired, the comrades felt competent to proceed. Always eager to be off, they decided in favor of the caravan to depart first…though it was modest in size. Borad, the caravan master, agreed to take them for a reasonable fee. He was also pleased that the 'traveling actors' were well-armed and skilled in the use of weaponry. The amiable fellow assured that he had secured an armed escort of a dozen men. The caravan was to carry over three hundred travelers, but hopefully, raiders might consider them too insignificant to prove tempting.

"We may likely escape their notice," predicted the caravan's leader. "I have heard rumors that a vastly richer group will follow within several weeks, headed to some festival or wedding somewhere to the east. Now, *they* should prove a tasty target."

Meanwhile, Rupert counted the days until their desert journey might begin. He delighted in his friends' transformation, brought about by their dark disguise. Hearing them speak constantly in the languages of Raja-Sharan or Kashkara also aided in the belief they were truly developing different selves. It gave Rupert a matchless sense of freedom. King Ryker and his menace seemed a universe away.

And so their trek through vast wastelands finally began. From the very first day, high atop his swaying mount, with Raja and Majesty gamboling alongside, his beloved companions about him, Rupert felt alive and at peace. In the weeks that followed, the desert world would indeed have much to teach him. And Rupert, with all his heart, was most desirous to learn.

Chapter Twenty-Nine

Rupert's enchantment with the desert wastes continued unabated. Drego teased him, declaring the infatuation was due to his Raja-Sharani heritage. After all, the western quarter of that kingdom was pure desert; so the love of sand and sun was likely deep in his blood.

Whatever the explanation, Rupert counted each day a treasure. Knowing peril might lie ahead, he was all the more determined to savor his current happiness. Besides the glory of the sun-soaked days and the star-studded nights, Rupert relished the society of strangers as never before. The comrades had heretofore been compelled to remain aloof from those crossing their path. But now, that proved next to impossible. By and large, their fellow travelers were a sociable lot. It would have marked the comrades as odd indeed had they refused to become acquainted.

Rupert and Lira took special joy in the requirement of making friends. They remembered well to act the part of traveling players and the companions had adopted local names in order to more easily blend in. Rupert was now known as Razim and the youngest of their number was called Lamara. Most of their new friends were merchants or families on a visit to distant kin. Rupert had the strong suspicion some of the traders carried goods far richer than claimed, while understanding why they might prove less than forthright. Borad warned that robbers sometimes posed as ordinary travelers in order to steal from their fellow passengers.

At any rate, the companions were delighted to let down their guard. When it became known they were entertainers, there was an instant request they perform that very evening. Drego, perhaps alone among the adults, felt it an excellent idea and immediately agreed. After all, he reminded his reluctant circle later on, they must always be willing to prove their identity. And so, the companions sang songs from their ever-growing repertoire, while Drego gave an impressive display of juggling to boot. The performance was deemed a success and to the chagrin of Liam, Daniel, and Morley, their audience declared they must entertain on a regular basis. Rupert, Lira, and Drego, however, were delighted to accept.

Again that night, Rupert lay awake for several hours. Sleep was often not swift to come, despite the full days of riding or walking through the burning sands. The canopy of heaven continued to dazzle anew each time he beheld it. There could be nothing more glorious… making sleep seem a sorrowful waste. But finally, rest did come, though well after midnight.

However, Rupert's reluctant slumber was disturbed in the most shocking manner. Sounds of Raja howling, Majesty whinnying in a high-pitched panic, along with grunts and groans from the camels, caused him to go from slumber to sitting instantly upright. He struggled to comprehend what was causing the animals such distress. The boy felt the ground rumble beneath him and for a confused moment wondered if another earthquake might be the cause.

Swiftly, the prince was on his feet, as were his companions. Rupert was aware that cries of alarm and havoc were running the length of the caravan. In addition, from a distance but coming ever closer, were other cries…blood-curdling shouts of men on the attack. The truth struck Rupert like a brutal blow - the Raiders of Ribakesh were upon them!

The Golden-Eyed Prince reached for his quiver of arrows and strapped it to his trembling body. He then grabbed up his bow in one hand and with the other, snatched sword and dagger, shoving them into the sash fastened about his waist. Wordlessly, he witnessed his companions performing similar actions.

"Lira, stay back," cried her father. "Stay with Majesty." The other horses had been tethered, but Majesty had been allowed to roam free. The huge horse, snorting with ears pinned back, looked prepared for battle himself.

"They're coming...sounds like hundreds...horses and camels...do not shoot until you have a decent target. We must not fire wildly!" commanded Liam, attempting to take in everything at once. "Rupert, Lira, stay with Majesty and Raja. Get behind our saddles and keep down!" The camels had been relieved of their large saddles and the pile formed might offer some hope of protection.

However, Rupert would not obey. "No, I can shoot an arrow as well as any of you!" And without time for argument, he joined the men and stood resolutely beside them, while ordering Majesty and Raja to remain with Lira.

There were terrible screams everywhere - from the horrified members of the caravan, to their hired guards shouting directions, to the terrifying war-cries of the attackers. Each moment seemed eternal, yet each second passed with horrifying speed. How foolish they had been to believe a mere dozen guards would suffice! Every able-bodied male had taken to his weapons, but it was doubtful many were expert or experienced fighters.

Rupert's blood pounded in his ears, almost blocking out the chaos surrounding him. He strained to see if the marauders were approaching in a straight line, or instead had the caravan surrounded. Suddenly, a whizzing sound penetrated his consciousness. "Arrows!" he knew at once. The enemy, all mounted on horse or camel, were sending a hail of arrows flying before them. Rupert, with deliberation, removed one from his own quiver and prepared to take aim. The companions could no longer delay. They must fire now and hope to hit any of the approaching foe.

Without a word, the other comrades had drawn the same conclusion. More or less in unison, they let arrows fly. Rupert had a fleeting realization that he was firing upon fellow human beings; he who suffered agonies of guilt for having slain a single forest creature to feed his starving friends. Yet this was quite another matter. Kill or be killed was the only reality. Rupert must do anything within his power to protect the people and animals he loved so well.

The comrades could not know if their shots had found their targets. It would hardly have mattered, so great did the number of opponents seem. Their approach grew into a horrific cacophony. In another instant, a second volley fell about them. From Morley came a gasp and a cry. All turned in his direction…an arrow had pierced his shoulder. He fell back.

"Morley!" screamed Rupert, but Drego, who was next to the boy, restrained him forcefully.

"Rupert, you must keep firing! Morley's wound is not bad."

Rupert glared at Drego, but recognizing he spoke true, snatched another arrow from his quiver and fired again. Rupert knew his companions did the same, but it was as if they were placing drops of water upon a raging fire.

On and on the relentless horde came, until the sound of thundering hooves seemed to fill the world… accompanied by Raja's furious howls and Majesty's high pitched screams. Shouts of terror from along the caravan also assaulted their ears. Surely, this could not be real. Surely, this was some hellish nightmare!

As if in answer to those desperate thoughts, yet another volley of arrows descended. Lira, in a panic at seeing Morley unattended, made to rush to his side. Raja jumped up to knock her back down; by doing so, his body had been exposed to the onslaught. Multiple arrows pierced his back. A terrible, high pitched yelp escaped the powerful mastiff.

Rupert, hearing the ghastly sound, screamed, then screamed again. Yet once more, Drego prevented him from flying to Raja's side. He was not easily subdued, for it required all Drego's brute force to restrain the frantic prince. Rupert desired to grab his dagger and strike Drego dead for interfering.

In the end, it was Liam who took command. He shouted at the boy in black, stern tones.

"Rupert, they are coming! Remember yourself. Shoot! Shoot!"

Rupert could not disobey the voice of the man he loved so well, though his heart felt as if being torn from his body. Now the shattering sobs of Lira weeping for her wounded friends joined the nightmarish bedlam.

"Lira," cried Rupert. "Take Majesty! Go, run! Do not return until the fighting has ceased! Save Majesty! *Please*, Lira!" he begged again, this time using their native tongue, which they had not spoken for many long months.

"Rupert, you go too! Go with Lira now," begged Daniel above the frenzied din. The determined prince shook his head and fired again into the barbaric mob, now so close the boy could smell the rank odor of the horses, camels, and their darkly clad riders. The fire the companions had built hours before still burned, illuminating the hellish scene. The flickering images of approaching death added to the nightmarish quality of their desperate circumstance.

Grimly, Rupert prepared to fire once more, when a shriek from Lira made him turn swiftly about. Raiders had penetrated the camp and were attacking the comrades from behind. Lira, who had managed to mount Majesty, was pulled from his back onto the camel-back of one of the grisly murderers. Majesty, in a fury, sank his teeth into the leg of the rider, who screamed out in pain. But an instant later, it was Majesty who screamed, as three arrows struck him from the other side. The mighty stallion sank to his knees.

"No, this cannot be happening!" Rupert gasped. He raced in Lira's direction, but it was Daniel, firing arrows as he came, who first reached his daughter and her kidnapper. Rupert fired his own weapon at another marauder, but there were too many. In a horrifying instant, Daniel was struck in the chest. Rupert's adopted brother fell to his knees. Dropping his own bow, Daniel clutched at the arrow piercing his heart, while Lira screamed and Rupert froze.

It was Liam, sword in hand, who charged to his son's defense, but before reaching Daniel's side, another raider, mounted on horseback, rode him down from behind. In one horrible movement, he struck Liam's head from his body.

Rupert wailed soundlessly at the sight. Before he could further react, Drego slammed Rupert to the ground as a volley of arrows flew overhead. They had fallen next to where Morley lay. He was no longer alive… myriad arrows having penetrated his flesh.

Drego had now been wounded, allowing arrows that would have otherwise hit Rupert to pierce his own body. "Forgive us, Rupert," he gasped. "Destiny defeated us…we could not overcome fate." And with that, Drego, too, breathed his last. Lira's terrified cries could be heard growing fainter, as she was spirited away by the murderous band to a dark destiny of her own.

There was nothing left now. Arrows continued to rain down. The raiders had overrun the camp. Death was upon him. Yet Rupert would not perish at their unworthy hands. The Golden-Eyed Prince drew his dagger - the venerated object with carved silver handle and sheath, which dear Daniel had presented him upon his last birthday. Swiftly Rupert kissed it in loving tribute to his friend and to all his beloved comrades, who had followed his quest and had perished for his sake.

Almost able to feel the rank breath of his slayers upon his face, Rupert took the dagger and plunged it into his own heart.

The piercing pain of the blade caused the boy to cry out. His cries caused him to awaken. Rupert's eyes flashed open. There above him was the glorious, serene dome of the universe. He screamed again in terror, agony, and confusion, only to see, seconds later, the troubled faces of his precious friends surrounding him as Raja commenced licking his master's face.

"What ails you, my boy?" whispered Liam. Rupert reacted as if beholding a ghost, taking to his feet gasping.

He could yet feel the torture in his chest caused by his dagger. Yet, there was no blood - no screams or cries other than his own.

Several travelers, including Borad and a handful of hired guards, arrived upon the scene. "What is here?" demanded the caravan leader, sword in hand. But he and the others soon concluded nothing was obviously amiss.

"The boy had a bad dream, that is all," explained Daniel, wishing the intruders to depart. "He is prone to them. We apologize for the disturbance."

Relieved, the others returned to their campfires. Rupert, having not yet uttered a single word, at last comprehended the truth - he had indeed suffered a ghastly nightmare. Yet, he was not entirely convinced. Was *this* the dream…seeing his precious friends alive and well? Were they all, in reality, *dead*?

Rupert was guided to sit by the fire, a blanket wrapped about his shivering form, a cup of hot tea placed in his hands. Slowly, the fact they *were* yet alive penetrated his shattered being.

His family sat in a protective circle about him. "Can you tell us of your dream?" inquired Morley gently. "Whatever it was, we must hear of it."

"Yes," agreed Liam, "for your dreams are never without meaning. So let us know when you are ready to speak." He reached over and embraced the still-mute boy, hoping to pass his own strength onto his traumatized prince.

Rupert finally nodded. "I must tell you what I saw, though it shatters my very being to speak of it," he whispered. "Yet I promised long ago never to hold anything back. We can only hope what I foresaw was a warning only and that we may indeed be permitted to challenge our fate."

With that, Rupert took a deep, shaky breath and began to describe his unimaginable vision to his cherished friends.

Chapter Thirty

"Here is what happened," began Rupert. He was forced to pause; a huge lump filled his throat, making it difficult to speak. "Our caravan was overrun by raiders, striking in the dead of night. We were swiftly overwhelmed - vastly outnumbered. All of us perished, including Majesty and Raja. No, Lira survived. She was carried off by the marauders. We could do nothing against them."

After a prolonged, dismayed silence, Lira spoke. "I do sense you have more to report, but hesitate to do so before me," she observed correctly. "I will prepare our morning repast. For the day will soon break." With that, she embraced Rupert and moved off. He was astonished at her insight. How wise she was, yet how young.

Though Lira had departed, Rupert still hesitated. It was all too ghastly and gruesome – those images now permanently seared into his mind. How could he tell his dear comrades of their black fate? It was Daniel who broke into his silent dilemma.

"Come, Rupert, you must share *all* of your vision. Only then may we attempt to unravel its true meaning."

"Yes," agreed his father. "You were not meant to bear this burden alone. We shall take it up as well. So, dark as your words may prove, please enlighten us."

Rupert nodded. Taking another shaky breath, he commenced his narrative. He found words of terror and power to convey what had overtaken his family. He deplored recounting the vision, for he refused to deny it as fantasy.

Strangely, it *did* bring Rupert a measure of comfort to share the horrific details. He recognized anew that sorrows and burdens *were* meant to be shared. With another deep sigh and more than a few silent tears running down his face, Rupert concluded the recounting of his tragic nightmare.

"Well, I admit to having heard cheerier tales in my time," mused Morley, attempting to lighten the mood after a stunned pause. "Moreover, I'd have preferred to die a bit more heroically. See if you can manage better in your next vision!"

Rupert smiled shakily at his comrade, though further words would not come.

"I myself find this dream less than accurate," chimed in Drego. "I cannot believe for an instant that my last words would be about 'fate defeating us' or some such. True, my mother taught me of it, but I can't say I agree that 'destiny rules all.'" He, too, spoke with a measure of jest for the sake of his distressed prince.

"Whatever the cause of your experience, we can only be grateful for it," decided Liam. "Now we can prepare for what is to come. So you see, your dream may yet alter our fate!"

"Yes, your warnings concerning future events have always proved invaluable," agreed Daniel. "So, as trying as this ordeal was, we must thank whoever or whatever sent it."

Morley concurred. "It's true, Rupert. Your dream will save us, no doubt. So courage, my liege!" He concluded by moving to Rupert's side, wrapping one arm about his shoulder. "All will be well. Has it not always proven so thus far?"

Rupert regarded his friends. Their jaunty courage did indeed bolster his spirits. Perhaps they spoke true - this nightmare could indeed provide their means of salvation.

Lira summoned them to breakfast. Flat bread, dried fruit, and yogurt prepared from camel's milk, procured from one of their fellow travelers, were passed among them. Rupert, who felt his appetite might have deserted him forever, found he was able to partake. The sight of Raja, lapping up his own share of the slightly sour yogurt, somehow cheered the golden-eyed boy.

"We must speak to Borad at once to warn of what awaits."

"Did your dream tell of *when* this mayhem was to occur?" wondered Drego. Rupert shook his head.

"It was while traveling with this caravan. Our journey should end in two or three weeks, when we reach Badarahm. I have the terrible inkling the attack will come sooner rather than later...perhaps this very night. There is not a moment to lose. But will Borad credit my words?"

"We must endeavor to prove convincing," said Liam with a firm nod. "It might be preferred if one of the adults had the dream, but since your cries aroused half the camp, there's no avoiding the truth of the matter."

After having managed to down their repast, they stood as one and made for the caravan leader. They found Borad loading his balky camels. He began to smile in greeting, but changed expression upon observing the dark looks upon the companions' faces.

"Well, I see you've recovered, young Razim. However, your countenance appears far from cheerful, as do your friends' sour looks. What ails you?"

It was Liam who acted as spokesman. In as few words as possible, he conveyed that Rupert had received a vision the caravan would be attacked by the fearsome Raiders of Ribakesh. Liam added that Rupert possessed the gift of prophecy, which they had learned to value.

"Why, this is utter foolishness," the caravan leader exclaimed. "No offense to your boy, but you cannot expect us to credit a frightened child! It is small wonder Razim dreams of raiders. I myself warned of them the day we met. Moreover, there have been whisperings aplenty of their terrifying deeds at the nightly gatherings." The turbaned and bearded fellow smiled down at Rupert in a condescending manner. "Have no fear, lad; armed guards accompany us. They will not fail to protect you."

Rupert felt anger rise. Borad thought him a frightened child. He had no knowledge of Rupert's true identity or capabilities. Yet he *had* to convince the fellow somehow!

"Sir, I beg you heed the words of my friend. If we cannot find a way to defend ourselves, all will perish. I cannot speak more plain." Something of the boy's princely power conveyed itself to Borad. He gazed at Rupert with a keen expression.

"Even if your words were true, what more could be done? Our guards remain alert through the night. They know their duties."

"We must at least warn our fellow travelers," urged Morley, "and all must prepare defensive tactics. Perhaps we might camp in circular formation, preventing attack from behind."

Morley's suggestion, which seemed only common sense, struck Borad as unnecessary. "You will not alarm the others. Panic is not pretty. Besides, they would laugh in my face if a child's foolish dream was the cause. I will speak to the guards. That should prove sufficient." Borad mounted his camel, signaling for the day's journey to begin.

"He won't listen!" exclaimed Rupert in muted fury.

"To be fair, we can hardly blame the fellow," ventured Drego. "He does not know you. Yet we must keep your identity secret, alas!" He smiled rakishly at his prince, noting the grim look in Rupert's countenance.

"We must speak to the others ourselves."

"Lira speaks true," declared her grandfather. "This very night, let us prepare to entertain as before and give warning." And so, the companions were decided.

For once, the glory of the desert held no charms for Rupert. Perhaps this day would be his very last! He spent the long hours on camelback desperately seeking a way to prevent the coming peril. Privately, the boy feared that even if all *were* put on highest alert, disaster would still overtake them.

"*Think, think!*" Rupert urged himself time and again. "I cannot believe I received this dreadful warning for nothing. There *must* be a way out!" Then, a cowardly yet simple thought crossed his mind. Why, they could simply depart the caravan! The raiders might attack, but the companions would not be present. However, besides the gruesome guilt accompanying the stratagem, this cold-blooded plan would not succeed. If they were on their own, the raiders would still find them; they would still perish.

Sunset finally came. As the weary travelers gathered for their evening meal, Rupert and his friends presented themselves, declaring they would entertain. Daniel and Drego had instruments in hand and the comrades began a series of lively tunes…which drew almost all their fellow travelers to the campfire. They formed an appreciative audience. At last Liam, after prolonged cheers, gestured for silence.

"There is something I must convey. We have reason to believe we will soon come under attack. Perhaps this very night - certainly before reaching Badarahm. We have informed our leader of this, but he believes our hired guards will prove sufficient. Nevertheless, please see to it you are armed and on the alert. We will be vastly outnumbered and each moment will count!"

There was an intake of breath from the crowd as Liam concluded. Questions rang out. Then, before panic might spread, Borad angrily denounced Liam and his crew.

"The source of this forecast of doom is the boy Razim. He merely suffered a bad dream, as children will; his family takes such nonsense as prophecy. We are well protected. No need to fear."

Borad's words were greeted with a variety of reactions. Some were vastly relieved to hear childish fantasies were the source of the warning, while others believed well enough in omens and portents. Arguments erupted as Borad's choler grew apace. Finally, he ordered the troublesome comrades to return to their own campfire.

They reluctantly obeyed. At least, warning had been given. Rupert was now convinced many would remain watchful during the night. That was all he could hope for.

The comrades sat about their own fire, swallowing tea, weapons at the ready. Majesty and Raja were warned of encroaching peril and were on the lookout. Still, there remained no solution to the dilemma created by the superior numbers the enemy would possess.

"*How* can we defeat them?" Rupert muttered yet again. "I feel we are poor creatures helplessly awaiting slaughter." The boy noted Lira's stricken look and hastened to regain control of his emotions. "Forgive me, Lira. 'Forewarned is forearmed', as they say."

"We should make ourselves less vulnerable at the very least," advised Daniel. "Gather our saddles and pile them in a circle. We can take cover and prove less obvious targets." Clearly this was a fine idea. If only Rupert believed it would be sufficient! It was further agreed two of their number would remain awake through the night. Morley and Drego agreed to the task.

Rupert was convinced he would certainly not sleep. This desperate night, even the magnificent heavenly display provided no comfort. The stars appeared cold and distant; uncaring as to the fate of tiny beings such as himself and his family.

Eventually, Rupert did manage to doze off...but just as in his vision, the howls of Majesty and Raja brought him rudely awake. He experienced a moment's confusion. Was he dreaming yet again? But, no! Heart galloping, he witnessed his friends snatch up their weapons and shelter behind the circle of saddles and supplies, piled high about them.

Screams of alarm spread through the caravan as the thunder of approaching hooves pounded towards them. To Rupert, that sound spelled their doom. His mind's eye envisioned countless horses and camels bearing the dark-clad deliverers of death.

Then suddenly, out of nowhere, *Rupert knew!* Inspiration leaped up like a pouncing jungle cat. *He knew!* He sprang up and dashed to Majesty's side, Raja at his heels. Rupert gestured for Majesty to lower his head and the boy whispered in his ear. The glorious stallion whinnied in response, comprehending at once. Rupert threw himself upon his steed's back. Then, to the horror of his friends, the boy raced out towards the approaching attackers. Bow and arrow were strapped to his back, sword and dagger in his sash, but he made no move to draw weapons.

"Rupert!" Morley screamed, as the others joined in crying out stunned alarms. After a moment frozen in indecision, Daniel and Morley bolted from cover to make towards their prince. Instantly, Lira called out to them.

"Father, Morley, come back! Leave Rupert be! *I understand! I understand!*" Then arrows commenced to rain down and they were forced to retreat again to the circle of saddles.

Rupert remained alone, in the open, with Majesty and Raja. He drew his steed to a halt. The Golden-Eyed Prince seemed in a trance, gazing towards the murderous foe, hardly moving a muscle.

"What is the crazy boy doing?" cried Drego. The others turned to Lira, but she was also gazing unblinking in the direction of the marauders. The others turned from Lira to Rupert in wonder, weapons poised, to observe the outcome of Rupert's unfathomable strategy.

Rupert sat astride Majesty. Power and a glorious energy surged through him. The Golden-Eyed Prince and the golden stallion felt united as never before. Together they sent the same silent command again and again to the charging camels and horses – '*go back, go back, go back!*' For *that* was the answer Rupert had been seeking! He could not hope to move the black hearts of vile villains, but he could influence their animal companions.

The young prince drew out his sword, waving it aloft. Yet Rupert was aware of nothing but this message to these four-legged creatures he would always consider his friends. They were being forced into danger and possible death. He assured them they were truly free...not slaves of evil masters.

"*Go back! Go back! Go back!*" he now bellowed aloud. Arrows flew, but the bold prince was oblivious to that, as well as the horrified cries from his family.

These moments seemed to belong to another world. Rupert was *alive*, connected to the stars above his head, to the mysterious, glorious forces of life, to his power as a Golden-Eyed Monarch. "*Go back, go back go back!*" His command was carried by the winds into the night.

Then finally, another sound penetrated his being. It was the furious neighing of horses and the groans of dozens of camels. Curses from their riders next reached his ears. Urging their mounts onward, the murderous band found their animals rebelling beneath them, declaring destinies of their own.

Rider after rider was thrown to the ground, or atop mounts suddenly reversing direction, refusing to go forward. A number of the cutthroats thus found themselves on foot at the edge of the caravan. Volleys of arrows cut them down where they stood. Then back, back, the others were driven, against their will, by their own mounts.

Rupert viewed the miraculous scene from high atop Majesty's back. The glorious stallion reared up on hind legs, savoring their triumph. The young prince's enemies were fleeing before him! Rupert brandished his shining sword aloft in magnificent victory.

"*Go back, go back!*" the boy still whispered hoarsely. Then from his heart, he gave homage to his animal comrades who had heeded his words.

The valiant prince experienced a breathtaking energy – as if somehow encompassed by generations of Golden-Eyed Kings, hailing the last of their line in this transcendent moment of triumph.

Chapter Thirty-One

Rupert savored his sublime emotions. With one hand, he continued to wave his sword aloft, with the other, to stroke Majesty, giving thanks to his superb steed. His only regret; the sword in his hand was not that of King Marco, which remained hidden away with the other royal treasures. Yet now Rupert recognized *this* sword was also unique; a part of an uncanny and staggering achievement.

The Golden-Eyed Prince became aware of his family dashing towards him, shouting in wild jubilation. Rupert turned Majesty about and headed towards them, Raja racing by their side baying wildly. By the time Rupert reached his friends, an ever-swelling throng had materialized, waving their own swords in the air, crying salutations to the startled boy.

"Hail to young Razim!" one called out. "He turned back those devils with his magic sword!" proclaimed another. They mobbed Rupert, Majesty, and Raja, causing the stallion to rear back in an act of protection. Rupert's own friends were finding it impossible to reach his side.

"Step back!" cried Liam. "Do not crowd the boy so!" But none was swift to heed those words, so overjoyed with the marvel they had witnessed. Most had been too far off to actually witness what had occurred, but those who had were quickly spreading the word, though not necessarily with any great accuracy.

"*Lightning bolts flew from the lad's sword!* It sent those murderers fleeing in terror, let me tell you!" proclaimed one grateful merchant.

"I believe you are quite wrong," objected a middle-aged lady traveling with her family. "He quite clearly *put a curse* upon those devils - took the courage right from their evil hearts and reduced them to cowards on the spot!"

Rupert glanced toward his comrades, a look of bewilderment upon his striking features. The crowd had not even paused to inquire as to the truth of the matter…they seemed mightily content to provide their *own* versions of events. The boy observed Drego stifling wicked laughter as the rest looked on in good-natured bemusement. Liam's ironic expression encouraged Rupert not to take such goings-on to heart.

The caravan leader elbowed his way to the front of the frantic throng. "Ho, my boy, it appears I owe you the gravest apology," proclaimed Borad. "For your prediction of future events has indeed come to pass. And now it seems even greater magic is yours! How you overcame those murderous cut-throats, I cannot fathom. Clearly, we are in your debt and owe our very lives to you, my brave lad!" He bowed in tribute as many of the others followed. More than one even knelt before him.

At first, Rupert wondered in alarm if his golden eyes had suddenly become visible. Yet it seemed such was not the case. The survivors were merely paying homage to their boy-savior. All were awaiting words from their hero. With an approving nod from Liam, Rupert determined to speak up.

"I thank you for your gracious words. The simple truth is, from childhood, I have had the ability to communicate with animals. I was thus inspired to request the raiders' camels and horses turn and leave us unharmed. After all, the animals felt us no ill will... it was merely their cruel masters who forced them into servitude. As you can see, they harkened to my pleas." Rupert attempted to give his explanation an air of simple logic, as if his feat was nothing out of the ordinary. However, he did not succeed in that aim.

"*Why, the lad is beyond amazing!*" declared a rather wild-eyed young fellow. "He commands every creature to do his bidding! We see he is far too modest - for clearly, he owns the power to curse our enemies while causing lightning to strike at will!"

Rupert wished to protest against these wild ideas, but others took up even more fanciful claims and the boy's voice was soon drowned out by the crowd. He began to grow bewildered at this strange development.

Eventually, his family was permitted to reach his side. "You are all most kind, but the boy needs his rest. I ask you to return to your campfires, for it is yet several hours till dawn."

The gathering seemed unwilling to disband until Borad spoke. "Yes, let the boy be. We must depart at break of day, but upon the sunset, let us have a celebration worthy of our young hero." The thought of festivities the following evening caught the mob's fancy. They finally, after cheering Razim for a moment longer, did at last depart.

Rupert was much relieved to see them go and then suddenly recalled another reason for jubilation the following day. For the dawn would bring Lira's birthday!

Meanwhile, Morley pulled Rupert from Majesty's back, hoisting him upon his own shoulders. He bore his prince back to their campfire, with a prancing Majesty and Raja leading the way. At last they could revel in the evening's miraculous happenings in private.

After being settled down upon the ground again, Rupert received warmest congratulations from his loved ones. When Lira moved to embrace him, he instead grabbed the girl under her arms and whirled her about in the air.

"You helped us, didn't you, Lira?" cried Rupert. "I'm certain I felt your energy joining Majesty's and my own. Thank you and well done!"

Lira was radiant. "Yes, the moment I saw you ride out to face those horrible men, I understood your plan. I did my utmost to come to your aid."

Daniel looked joyfully down at the young liege, but then his expression grew sober. "Dearest Rupert, could *you* not also have sent your message from comparative safety as Lira did? Was it quite necessary to ride out and make yourself a target?"

Rupert stared up at Daniel, taken aback. The thought had never even *occurred* to proceed in that manner. "I...I perhaps *was* slightly carried away by the inspiration of the moment. I was so elated with the certainty of how to defeat the raiders, I gave no thought to anything else," he confessed, somewhat shamefaced.

Drego gave a hearty laugh. "Do not blush my boy, for you gave us a fine spectacle! Had you played it safe, the caravan members would not have witnessed your theatrics, nor would they have known to whom they owed their miraculous deliverance from death. I believe you are at heart a true performer! The legend of young Razim is born this very night!"

"A legend that will apparently take on a life of its own," agreed Morley with a grin. "For it appears that mere *facts* simply will not do! These folks are having a high-ho time concocting their own version of events."

By now the companions were seated about their fire, downing mint tea, exhilaration filling their hearts. Yet Lira had no desire to share in the notoriety of the night's happenings.

"Please, Rupert," she whispered. "Do not tell anyone I helped. I do not wish for unnecessary fuss. The tribute rightfully belongs to you."

"Spoken with true modesty," said her approving father. "Yes, let us leave Lira out of the recounting, for I fear that upon the morrow, you will be required to recite the tale more than once...though your listeners will likely insist on their own embellishments to the saga."

"I must conclude this begins a new chapter for us, dearest Razim," observed a thoughtful Liam. "No doubt members of this caravan will travel far and wide after reaching their destination. Word of this night's miracle will spread rapidly. Without doubt, the tale will continue to flourish by leaps and bounds," he mused with an ironic shrug of his shoulders.

"We must consider other consequences of this night's happenings," Daniel reminded them. "For the raiders will certainly learn to whom they owe their debacle. When they hear of Razim and his magical powers, will they avoid any caravan of which he is a member? Or consider him a target for revenge?"

"Either is possible," sighed Morley. "Though let us hope the very name 'Razim' strikes fear into their hearts...or the heart of any villain who might wish us ill."

"Do you think 'Razim's' fame might spread all the way to Raja-Sharan?" inquired Lira.

"No doubt," replied her father.

"Why, that is wonderful! For we had no way of gaining admittance to the royal palace. If they have heard of Razim and his doings, then the royal family might invite us for a visit!"

Lira's family turned to the girl in surprise. None had thought of that.

"Lira, you are brilliant indeed!" declared her grateful prince. "For as vagabond performers, there is little to recommend us. Yet they might be curious to meet someone of whom they've heard many an absurd tale."

His friends laughed heartily. "Well, once we reach Raja-Sharan, your golden eyes might prove to be visible to many or a chosen few," ventured Liam. "That would, in itself, be our price of admission to the fabled pink palace. If not, we are required to search for another way to reach your kinsmen. The fable of Razim might provide the opportunity. So when we celebrate on the morrow, let us not attempt to dissuade exaggerations and flights of fancy. In the end, it may serve our purpose."

At last Daniel suggested they take what rest they might, for the following day would likely prove a trying one. Rupert, with waves of energy still coursing through him, knew sleep would arrive only with difficulty.

When Lira carried away their cups of tea, Rupert reminded the others of her birthday. He meant to inform Borad, so the coming celebration would in her honor, as well as for his own victory. Joyful as he was at this night's astounding events, he had already garnered more than sufficient accolades.

Later, Rupert stretched out under the canopy of stars, his blazing golden eyes regarded them with awe. He imagined the most dazzling lights were his own majestic ancestors, looking down in approval. He smiled at his own foolish thought, yet it brought comfort to think that, wherever they might be, they were proud of him and esteemed his actions.

The following day, Rupert found a moment to confer privately with Borad concerning Lira's birthday. He responded with pleasure, promising to spread the word. Rupert believed she had forgotten and so anticipated her delighted surprise at day's end.

And a great celebration it was! As soon as the caravan camped for the evening, Rupert and his friends were summoned to join Borad at his huge campfire. Every traveler gathered round. First Borad insisted upon hoisting Rupert to his shoulders, allowing the crowd to again give him a rousing cheer. The boy could observe their expressions...some regarded him with joy and awe, others with looks almost fearful. They did not comprehend how he had accomplished the miraculous. There were even those who believed he might commune with dark forces. That, too, would be woven into the legend of Razim.

After enduring more tributes foisted upon him, a startled Lira was called to join Rupert, who announced that this was his sister Lamara's eighth birthday. She blushed beautifully while receiving cheers of the throng, as well as embraces from her family.

Soon a feast was presented, and singing and dancing the order of the evening. The comrades were habitually called upon to entertain, but this night they were permitted to be the audience. Gift after gift was presented to the overwhelmed girl, who was a very pearl of perfection in the eyes of her new friends.

"This is far too much," she protested, but understood that to refuse would be considered the height of rude behavior. Soon, a small mountain was heaped before her...dozens of bright silken scarves, vials of scented oils, sandalwood ornaments for her hair, bangles of every description...enough for a dozen young ladies. Lira then had a very happy thought. Along the way, they would undoubtedly encounter many kind and helpful strangers. She could pass on her gifts to them! The idea pleased the unselfish girl very much.

At length, it came time for her own kinsmen to present tokens obtained in the bazaars of Ribakesh. Her father gifted her with a necklace of silver, studded with several small sapphire stones...the very color of his daughter's eyes. She gasped in delight and immediately placed it about her neck. Her grandfather presented her with what she assumed was another necklace, but it was instead something to be worn in her hair. Liam went on to explain that the ladies of Raja-Sharan were said to wear bejeweled tresses as a matter of course. Lira happily received the gold and ruby ornament, immediately planting it in her wildly curling, artificially darkened tresses.

Morley, now somewhat abashed, presented her with a lovely silken scarf. He had no way of knowing, when he'd purchased it weeks previously, that an entire caravan would be presenting her with birthday gifts, including a multitude of silken scarves. But she declared herself very well pleased with the turquoise and red-fringed article.

Drego was next and presented a perfect gift – a tambourine! Now, Lira could play an instrument whenever they performed and she was absolutely delighted. Lastly,

Rupert presented his precious sister with several books written in the language of Raja-Sharan, tales and legends of that kingdom dating back many years…lavishly illustrated. He knew the girl would love them. The sight of Lira's eyes lighting with delight confirmed his hopes.

She stood to embrace her loved ones. Then grabbing up her tambourine, she shook it in the air, summoning them to their feet.

"Let us give thanks to the victory of last night!" she proclaimed. The beauteous lass began to sing and dance to a haunting tune which originated from Raja-Sharan… the land in which they placed so much hope. Her family, not resisting her infectious joy, joined in, with all the caravan members clapping along to the exotic melody.

Rupert experienced another moment of infinite bliss. He could not help but recall Lira's last birthday, seemingly from a distant past. For how much had occurred since that amazing night; the night he led his friends to his cottage in the forest, seeking shelter from the pursuing army of King Ryker. That very night Rupert had finally shown the comrades his royal treasure and revealed to all but Lira the secret of his golden eyes… that he was the one true heir to his kingdom's throne. Then when he'd slept, he'd been given a mysterious vision, instructing that their destination should be the homeland of Queen Khar-shar-leen - the fabled land of Raja-Sharan.

Thus began their prophetic journey and very perilous indeed it had proven to be. How many incredible and unforeseen obstacles had been theirs to overcome!

That myriad hazards lay before them was undeniable. Yet overflowing with rapturous, new-found confidence, Rupert was convinced they would surely conquer any gauntlet fate might dare throw in their path.

Chapter Thirty~Two

The following days were strange indeed for Rupert. He had wished the victory over the fearsome raiders would soon fade from memory. However, events proved quite the contrary. The curiosity of the caravan members concerning their boy-hero appeared insatiable. He was constantly gaped at, pointed out, and served as subject for the wildest speculation.

"I must confess to be truly perturbed," admitted Rupert to his companions during a rare peaceful moment. For one result of 'Razim's' notoriety was that they were constantly in demand to share meals with new-found friends. Since it was considered rude to refuse, there remained little time to commune in private. Rupert took advantage of one such opportunity late one evening, after taking dinner with a retinue of well-wishers.

Daniel smiled at his prince and made answer.

"Rupert, you have saved the life of every man, woman, and child making this journey. This is a fact you cannot erase from their hearts as long as they live! Moreover someday, when your *true* identity is revealed, you will be held up as a hero for countless thousands of your subjects. Thus I fear your days of anonymity are rapidly drawing to a close."

These were not welcome words to Rupert, but plainly they contained much truth.

"Do not forget, your fame will aid in gaining access to our allies. So it is a blessing, though a mixed one to be sure."

"Drego knows whereof he speaks," chimed in Morley. "After all, he has experienced a degree of fame himself, being a performer of some note. Though it appears he rather *relishes* notoriety, unlike you, Rupert."

"Well, they don't make up crazy stories about Drego," chimed in Lira. "I suppose it is because people must admire heroes, so the marvel of their deeds is increased in the telling."

"Indeed," Liam said to his liege. "Rupert, be you hero or king, your deeds...your *life*...will no longer be merely your own. Accept this, and do not bemoan it. It is your fate, after all."

Rupert smiled in his mentor's direction. "What, do *you* now speak of *fate?!* I remember well you decried the very notion not long since."

Liam nodded in mock solemnity. "It is a foolish man who refuses to learn what life offers to teach him.

However, I have in no way made up my mind on the matter."

Their observations continued for some time, all relishing the opportunity to converse freely. The companions had assigned Majesty and Raja to stand guard, thus providing ample warning should anyone draw near. It was only in these stolen moments they dared use their true names rather than their adopted ones. In addition, they had long refrained from speaking their native tongue. The comrades now spoke exclusively in the language of Raja-Sharan or Kashkara. That fact, as well as their altered appearance, allowed their fellow travelers to take them for citizens of those regions.

Other than the continuous, albeit unwanted attention, the companions passed the next few days without incident. Then, one week after the defeat of the raiders, the caravan came upon an oasis. They had stopped at several sites along their route, but this one proved sizeable.

Intriguingly, theirs was not the only caravan halted there. Indeed, two other groups had broken their journey...one traveling from the north heading south, the other from east to west.

There was water aplenty to share. However, Rupert soon found cause for concern. Those who challenge the desert wastes tend to be a sociable lot, eager to exchange information of conditions to be encountered. The caravan leaders, as well as most of the travelers, soon found themselves eagerly engaged in converse. No more than a moment had passed before Rupert and his friends heard the name of 'the miracle-boy, Razim' on every lip.

Rupert sighed, wishing he could make himself invisible. There were close to a thousand people among the three parties and it appeared he was the focus of every astonished gaze. Fingers pointed in his direction, open-mouthed stares greeted him and some even bowed low as he strode past. His friends did their best to shelter their prince from notice, but that proved impossible.

However, matters soon grew worse, at least in Rupert's opinion. The boy had done his best to keep his face turned to the ground, but he finally looked up to see Borad leading two men in his direction. He introduced them as leaders of the other two groups of travelers. They stared down at Rupert with shining eyes.

The taller of the two addressed him. "I must admit, I was hardly able to credit the truth of the tale being recounted, young Razim. Yet, I've known Borad here for many years and I've never known him to speak false. How a mere youth came to defeat the murderous raiders, I can hardly say. Now I, for one, salute you!" The fellow touched his hand to his chest, then his head, then nodded to the boy.

"I was able to turn back their mounts, nothing more," sighed Rupert for what seemed the hundredth time.

"As if *that* were an every-day occurrence!" declared the other stranger, a fellow with skin burned darkest brown and creased by the sun. "May I also offer my congratulations and offer you the sum of one hundred pieces of silver to accompany my own caravan on its way south. For my train transports many valuables, making us a likely target. Word of your presence should turn back any who would dare menace us."

Rupert regarded the man, aghast. "Sir, do not speak of such matters to me! You *cannot* offer me payment in exchange for protection. You put many in danger by doing so." The young prince experienced a churning agitation. Liam, putting a calming hand on Rupert's shoulder, spoke up.

"Razim is quite correct. If word should spread that you paid for the boy's help, caravans near and far would be open to every desperate or dishonest lad who could hope to pass himself off as the real Razim. For who but the comparatively few gathered here know his true appearance?"

Morley, too, with growing choler, struggled to control his temper. "If false 'Razims' agreed to accompany other caravans for profit, countless lives could be lost if the raiders attacked. Those cut-throats would target the imposters, slaying lads whose only true crime was greed...or perhaps an earnest desire to support their loved ones. At any rate, you must *never* make it known you offered Razim payment. What he did, he did for only the most noble of motives. You must not dishonor that fact."

All three of the caravan leaders regarded Morley, then Rupert, more than a little shamefaced. The sun-withered man who had made the spectacular offer spoke again.

"Do forgive me, young sir. I meant no disrespect. Please believe me for that. Accept apologizes for my over-zealous wish to safeguard my people."

"I do understand," responded Rupert gravely. "But, please sir, give me your word the offer remains secret."

"Not so hasty," interrupted Daniel. "For were it known that payment *had* been offered, but instead stoutly *refused*, it should serve to prevent imposters from exploiting treasure from other caravans."

Rupert smiled gratefully at Daniel. He immediately saw the wisdom of the latter's idea. Spreading the word that 'Razim' had flatly refused payment would better serve the purpose. The three captains began to spread the news within moments. Unfortunately, it had the undesired effect, at least to the young prince, of making him appear all the more noble, causing his reputation to grow apace as the story spread to every member of all three caravans within the hour.

That night, Rupert and his kin could not avoid being feted by the enormous gathering. All thousand souls demanded to hear of Rupert's heroics...even those who had heard it recounted many times. Since Rupert could in no way avoid the telling, he made the best of it by insisting he and his friends conclude with entertaining their audience. After all, it would not hurt if their reputation as performers also preceded them to Raja-Sharan. And so, despite his reluctance to claim the rightful mantle of hero, he managed to finish the evening in improved spirits.

By morning, the three caravans had gone their separate ways. Relieved, Rupert began to savor a measure of elation. In only a few days they should reach Badarahm! It was scarcely credible. For that kingdom was the very last to be crossed before arriving in Raja-Sharan; the land which had appeared as an ever-elusive mirage, always far upon the horizon, a place of legend - not quite real. Yet now, their goal was almost within sight!

Late that evening, the comrades consulted their precious map, although in truth, they had largely committed it to memory.

"Badarahm is not large," whispered Lira enthusiastically, "at least as it runs east to west. It should not take very long to cross, is that not right?"

Indeed, it was true that Badarahm covered a sizeable territory running north to south. However, it was only several hundred miles across, at least in the area the companions would face. They could reasonably hope to make that journey in a week or two at most.

"I can hardly credit it," declared Rupert in an excess of joy. "We are so nearly there. Surely, *nothing* will stop us now!"

His adopted family smiled in wonder at their prince. Indeed it *was* miraculous beyond comprehension they had come so far.

"We must carry on with caution, as always," amended Daniel, "though we have cause to be hopeful with our miracle-working king to guide us! Moreover, it is only a matter of days until your birthday…so we will have further reason to celebrate!"

Rupert regarded his comrades, euphoria filling his heart. He could never fully comprehend how these loving, loyal, astonishing beings had come into his life. He acknowledged he was nothing without their guidance and care. It hardly seemed possible they were not related to him by blood. For blood kin could hardly deserve a closer place in his heart.

It came to pass that three days later, the caravan reached the border of Badarahm. A dozen guardsmen, clad in long purple robes and black sashes, made way as the travelers entered their territory. Purple and black banners fluttered in the wind at the crossing point. They had experienced only the most desultory of searches. Caravans were no rarity and so were regarded with little suspicion. Again, the companions relished crossing into new territory unchallenged...something that had hardly been the rule in past experience.

The trek's final destination was not the border itself, but the town of Barzak, located approximately ten miles further on. There Borad would, after a few days rest, guide another group of travelers back in the direction from whence he'd come.

Rupert recalled well what he had heard concerning the Kingdom of Badarahm - a land where the dead ruled the living. The thought filled him with trepidation, but also an overwhelming curiosity, a certain dark excitement. For the Golden-Eyed Prince could not but wonder if the dead would indeed have a message for someone longing to unravel the perplexing web of his ultimate destiny.

Chapter Thirty~Three

Barzak teemed with activity. Situated on a river running the length of the country, it was a major center for trade and travel. As the camels lumbered through the town gates, the travelers were greeted by a throng of locals offering everything from lodgings, to a mountain of merchandise, to guides promising the finest in local cuisine. Rupert and his friends surveyed the chaotic scene somewhat overwhelmed. A dozen voices addressed them at once.

"Let us take advantage of the offers to board our camels," shouted Drego over the din, for it had been agreed to keep only horses with them while they sought suitable lodgings. They would remain in Barzak several days, inquiring after another caravan to join, but that was not all. They had come so very close to their destination.

It was imperative to gather as much information as might be had before proceeding onwards. They would also hope to learn more of Badarahm itself, for knowing better the land they must next traverse could only prove useful.

Dismounting their odorous beasts, Liam rapidly made arrangements for their board with one of the eager solicitors. The party then led their horses through the masses of people until they'd located Borad. They proceeded to say their farewells and Borad appeared very sorry to see them go.

"You have provided us with a miraculous deliverance, young Razim. May you and your loved ones continue to be blessed by fate and may your destiny be one of resounding greatness!" The fellow clasped hands with the companions and watched as they turned to go. He knew he would carry their image for all his lifetime.

The party proceeded through the throngs with wide eyes. An enormous bazaar was set up immediately within the imposing city gates. Alien spices pervaded the air and Raja was not the only one to sniff with curiosity.

"May we eat soon, Father?" wondered Lira. "For it is near noon and I'm eager to sample the local fare."

"Let us first secure lodgings. We surely do not wish to stop at an inn, where privacy may be at a minimum." They realized the necessity of safe quarters in order to speak openly, but for another reason as well. Drego required they dye their skin again...and all but Rupert and he would darken their fair hair as well. Such activities necessitated isolation from curious eyes.

As they wandered through the thriving bazaar, the need for security became even more acute. Leading their horses through the narrow alleyways, Raja glued to his master's side, Rupert found himself the target of many a pointed finger and rash comment. Evidently, reports of Razim's dramatics had taken mere moments to disseminate. They became surrounded by curiosity seekers, well-wishers, and those offering free meals, accommodations, and gifts.

The companions were greatly put out, wishing it possible to regain a measure of anonymity. But that was easier said than done. It became a daunting challenge to move through the pressing crush. Raja and Majesty determined to protect their friends. The warning growls from the huge hound, along with the sight of the powerful stallion rearing on hind legs, did provide a measure of breathing space.

It was at that uncomfortable juncture that a young fellow managed to reach their side, leading his mount. He took Liam by the arm.

"Do come with me, sir. My father bids you be his guest. We reside on the outskirts of Barzak and may promise all the security you might wish."

The companions regarded him in surprise and no little measure of suspicion. Yet the youthful stranger, clad in dark robes and white turban, seemed eager to be of assistance. Moreover, it was plain they required rescue from the suffocating throng. The comrades exchanged glances and nodded. They mounted their horses and followed after their rescuer, who was able to at length break free of the exasperating horde.

As they made their way from the bazaar, Rupert noticed that, besides the many stalls offering up every sort of merchandise, there were a number of dark blue tents scattered about. No goods were visible from the outside. However, each tent featured a representation of a single eye painted above the entrance.

Rupert experienced a chill of curiosity as they hastened past. He had the strongest intuition that those claiming the power of communication with the dead were concealed within. The Golden-Eyed Prince vowed that, whatever the objections, he would find a way to consult such a one before departing Badarahm.

They had gone no more than two or three miles from the city gates when their guide turned down a quiet side-road. In the near distance was a fine house of white stone, but it was at a smaller cottage where they were drawn to a halt.

"You are most welcome to stay in my dwelling, which you see yonder. However, I believe you'd prefer to be left to yourselves after the constant attention thrust upon you. We have guardsmen patrolling our grounds. I can assure you will be unmolested here. Feel free to treat this cottage as your own for as long as you wish. For it is not often we are privileged to honor heroes as our guests."

The companions regarded their young host in puzzlement. "We have but newly arrived in Badarahm," declared Morley, giving him a narrow look. "How is it you know of young Razim's deeds already?"

"My father was told of it in a vision several days since," came the unexpected reply. "He was summoned away on a family matter and so bid me welcome you in his stead. You'll find the guest house well-supplied, but send word if you lack anything at all. And now, I will take my leave. My name, may I add, is Andrak. I am honored by your blessed presence."

They watched him turn his horse towards the main house, undeniably taken aback. He had so casually claimed to know of their existence before any caravan could have spread the news. Andrak spoke of his father's 'vision' as if it were the most common of occurrences. Indeed, Badarahm was already proving to be more than a little mystifying.

Wordlessly, Rupert and his party entered the cottage. It was ideal to their purpose…a large corral and stable provided shelter for their horses and the house itself, which consisted of four rooms and two fireplaces, seemed luxurious to the weary travelers. They discovered the larder well-stocked. Perhaps best of all, a well lay outside the back door, assuring an ample supply of water, so necessary for the process of dyeing their skin and hair.

"I do not understand how it happened, but it seems we've landed in exactly the perfect spot," observed Drego with a hearty laugh. "A few moments ago we were being overcome by mobs of Rupert's admirers…and now, we've perhaps found the one place where we might enjoy a measure of peace and quiet!"

"Yes, it is fortunate, though more than a little unsettling," confessed Daniel. "I feel as if I've awoken from a dream and now experience some degree of confusion."

"Shall we now expect to *always* find ourselves surrounded by Rupert's admirers? I admit I begin to enjoy it less and less," sighed Lira.

"We must discover new methods of disguise," declared Rupert firmly. "For the chaos that greets us will surely hamper our freedom, which would prove most trying."

"Let us not forget our goal - to reach Raja-Sharan and gain access to the royal family there. That would not be easily done without your new-found fame," Liam reminded his prince. "Yet perhaps we *will* find means to travel undetected when the need suits us."

"Even *I* hope that proves possible," declared Drego. "Fame, it appears, can be most vexing."

The comrades exchanged rueful smiles, but as they luxuriated upon comfortable cushions surrounding a low-legged table, they acknowledged they would enjoy a measure of comfort and luxury after long weeks crossing the desert wastes. Liam and Lira saw to preparing a hearty meal while the others tended to the horses. Before long, they partook of a fine noonday repast, one flavored with hot spices new to their experience. All but Morley and Raja found favor with it. They contented themselves with generous helpings of delicious flat bread, as well as lavish piles of mouth-watering fresh fruit. All were in high spirits at the thought of Raja-Sharan, now so very near.

It was then that Rupert revealed what newly occupied his thoughts. "I mean to take advantage of our time in Badarahm. I wish to consult one who is able to converse with the dead; for who is to say that a vital message from my honored ancestors might not be revealed?"

His family regarded him, aghast. "Rupert, you *cannot* be serious! It would be foolishness itself and far too dangerous. Those people are undoubtedly frauds," shouted an angry Liam.

Rupert proved obstinate. "If they are frauds, how could they be in any way dangerous? If they could see nothing of my true identity, we would know instantly. Yet what if…what if they *could* communicate with King Marco or Queen Khar-shar-leen or any of my kinsmen? How could we shun that possibility?"

Liam was the least likely amongst them to believe in such matters and he continued to scowl at his prince. However, his son appeared more open-minded on the subject.

"Rupert is right. A fraud could do us no harm, while a genuine 'spirit-talker' - or whatever such people are called - could provide a chance to gain intelligence."

"I, for one, am open to such things," Drego readily confessed. "My mother has communicated with me and come to our aid. However, Rupert, you have long been blessed with 'messages' or 'intuitions' from somewhere. Thus, if your royal ancestors wished to contact you, why not do so directly? Why an intermediary?"

"I have no answer for that. Perhaps I lack the gift that makes it possible. Therefore, why not consult one who possesses that ability?"

"Rupert, you are forgetting one thing," said Morley with some degree of agitation. "Suppose this person *is* able to discern who you really are, by way of messages from the beyond or some other method. Who is to say your secret would be safe with him...a stranger. Our very lives depend upon your true identity remaining concealed. What say you to that?"

Silence greeted Morley's words. The truth of the matter was beyond dispute. If a soothsayer recognized Rupert as a Golden-Eyed King, their lives would be in potential peril, for he could sell the information to whomever he wished.

"Morley speaks accurately," chimed in Lira gravely, "but everything we do is a risk. What if Rupert could learn where his parents might be? Why, they might even be alive somewhere! Isn't that worth knowing?"

Again, no one spoke. After a long pause, with Rupert's heart written plainly upon his striking features, Liam responded.

"I do not wish to crush your hopes, my boy. Since we are to remain here a number of days, let us decide nothing in haste. At the very least, let us sleep on the matter."

After those sensible words, the talk turned practical. Drego insisted the dyeing of hair and skin should proceed without delay. None objected, especially since their bodies were admittedly caked with multiple layers of sandy grit and grime from their endless desert sojourn.

"Imagine being clean again! I fear my hair smells of camel, which is not my favorite fragrance," Lira concluded with a giggle. It was thus decided to renew their disguise that very night. However, other matters continued to concern Rupert.

"We must not fail to gather all available intelligence concerning Raja-Sharan. But how are we to accomplish this? We are followed everywhere, with sensible converse unlikely to be encountered."

"I might venture out on my own," suggested Morley. "I'll not attract as much notice as my prince, I'll warrant you." Rupert was not pleased at the idea.

"Thank you, Morley, for the thought, but I refuse to remain confined in this cottage. Perhaps it is time to take up feminine disguise once more. I notice many local ladies wear a veil. Would you men not care to join me so we might walk about freely?"

His friends regarded him, expressions ranging from amusement to pain. "Please, Rupert, not again! Surely, once was enough on this mad journey," declared Morley.

"Ah, but 'tis a fine idea," stated Drego, who had not been among their number when they'd been forced to adopt disguise - the men as women, Lira as a boy. "Where is your loyalty to your liege?"

Lira gave her declaration of approval, but again Liam suggested they postpone any decision, though recognizing somehow his prince would have his way and walk freely among the citizens.

Evening approached. A never-ending supply of water was drawn from the well. The comrades were able to cleanse themselves, making good use of the fragrant sandalwood soap Lira had been presented upon her birthday. After prolonged scrubbing, they were clean for the first time in long memory. Following that, walnut dye was applied to skin and hair. By morning, their appearance would be as desired.

However, as they sat before the glowing fireplace, Raja came to a sudden alert. The sound of many horses approaching could be plainly heard. Alarmed, Rupert raced to the window and gasped. Half-a-dozen guardsmen, mounted on fine steeds, halted before the door.

"Soldiers!" he whispered, not knowing what threat they might represent.

Damp hair hanging down their backs, the companions were but half-clad and barefoot. Upon a bold knocking against their door, the men grabbed up their weapons as Rupert took out his dagger. However, it was Drego, with nod to the others, who chose to answer. His hair had not been dyed and his disheveled appearance was still the most presentable of the group.

Stepping forward, he opened the door a crack, his sword concealed from view. The soldiers were dressed in dark purple garb, long robes with black sashes about their waists. Black turbans covered their heads. Their horses' saddles and bridles were of similar hues. All were well armed, but their weapons remained undrawn.

"Forgive my intrusion, sir," began the spokesman, a tall fellow of about thirty. "I am told I might find the boy Razim here." Drego, suspicious, made no reply. "We are men of His Greatness, the Raja Manzar. My lord bids me welcome you to his kingdom and wishes the honor of your presence on the morrow. His palace is not ten miles distant. If you agree, my men and I shall return at the noon hour to escort you."

Those within the cottage could hear the soldier's words and were, one and all, struck with astonishment. A royal invitation! Just what they had hoped might occur upon reaching Raja-Sharan. They knew nothing of the ruler of Badarahm, but could imagine no reason to refuse the summons. Indeed, it might be looked upon most unfavorably should they do so.

Drego gave a swift look to his companions, who indicated dazed approval. He voiced their assent; they would indeed be honored to attend upon their royal host. With that the soldiers withdrew, leaving the companions regarding one another in dazzled wonder.

Now, their journey had taken yet another most unanticipated turn. And Rupert, standing with dripping hair and in stunned disbelief, could hardly wait until the morrow.

Chapter Thirty-Four

The companions, aflame with curiosity, followed their escort down a well-traveled road. The soldiers had appeared at the promised time, though Rupert and his friends had been ready and waiting for hours. They had dressed in their best, as humble as those garments were, for they owned nothing finer than the simple robes worn while crossing the desert. Lira insisted each wear one of her recently acquired colorful scarves about their waists. Rupert chose to make use of the silken one of marvelous golden color, heavily fringed at the ends, a gift from Lira upon his last birthday. The color almost exactly matched his golden eyes. To the young prince, it represented a secret talisman to his true identity.

Rupert, much to his exasperation, found himself recognized by passing citizens as they made their way towards the palace. The presence of these guardsmen could only have one meaning to the gawking throngs - young Razim was being honored with a royal summons! Alas, that could only result in Rupert's notoriety growing to even loftier heights.

Fortunately, the Raja of Badarahm's men did their job well, keeping the curious from mobbing the boy and his family. Rupert was able to ignore them for the most part, for he was well and truly lost in his own reflections. How had it come to pass they were on route to a royal castle?! He stole looks at his companions, who wore similar bemused and bewildered expressions... though a look of blatant amusement lit Drego's virile features. Rupert could not but wonder what, if anything, the local sovereign would know...or *wish* to know...of his true circumstance. Should Rupert dare reveal that he was a fellow king? He had discussed the dilemma with his friends the evening before, though no firm conclusion had been reached. Liam counseled extreme caution and clearly, that was the wisest way to proceed.

The trek to the fortress was not long. The escort eventually turned off the main route, guiding their guests to a more secluded path, well guarded by purple-and-black-clad servants of the Raja. After another mile, the royal dwelling came into view. The comrades gasped, for they had seen nothing like it before.

It was a formidable structure, several stories in height, marked by high towers at each corner, with rounded turrets at the tops. The palace was made of glistening white stone, which gleamed blindingly in the desert sun. Purple and black banners fluttered from the rooftops and towers.

They entered a vast courtyard where elaborate fountains flowed and there they dismounted. The horses were left behind. The guests, including Raja, who had received permission to accompany them, were shown into the impressive edifice.

The floors were cool, white marble, assuring relief from the unrelenting desert heat. The many tall windows were shaded to keep out the brilliant sunlight. The walls, painted in a light purple, featured marvelous representations of life in the kingdom – desert caravans, moonlit nights with beautiful ladies dancing under the stars, and brave deeds of the royal family itself.

The party was invited to remove their shoes and then progressed through several inner rooms. Each was luxurious; lavishly, yet tastefully adorned. Myriad attendants scurried this way and that. Rupert and his friends attempted to absorb everything before them. It was a challenge not to feel overwhelmed.

At last, they arrived at a spacious, high-ceilinged chamber. The walls and floors were of shining white marble, inlaid with swirls of gold. Outside the opened windows and doors was a marvelous fountain, flowing with water, shaded by luxuriant foliage. The atmosphere provided a peaceful oasis from the searing outdoor temperatures.

The comrades were beckoned to take a seat upon colorful low divans arranged throughout the chamber. With that, the guardsmen withdrew, leaving the young prince and his friends exchanging mute looks of anticipation. Somehow, none dared speak. They had only a moment to wait before graceful servants, male and female, beautifully clad in dark purple silks, entered, bowed to their guests, then turned towards the open doors leading to the courtyard. Upon hearing the approach of footsteps, they fell to their knees and touched their foreheads to the floor.

An instant later the Raja of Badarahm appeared. He moved to a raised dais, heading for a marvelously carved chair of dark wood, tufted with deep purple velvet. He stood for a moment, smiling down at his guests.

Rupert stood frozen, unaware of how one comported oneself in the presence of royalty. Though unprepared, the boy with golden eyes acted first. Following the actions of the servants, the prince fell to his knees and touched his head to the cool marble floors. His companions followed suit, though more than one felt it unseemly for one king to bow so low before another.

The Raja Manzar spoke his first words. "Arise, my friends. Do be at your ease. I am indeed pleased to welcome you to my humble home."

The party arose as one and stood before the monarch. He made a fine impression to their eyes. Manzar was a young man...certainly no older than Daniel or Morley...in his mid-twenties at most. He was of medium height and of slender, almost frail physique. Yet his appearance nevertheless was most pleasing. The young ruler had handsome features, a golden-brown complexion, setting off his fine, dark eyes which shone with intelligence and humor. He wore a turban of light purple, with a stunning red ruby in its center. His long black hair hung down his back from beneath the head covering. He was clad in a purple tunic reaching his knees, along with black fitted trousers, both made of the finest silks. A black sash was about his waist and his fingers bejeweled with magnificent gold rings featuring precious stones of red, blue, and green.

The Raja stepped down from the dais and approached his guests. Rupert's heart was pounding. He attempted to recollect that even a king was an ordinary being, that he himself was one after all. Yet the boy knew this was an unforgettable moment and would not attempt to curtail his emotion. Rupert wished to address his royal host, but recalled it might appear unseemly should he, a mere youth, speak first. Fortunately, Liam found his tongue.

"It is you who honor *us*, my lord," said the greatly intrigued Liam. "It is our pleasure to wait upon you and be of service."

The Raja came close, looking them over one by one. Rupert felt himself blush, though he knew not why. He feared that perhaps this king could see through their disguise. Though now all sported dark hair and complexions of light golden brown, the prince felt exposed.

Manzar smiled. "I must admit I have heard many tales of you already. Yet, I confess to be taken aback by your marvelous appearance. I supposed talk of your dazzling looks to be inflated fable. Yet I see it is true. I have seldom seen children of greater beauty. Even the men amongst you are a rather handsome lot."

Drego spoke. "My lord, the young ones are clearly extraordinary. As for the rest of us, we're no great matter to speak of!"

Rupert swallowed at Drego's casual humor. Was that any way to address a monarch? However, it appeared the Raja took no offense. Indeed, he gave hearty laugh.

"And who might this giant be?" Manzar inquired of Rupert, indicating the hound at his side.

"This is my faithful friend, Raja," he replied before almost choking at his words - for his dog had the same title as the king! But again, the Raja took no offense and laughed once more. He was clearly someone who did not care to stand upon ceremony and proved eager to put his guests at ease.

"Come let us sit by the fountain, for it is a favorite spot of mine. I hope you are not disappointed at the modest proportions of my home. This is by no means my main residence, which is located several hundred miles to the north. I spend time here but infrequently. Yet I do enjoy my visits, since it was a favorite also of my father, the most honored Raja Zangor, who departed this world not long since."

"Is that why everything is so dark?" inquired Lira, speaking in Veshti, the language of Raja-Sharan, as they all were. "Are you still in mourning for your noble father?"

The others wished to hush the girl, concerned her words might give offense - either to the Raja or his decorators. But again, the friendly monarch beaned at the radiant lass.

"You are quite correct, my dear little beauty. During the official year of mourning, we are required to wear dark clothing and keep our homes draped with somber hues. Though here in Badarahm, we *always* maintain a number of rooms in dim shades, for it makes it easier for the departed to communicate with the living. It is said they are not attracted to overly-bright surroundings."

The words of the Raja were spoken in the most casual of tones, but of course, they had a marked effect upon the companions. The gossip was clearly true...here in this land, even the rulers spoke of communion with the dead as if it were no more extraordinary than with the living! Again, Rupert found himself consumed with curiosity.

The Raja saw his new friends at a loss and endeavored to put them at their ease.

"Come, you must be hungry and thirsty after your journey. Let us partake of our modest repast and become better acquainted."

Manzar clapped his hands. Immediately there materialized a bevy of servants bearing quantities of food which they spread upon a round table before the refreshing fountain. A place was even provided upon the ground for Raja. The meal looked delicious; the Raja assured that he knew none would partake of meat and all had been prepared according to their desires.

They may have been too overwhelmed to speak, but they were able to eat. All were curious as to what a monarch might serve and the companions found the menu lavish and mouth-watering. There were mounds of rice, along with vegetables cubed and cooked in hot spicy sauces, flat breads of every description, yogurts, mountains of nuts, thin soups made from lentils or beans; the courses seemed never-ending. Even the hearty appetites of the companions were challenged to do justice to it. The desserts featured half-a-dozen choices, including something they had never before seen - cool sherbets made from mountain snows, sweetened with fresh fruit and honey. It was almost as delicious as chocolate in Rupert's opinion.

The Raja gave his guests leave to dine without demanding much conversation in return, hoping they might feel more at ease as the moments passed. Indeed it was true that Rupert began to relax. As the meal was completed, the multitude of dishes cleared away, and iced mint tea served, the host spoke up again.

"I would be most honored, young Razim, if you would relate in your own words your remarkable rescue of the caravan from disaster. It is a tale almost too amazing to credit and I relish the opportunity to hear of it from its true source."

Rupert could hardly refuse. Therefore, he was obliged to recount the episode in simple yet eloquent terms. He truly disliked being made much of, feeling more and more a fraud as time went on. However, his noble audience was not of the same mind.

"Young Razim, being of royal blood is a matter of fate or accident of birth. Yet I believe *true nobility* is a matter of one's deeds. Therefore you, my young friend, *are most worthy of your royal roots!*"

The words caused stifled gasps from his audience. They were clearly astonished that the Raja should refer to

Rupert as possessing royal blood. *How could this be?!* The companions, from long habit, greeted the sovereign's words with trepidation. Could this be but a trap? The silence lengthened. At last Rupert spoke.

"My lord, I am most humbly flattered by your gracious praise. Call my deeds noble if you must, but I am bewildered you declare my blood to be royal. Are you perhaps making a jest?"

"I confess, Razim, that I owe my good information to my dear father, the late Raja, who spoke of these matters only three days since. He assured me that a boy-hero was soon to enter our land and that upon his fate many lives would depend, empires might rise and fall - indeed, the destiny of Badarahm itself would be determined by his future actions."

Rupert beheld his royal host, aghast. His comrades were no less stunned. None knew how to reply, or indeed, if they should speak at all.

"I must add one more thing my departed father conveyed. He assured me that you and I, young Razim, share a bloodline. We may be distant relations to be sure - but if true, you must be of noble origins. If you have been unaware of this fact, I assure you, my wise father certainly knows whereof he speaks."

Rupert cleared his throat. At length he found his voice, after a furtive glance at his greatly disconcerted friends. "But your revered father has passed away, is that not so? Did he speak of these matters before his demise?"

Manzar regarded the striking, bewildered, guarded youth before him. "Yes, that is true. His death occurred almost ten months since. However, perhaps you are familiar with the customs in my land. We have gifted ones who communicate with those passed on...if their spirits are willing to speak. Is that not the tradition in your realm? And where, may I ask, *is* your land of origin? For most of you have dark hair and golden complexions, but light eyes. That speaks of mixed blood, does it not?"

Rupert did not dare to respond. He stood mute. Then Daniel gave an answer previously agreed upon.

"Why, my lord, we hail from the land of Gitano. It is very distant and the population contains those of varied origins. So yes, we are of mixed parentage."

The young Raja looked directly into Daniel's sapphire eyes. He was skeptical of the tale, but would press them no further.

"Well, this much I can tell you," Manzar went on. "Royal ladies from Badarahm have married into other noble families for countless generations. The lands of Ribakesh, Raja-Sharan, Kashkara, Bithora, Saldama, and many others contain the blood of our princesses. So I believe if we might *truly* trace your origins, young Razim, we would discover a noble lady of Badarahm as one of your kin. For my father tells me that your fine friends are not of your blood."

Rupert was appalled. How could this man know so many of his secrets? Though what he said might prove true enough. Certainly, if a royal lady of Badarahm *had* married into the ruling family of Raja-Sharan sometime in the past, then he might indeed be a distant relation to the Raja standing before him. Yet how could Rupert's future actions affect *this* kingdom or any besides his own?

He could not begin to speculate, while desiring greatly to speak freely to his friends. How difficult it was to hold his tongue! A thousand questions longed to burst forth.

"I do not expect you to credit my words," assured Manzar, "for I must conclude you do not share our custom of speaking to the departed. Therefore, I would be delighted to summon my royal communicator, so that you might speak to your kindred and confirm what I have said."

The astounding proposal took the comrades by surprise. Each had lost loved ones and could hardly imagine reunion with them might be had for the asking. Liam could speak to his wife, Morley to his brothers who had perished in the service of King Ryker. Lira could hear from her mother and Daniel his wife. Drego could perhaps find his parents once more. And Rupert...could he *truly* talk to King Marco? He could barely comprehend the magnitude of the offer.

A staggered silence followed the Raja's enticing offer. Surely, this was not to be decided upon that instant. All turned to Rupert, who had so recently expressed a fierce desire to speak to his departed kin. But now, he hesitated. Some inner voice cautioned against this; that a better opportunity might present itself, one that would carry with it no doubts. One that would *not* include an intermediary.

Thus, almost unbelievably, Rupert bowed his head to his noble host and spoke: "I thank you with all my heart, my lord. Yet I must decline your gracious offer." The words burned his tongue, but Rupert knew he was right. He could sense his friends standing beside him breathing a huge inward sigh of relief.

After that, the golden-eyed boy felt as if an enormous weight had been lifted from his shoulders. Intuition conveyed he had passed some sort of test, though he could not say exactly what or why. Somehow consoled, he smiled at his host with gladness and a measure of serenity.

"I thank you again, as do my friends. Perhaps we may be of service to *you*. May we not perform in exchange for your graciousness?" The companions had indeed brought their instruments, thinking that the royal summons had been connected to their growing reputation as entertainers of note.

The Raja shrugged. Clearly, his guests were determined to keep their own counsel. Declaring he would be pleased to view their performance, they proceeded to delight Manzar with their favorite melodies. Meanwhile, Rupert could not help but note the young king rarely left off observing him. The Golden-Eyed Prince felt this man knew more he was not yet revealing. However, Rupert could hardly fault him for that…for he himself had kept back all he might have chosen to reveal.

After a pleasant interlude of music, the Raja held up his hand. "Delighted as you have made me, I fear royal duties beckon. However, before you depart, I wish to offer one other service I hope you will take advantage of. I believe it is true your journey continues by caravan to Raja-Sharan - and that your identity as the hero Razim will prove a hindrance?"

Liam smiled at the understanding Raja.

"Yes, indeed, my lord, we fear that Razim's reputation will create undesired attention. Yet what remedy is there for that?"

"Just this. The next caravan departs for that destination in five days. How would it be if I arranged for my men to escort you instead? You would arrive in very good time and would not be molested along the way. You could enter Raja-Sharan in anonymity, as I believe you desire. Likewise, I could see fit to delay the caravan several days further. You should thus have at least a week in your new land without tales of Razim inhibiting your actions."

The companions were delighted at the thought. To be able to move about freely would be a fine thing and much to their purpose.

"My lord is too kind," exclaimed Daniel, while the others added their own words of heartfelt thanks.

"Then let us have you depart on the morrow near midnight," suggested Manzar. "None will be about to observe your actions at that hour. I shall have my soldiers call upon you, and you men shall don their uniforms as well. As for young Razim and Lamara, we shall find you suitable camouflage. Is that agreeable?"

The companions were again profuse in their thanks. The Raja had only one request...that the companions dine this evening with their host who had offered them his cottage as a haven. To leave without honoring him would be considered a great breach in decorum.

"Of course we shall be delighted to comply," agreed Liam speaking for the others.

Then quite abruptly, it seemed, the royal audience was at an end. With a gesture, a servant appeared to guide the guests back to their horses. Before they took their leave, the Raja gestured for Rupert to come to his side. He whispered very briefly in the boy's ear. The young prince stood stock still, growing pale under his dyed complexion. With that, as Rupert and the others bowed low, Manzar vanished into another room, the white silken curtains fluttering behind him in a sudden breeze.

The companions were consumed with curiosity. What could the Raja have said to their liege? But there was no opportunity to speak while a dozen guardsmen escorted them back to their cottage. In fact, the presence of the guards proved a necessity, as word of the royal visit had spread, causing many hundreds of people to spontaneously line the path, shouting Razim's name and cheering him on.

It was when at last they were delivered to their cottage that privacy was theirs once more. The captain of the guard, before departure, announced he would return the following evening upon the eleventh hour. The guards also produced gifts the Raja had sent as a farewell to his new friends. Each received one, wrapped in cloth of dark purple. Taken aback, Liam and Rupert urged the soldier to make proper thanks to his master.

The Raja's men then departed. The party entered the cottage, gifts in hand. A mere few hours had passed since leaving their shelter, but each felt something profoundly odd and momentous had occurred.

"Tell us, please! What did the Raja whisper to you?" begged Lira, expressing the thoughts of the others as well.

Their Golden-Eyed Prince turned to face them. He could barely utter the words.

"The Raja said his father instructed him to pass on one word to me. That word was '*Rupert!*' Somehow, he knows my true name!"

Chapter Thirty~Five

Rupert's friends regarded him in stupefaction, along with a measure of suspicion.

"*How could he know our true identity?!*" gasped Lira. She turned to her father as if he might somehow hold the explanation.

"Not so hasty," Daniel replied. "We have been perhaps too careless in using our true names when enjoying private converse. It is not difficult to imagine we were overheard, and the information passed to the Raja."

"The more I ponder our royal interview, the less satisfactory it seems," added Liam. "If he indeed knows of Rupert's secrets, why did he not plainly state so? Why speak in portents and riddles?"

"Moreover, if his royal father communicates from the grave, why did he not reveal that Rupert possesses the title of *king*?" added Morley, stymied.

"We can presume the Raja does *not* know Rupert's true lineage, else he would have announced the fact," opined Drego flatly.

"Wait, for we can make no assumptions," broke in Rupert. "We can hardly blame the Raja for being less than honest, for *we* are certainly guilty of that very crime. We admitted nothing. Perhaps, if we had, His Majesty might have proven more forthcoming."

"All this again is speculation," declared Liam. "The Raja seemed to know much, and yet little. He knew Rupert's name, while claiming he had royal blood somewhere in his veins. Also that we are not Rupert's real kin. Yet, he did *not* know of Rupert's true origins, the name of our homeland, or that he has golden eyes. This is most unsatisfactory! We were likely correct in confessing nothing to him."

"Yet the Raja predicted Rupert would affect the destiny of many lands, including Badarahm. If true, why be so obtuse?" pondered Daniel.

"Perhaps the answer lies in the gifts he's given us," declared Lira sensibly enough, but simple eagerness to see what the Raja had presented them made the girl eager to examine the parcels.

Her father laughed. "Yes, sweetheart, you are right. Perhaps there might indeed be some clue contained within." Daniel looked to his friends, apparently suddenly curious themselves.

The companions sat down before the hearth, carefully unwrapping the parcels. However, the contents puzzled them even more. For each contained a suit of clothing. The men had been given high-collared, fitted-sleeved tunics which reached almost to the knee. The front was fastened with a number of buttons. They were in a variety of colors, embroidered with simple patterns. The trousers were loose fitting and of darker hue, gathered at the ankles with more fastenings. Lira's gift consisted of a jacket with a rounded neckline and flowing sleeves. At first, she thought it also featured a full skirt. Upon closer examination, it appeared that it was, in fact, billowing trousers.

Lira was delighted. "See, it has the modesty of a skirt, yet very practical too, for I shall be able to walk and ride freely." She also admired the deep rose color of the jacket, which had many cloth-covered buttons down the front. But the girl could plainly note that the others did not share her pleasure.

"This is most vexing," sighed Rupert, examining the garments. "What an odd gift for a king to bestow upon those who are to determine the fate of his nation!"

"Perhaps he's just a very practical fellow," said Morley with an ironic shrug. For the fabric was not even fine silk, but instead a sturdy, serviceable cotton. Certainly, it was by no means luxurious.

"Yet, we must still thank His Majesty, for this must likely be apparel common in Raja-Sharan. It will at least save the necessity for making such purchases as soon as we cross the border. In truth, our supply of money is dwindling." He spoke with humor, but his words alarmed Rupert. What *would* happen when their funds ran out? He could only hope that aid from his Raja-Sharani relatives would appear long before that might occur.

Further speculation on the cryptic actions of the Raja would have to wait. The companions had much to accomplish before departure on the morrow. Daniel went to the main house to announce their intentions to their host, requesting they dine with him that evening. That done, they had a long list of items to attend to, including cleaning of weapons, washing a mountain of clothing in the well waters, and replenishing their supplies.

After a busy few hours, they proceeded to the main house for a dinner of thanks with their host Andrak. The fellow seemed discretion itself. He obviously knew of the royal summons, but asked no untoward questions. The evening passed a bit awkwardly, yet pleasantly enough. The companions presented him with sandalwood soaps and incense that Lira had received upon her birthday and Andrak seemed well pleased. After offering any further assistance should they require it, their enigmatic host bid them a good night and a safe journey.

The following day was filled with activity. Towards noon, a guardsman of the Raja appeared, delivering the companions' camels, along with uniforms the men in the party were to wear. They were received gratefully. Lira later laughed to see her family and friends dressed as the Raja's men.

"You all look quite dashing," she observed with pleasure. "However, what of Rupert and myself?"

'I'm certain the Raja has something in mind," replied Rupert. "We shall have to be patient until tonight." The young liege could hardly wait for darkness to arrive. For it meant their journey to Raja-Sharan would begin again...the *final* steps in an astonishing odyssey!

At last, the moment came. The companions had been ready for several hours. None could follow Liam's sensible suggestion they attempt sleep, though clearly they were meant to travel through the night. The king's troop appeared in a timely fashion. Soon the men were mounted on camel back, but Rupert and Lira were left in puzzlement.

"We have not forgotten you, young friends," said the captain, named Zarkahn, with a smile. He indicated the camel upon which Daniel sat. On either side of the beast were hung two huge baskets. "You must conceal yourselves until we have put some distance between ourselves and the city. The Raja, my master, wishes it so."

Rupert felt a surge of indignation. 'Hide in a basket' indeed! But Lira was of another mind.

"How exciting! Don't you agree, Razim?"

Clearly, 'Razim' did not. The chuckles reaching his ears from Drego's direction did not improve matters. The soldiers lifted each of the young travelers into one of the baskets, though Raja did not favor the action, nor did Majesty. Rupert had to reassure them there was nothing to fear. And with that, the party set off.

They did indeed travel through the night, stopping only twice to make certain Rupert and Lira were not too uncomfortable. Lira, in fact, managed to fall asleep, though her prince was not so fortunate, since he spent much of the night grumbling unhappily to himself. However, when dawn finally broke they halted, allowing Rupert and Lira to emerge from their cocoon.

Rupert stretched his legs gratefully as a relieved Raja romped by his side. His golden eyes surveyed the scene, finding no sign of others upon the road. "I hope we are now safely away," he said to Zarkahn. The young captain assured that this was so.

After a hasty meal, the party continued. Now, atop a camel and free to enjoy the exotic surroundings, Rupert knew a growing elation. They were truly on their way; only a week or so to reach their goal. It was almost beyond credence!

How the Golden-Eyed Prince wished to share his feelings with his friends, though discretion must be their watchword. He turned to each with a radiant smile. His adopted kin could easily read his thoughts, for they were not so very different from their own.

The party made good time each day, beginning at dawn and hardly pausing till sunset. Rupert was delighted at the swift pace. He took note that the terrain was changing. The stark true desert was giving way to more frequent sights of scattered greenery and watering places. The weather began to noticeably cool as well.

"If we meet no obstacles, you should expect to reach Raja-Sharan in about five or six days' time," came the welcome words from their leader after less than a week had passed. The companions had become acquainted with the captain, finding him a capable and agreeable fellow. The dozen soldiers that accompanied him seemed a good-natured lot as well. Rupert and his friends, grateful for their help, chose to thank them by entertaining each evening with song. Their escort returned the favor, with music native to Badarahm. The companions were delighted. Rupert was especially pleased to acquire even a few words in yet another foreign tongue.

The following night, Rupert dreamed that quicksand lay in their path. He lost no time in warning the soldiers, who proceeded with great caution. The prince was convinced that the peril faced them only upon this day, so if it could be avoided, they would be then safe.

After traveling for several hours, Rupert grew aware that danger was near. He caused the party to follow a circular path instead of their usual straight line. By day's end, they had arrived at their campsite in safety. The soldiers thanked Rupert, but with a quizzical look.

Drego had been amused at the day's events.

"Perhaps you *did* spare us from tragedy," he explained to the bemused boy. "Yet since nothing untoward *did* occur, we shall never *truly* know."

Morley, too, was diverted. "Yes, avoiding danger altogether is not nearly as dramatic or satisfying as miraculous escapes!"

"Yet this day *may* someday become part of the legend of Razim…but perhaps not without some creative embroidery. It may be reported you personally pulled out several camels and a soldier or two from a horrible death by quicksand!"

Rupert was able to laugh at Daniel's prophecy, content that danger *had* been averted. It mattered not what the soldiers felt. Dramatic the day's events might not have proved. However, he remained confident that the warning had been quite real, and was very glad to have heeded it.

The following day was Rupert's twelfth birthday. He'd awoken just after midnight, euphoric, and consumed with diverse thoughts. He could not but reflect on his bizarre upbringing - isolated in the forest with his inscrutable grandparents…who had vanished forever the moment he'd discovered the royal treasure. What an enormous turn his life had taken after that! He could hardly comprehend the people and events encountered. Could he *truly* be the same person? So many questions had been answered, yet a multitude of mysteries remained.

Rupert wondered where he might be one year hence. Would he be returning to his native land, army in tow, leading them to free his homeland? Yet he must not look too far into the future. First would come the momentous meeting with his royal kinsmen in Raja-Sharan. For upon their promise of aid, all depended.

After greeting the dawn with a joyful gallop on Majesty's back, Raja beside them, Rupert returned to find his friends awaiting with their warmest congratulations. Their existence had changed profoundly upon crossing paths with Rupert - their former lives of empty despair were now filled with hope.

Celebrations had, of necessity, waited upon the evening, when the companions might be at their leisure. Oddly, the soldiers were somehow aware of Rupert's birthday, inviting the party to share their fire, entertaining with traditional songs from Badarahm, accompanied by small tokens for the youthful hero.

It was therefore growing late when the comrades finally withdrew to their own fire to celebrate in private. Each had an offering for their prince, ranging from a topaz ring from Liam, the stone the very color of Rupert's golden eyes, to a flute from Daniel, knowing the boy wished to learn, admiring the haunting tunes that the giver so flawlessly produced.

After thanking them, while taking care he was not observed by the soldiers, Rupert startled his companions by kneeling before them. Bowing his head with humility and grace, the prince gave thanks for their love and companionship, acknowledging his life would be meaningless without them. They protested, knowing they should bow before *him* instead, but Rupert would not be gainsaid. Then he arose, embracing each of his friends, tears of happiness glowing in his magnificent eyes.

They finally slept until another dawn broke. Only two more days were to pass before reaching Raja-Sharan! Their excitement was difficult to contain. However, as they camped the following evening, a most unexpected event unfolded. Zarkahn, the captain of the troop, approached their fire.

"I bring greetings from my master, the Raja. He instructed me to speak with you when we neared your destination. He believes it is true that you have little information concerning Raja-Sharan. Is that not so?"

"That is indeed the case," responded Liam. "All we know are of happenings long in the past. If you have more current news, we would be grateful to hear it."

"Then I will inform you according to my master's instructions." All were seated about the fire, sipping mint tea. Zarkahn joined them. He began his narrative with an audience of eager listeners.

"Raja-Sharan was a kingdom upon which destiny smiled for many long years. A series of goodly rulers guided their noble land for generations. They were, by and large, able to maintain peace with their neighbors. Thus, their country prospered. However, it is said that those whom fortune favors will eventually be required to pay the price. And indeed, fate turned a cruel face towards Raja-Sharan; for in this world, all things must eventually come into balance.

"Firstly, not half a year since, the noble Raja, Bardor by name, died unexpectedly. His Majesty was reported to have been resting in his garden when a poisonous viper struck. There was no remedy or rescue. Of course, the nation was much grieved.

"However, all was not lost. The Raja and Rani had two fine sons, the eldest being sixteen, the younger fourteen, as well as a daughter of twelve years. The elder of the sons, Marjara, now took the crown. His mother was a good and noble lady, well able to guide the youth through the tragic nature of his coming to the throne, though her own grief was great indeed.

"Sadly, the sorrows of the royal family had hardly begun. Not one month after the death of his father, the young Raja took his morning ride upon horseback. He raced ahead of his companions as had been his custom, only to be later found dead of a broken neck.

"The second tragedy in such a short time threw the Raja's family, as well as the entire kingdom, into darkest grief. The double loss of husband and child was likely too heartbreaking for the noble queen. Three days after her son's demise, the Rani was found dead in her chamber. Some believed she perished of a broken spirit, while others claimed she had taken poison. There was even speculation that she had been murdered. For wild stories now were upon every lip. It was clear at the very least, that fate had decided to demand payment for so many years of success upon the world's stage. Others concluded an enemy had put a curse upon their royals - and thus upon the kingdom as a whole.

"Now, the fact remained that only one heir to the throne existed. The youngest son, Bajra, now found himself an orphan, aged barely fourteen, with a throne to protect, as well as a beloved younger sister, the Ranila Paraminda, to safeguard. Of course, a host of royal advisors crowded about them, but the young Raja, shaken by the terrible calamity that had decimated his family, was clearly overwhelmed.

"One thing was certain. Barja must immediately marry, so a royal heir might be produced. The boy was the last male of his line. If he were to die with no successor, disaster and chaos awaited.

"Fortunately, before his death, a royal marriage had been arranged for his elder brother, with a princess of the land of Saldano. She had already departed towards Raja-Sharan with a large retinue. The new Raja's advisors instructed that her people be informed of recent events...proposing the marriage take place instead with the younger brother.

"However, the news was received by the bridal party with horror. Clearly a curse of fate was upon the royals of Raja-Sharan. As a result, the marriage contract was now to be considered null and void. The bride and her escort returned at once to their homeland.

"Matters were at a terrible pass. All efforts to seek another bride proved in vain. What was to be the fate of the kingdom if no heir could be produced?

"At this dark moment, an offer of marriage arrived from a far-off land…but it was a strange one indeed. For the offer was not of a bride for the Raja, but instead a husband for his younger sister. Moreover, the groom made the unprecedented proposal to travel to Raja-Sharan for the wedding. Never had anyone heard of this! A bride always traveled to the land of her husband. This remained true whether it concerned a peasant girl going to the next village, or a princess of royal blood journeying to a distant kingdom.

"However, the royal advisors could not afford to be overly fastidious. If indeed this marriage were carried out without incident, it might convince the world at large that any curse was indeed over. After that, a wife might be successfully sought for their Raja. In the end, that was all that mattered.

"Thus, the offer was agreed upon. The foreign prince is now said to be on his way. Perhaps that royal wedding would bring new hope to a most beleaguered land."

The captain completed his narrative. He could not help but observe the stunned expressions on the faces of his listeners. However, he stood to go, sensing they might desire to converse in private.

"Just a moment," demanded Liam. "Who is this prince who travels from afar? What is his country?"

"He is called Jezra, and his kingdom, Zahira. I know little of that land, nor does my liege, else I would tell you of it. Now you are aware of all I have been instructed to share with you." With that, the captain bowed and returned to his men.

"This is most terrible and unforeseen," cried Rupert, while remembering to keep his voice low. "I had never imagined my kindred in Raja-Sharan would be facing such trial and turmoil."

"Indeed," said Liam, stricken. "Moreover, I am not a great believer in 'fate'. My suspicious heart is convinced your family has met with acts of treason; to have so many royals wiped out so swiftly, leaving mere children to deal with what evil faces them!"

Then all eyes went to Drego. His fine-looking features were contorted with rage.

"You do not begin to know how right you are!" he hissed. "For clearly you know nothing of Zahira, but *I do!* It borders Gitano, my father's homeland. You may remember my recounting that, as a child, my family was forced to flee before ruthless invaders. They came from Zahira; that kingdom being recently overthrown by those same savage men."

"And so Prince Jezra is your enemy?" asked Rupert, wondering again at this terrible turn of events.

"He is far more than that, my prince. He is *your* greatest enemy as well! For the invader who drove out my people was called Bara - this devil was younger brother to Zorin, the very monster who slaughtered all your Golden-Eyed Family and threw your kingdom into hell!"

Rupert and the others regarded Drego in stunned disbelief. *This could not be!* The prince, who was even now coming to marry the Raja-Sharani princess, was kin to Zorin, and his son, King Ryker! Rupert and his friends had fled to the ends of the earth to escape their web of evil! Yet now, the companions found themselves facing a menace that threatened like a volcano building towards a shattering explosion.

"Drego, this can mean only one thing!" cried Daniel. "The prince from Zahira and his clan are behind the disasters befalling the royals. This can be no coincidence. Jezra means to seize the throne of Raja-Sharan, by marrying the princess and then doing away with her brother. There can be no doubt!"

"Would he be allowed to rule?" asked Lira in a tremulous voice. "He isn't a real member of the royal line."

"Ha!" cried Rupert in great bitterness. "Is King Ryker, or his filthy father Zorin, a true Golden-Eyed Ruler? *No!* They murdered them all and took over my kingdom, slaughtering any who opposed."

"Rupert must be right. For the same occurred in Zahira. The king and his children were poisoned, then in the chaos that ensued, the country was overrun...just as in *your* homeland, Rupert." Suddenly, another horrific thought caused Drego to utter a dark curse. "Rupert, hand me the map!"

Reaching into his tunic, Rupert quickly produced it. Drego pointed out their homeland, then Raja-Sharan, lying in a direct line far to the east. Zahira lay between them, to the south. If a line were drawn connecting the three kingdoms, it would form a perfect, inverted triangle. Rupert grasped Drego's point at once.

"It appears that not only Raja-Sharan may be in mortal danger. For if it is taken by these black-hearted devils, what is to stop that band of murderers from attempting to conquer all lands between their three kingdoms! They could someday rule half the world!"

The others beheld the map in growing dread and dismay. None could dispute these evil, soul-less cut-throats would not wish to swallow up as many territories as possible. *Now* Rupert comprehended only too clearly the Raja of Badarahm's words - that on Rupert's actions, the fate of *many* nations might rise and fall, including the Raja's own! But how might one stripling prince and his tiny band of friends prevent this coming catastrophe?

"Yes, we must presume the very worst," declared Liam, "and be on our guard. We arrive in Raja-Sharan upon the morrow. We shall not permit the tribe of King Ryker to doom another kingdom to massacre, slavery, and despair. We must give warning without delay!"

With that, the companions spent half the night in contemplation of the dark and dreadful turn their path had taken. All had long counted upon Raja-Sharan to give reality to their mission of receiving aid for their homeland, allowing Rupert to ultimately reclaim his throne. Yet now, far more immediate concerns lay on their path. They must save what remained of Raja-Sharan's royal family. It was also their only hope of saving themselves.

The next day near noon, the guardsmen took their leave. They were not to cross the border, having business for their master in the north. Rupert and his friends thanked them with all their hearts, then continued eastward. The border lay a mere three miles distant. Finding it with no obstacle, the party crossed over after a cursory examination by men clad in dark blue robes and golden sashes about their waists.

Thus, Rupert and his adopted family set foot upon Raja-Sharan's soil with little ceremony. Their hearts should have been bursting with joy, having overcome so extraordinarily much to arrive at the end of this epic journey. However, the report of this kingdom's recent fate had turned hope to desperate fear and fury. Still, Rupert wished he might dismount Majesty and kiss the ground under his feet in gratitude. For the fact remained that the companions had reached their destination alive, strong, and united.

The road was eerily silent, despite the appearance of a number of travelers. The atmosphere seemed to reflect the shock and loss of recent days. The comrades did not exchange a single word. However, a brief time after entering this almost mythic land, something unexpected did occur.

A narrow path veered off to the left. Out of nowhere, Rupert experienced a powerful force pushing against him. He drew Majesty to a sudden halt, causing the great stallion to rear up. The Golden-Eyed Prince now felt a desire beyond all things to venture down that lane.

Wordlessly, Rupert turned Majesty. His friends called out to him, but received no answer. They were forced to follow, exchanging quizzical and guarded looks.

It was not long before Rupert turned once more to head for a dilapidated, thatched roofed abode located to one side of the path. He and his companions drew up before it.

Rupert found himself quite unable to move. Heart pounding madly in his chest, the golden-eyed youth grew dizzy and faint. He struggled to contain his wild, bewildering agitation. Then after a pause, the door of the cottage silently swung open. An elderly man and woman emerged. Greeting the party with enigmatic smiles, the couple bowed low before the young prince. They then arose.

And standing before Rupert were his grandparents!

Made in the USA
Charleston, SC
18 August 2012